TASLIMA NASRIN
SHAME

A Novel

 **Prometheus Books**
59 John Glenn Drive
Amherst, NewYork 14228-2197

Published 1997 by Prometheus Books

01 00 99 98 97   5 4 3 2 1

Library of Congress Cataloging-in-Publication Data

Nāsarina, Tasalimā.
   [Lajjā. English]
   Shame : a novel / Taslima Nasrin ; translated from the Bengali by Kankabati Datta.
      p.   cm.
   ISBN 1–57392–165–3 (cloth : alk. paper)
   I. Title.
PK1730.3.A65L3513   1997
891.4'437—dc21   97–27653
                                                CIP

Printed in the United States of America on acid-free paper

Contents

Preface

In December 1992, a 450-year-old mosque was razed to the ground in India by a mob of fanatic Hindus. They claimed that this particular mosque was built after demolishing a Hindu temple which had been built earlier on the same spot in honor of Rama, an incarnation of God. Rama is actually the hero of a world-famous Indian epic, the *Ramayana*. Naturally, sensible and clear-headed people, who consider the *Ramayana* an outstanding work of art, nonetheless think Rama is actually an imaginary character. Likewise, most modern historians and archaeologists are of the opinion that no particular site could be identified as his birthplace. They also say it is difficult to ascertain whether this particular mosque was built after destroying a Hindu temple of worship. But a number of Hindus were determined to do away with the mosque, and with the support of ultranationalists and the rightest Hindu party called the Bharitya Janata party and their various front organizations, they accomplished their task. The motivation behind this atrocious act was that it would pave the way toward establishing "Hindu Raj" in India by replacing the secular constitution which gives equal rights to Muslims, Christians, and believers of other faiths. There are millions of Muslims in India. They were naturally shocked, and came out in protest. Therefore, riots broke out in different parts of the country. Widespread violence and devastation took their usual toll in terms of life and property.

The British carved a country, which is Bangladesh today, out of India as a part of Pakistan. The other part of Pakistan was at least one thousand miles away in western India. The logic behind this partition was that the Indian Muslims needed a separate homeland for themselves. However, the fact remained that, even after this partition, millions of Muslims remained in India. Another thing became obvious within a few years. The Muslims in eastern Pakistan realized to their horror that the Muslims of western Pakistan were subjugating them. There was no affinity between the language, culture, and way of life of the two people. Religion was the only bond, but co-religionists did not mind oppressing their fellow Muslims living in the eastern part of the country. They systematically tried to destroy the language and culture of the Muslims in East Pakistan. Naturally, at first there was resentment and, finally, a revolt. Bengali nationalism was roused and after a bloodbath, the Republic of Bangladesh was born in 1971. I was just nine years old when my country got its freedom.

Bangladesh is predominantly a Muslim country, but there are at least ten million people living there who are Hindus. Besides the Hindus, there are Buddhists and Christian minorities as well. Previously the mosaic com-

8

prising the various minorities was more colorful. During the partition of India, millions of Hindus left for India with their families, leaving behind their ancestral home, farmland, and whatever they possessed. Similarly hundreds of thousands of Muslims migrated to East Pakistan across the border from the Indian part of Bengal.

During Pakistani rule, this flux of Hindus occurred periodically. Comparatively fewer and fewer Bengali Muslims migrated to Pakistan from India. Perhaps the last time it happened was in 1964. After the emergence of Bangladesh, as a secular, democratic, socialistic republic, the founding fathers of the nation thought that nobody would ever be able to play with the minorities of the country. They knew that the Hindus had also suffered under the Pakistani rulers, and had shed their blood to overthrow these tyrants. They were given equal rights with the Muslims and allowed to live with dignity. But unfortunately, with the destruction of the mosque in India, the Hindus suddenly found themselves caught in an altogether different situation. They became the targets of Muslim fanatics. In protest against the nefarious act of demolishing a Muslim place of worship in India, their houses and business establishments were attacked and places of worship demolished, as if it were the Hindus of Bangladesh who were responsible for the demolition of the mosque. One of the consequences of the partition of India was that, if anything undesirable happened in one part, the other parts reacted immediately. As a result, a religious riot in India meant a religious riot in both parts of Pakistan. We had thought that it would be different after the formation of Bangladesh. We had thought that whatever happened in India, or any other part of the world for that matter, it would not affect the country's social structure. We had thought that Hindus and Muslims who had lived side by side for centuries would not be affected. We had shared the same culture, literature, and both had contributed to the growth of the Bengali language, literature, and culture. Both had contributed to the economic growth of the country, too. But in that black December, to my horror I found that around me, unexpected things were happening. Hindus were being persecuted by the Muslim fanatics through no fault of their own. Mobs were hunting them. Helpless people did not know how to save themselves or the honor of their women. They were bewildered. The police could give them little protection. The secular politicians and intellectuals were also, in a sense, dazzled. Of course there were protest marches, peace missions, human chains, articles and editorials pleading for peace and order. But it was the fanatical fundamentalists who had a field day during those troubled times. I was horrified, I was agonized. I felt outraged, and the reaction was this little book, *Lajja* (*Shame*).

I was in a hurry. I did not know what to do, but I felt I must protest, and I must make this protest known to my people. The book was written almost in a trance. It was ready for the press within just a few days. I handed over the manuscript to a publisher and felt relieved. The book was published in February 1993. I was fortunate because, in retrospect, I feel it would have been very difficult for me to publish a book like *Lajja* in Bangladesh had there been no courageous publishers there. More than fifty thousand copies of the book were sold out in a very short time. Suddenly a government order was issued and *Lajja* was banned in Bangladesh. The argument in favor of this ban was that this book was a threat to social peace and tranquility, that it might endanger the relation between the two communities, and so on. After that, the events took a different turn. Pirated editions started to surface in the Indian part of Bengal. *Lajja* became a best seller in India on the black market. To my horror, I heard that the Bharitya Janata party, the very people who led to the demolition of that mosque, and whose followers were primarily responsible for the riots in India, took up my book in support of their subversive ideas. They translated the book into Hindi, and serialized it in their journals to rouse the sentiments of the Hindus against the Muslims. They said, "Look, here is proof provided by nobody else but a Muslim writer who has shown how Hindus are persecuted in Bangladesh today." Naturally, in my country I was accused of being an agent of Hindu fundamentalists in India. Some fundamentalist newspapers and journals in Bangladesh spread the canard that I had received millions of takas from Hindu fundamentalists for writing the book. Even my friends started looking disapprovingly at me.

The book had two sets of critics. The literary critics who had praised my poetry or essays found it wanting. They said that it was no work of literature. Even the friendliest critic could only tell readers that the book was an important testament but still fell short. The second set of critics, both in Bangladesh and in India, were not just literary critics, but socially alert writers and journalists. Those who belonged to Bangladesh thought not only that it was a bad book but also that the timing of its publication was bad. I had done a disservice to Bangladesh, especially to the progressive forces who believe in secularism and democracy. "Did we not oppose the fundamentalists who were inciting the mobs to oppress the Hindus? Were we not outspoken against them in newspapers and periodicals? Had we not organized marches and meetings?" They felt I had let them down, and that by providing a handy propaganda item to the Hindu fundamentalists in India, I had indirectly helped the Muslim fundamentalists to organize themselves. The fringe of the radical left went further. They dubbed me an Indian agent in Bangladesh, called me names, and declared that I was paid handsomely for denouncing my own country and people. This sort of criticism was heard in India, too. A segment of the leftist intellectuals there accused me of having helped the Hindu fundamentalists, and of putting down the progressive leftist forces of Bangladesh who were fighting the fundamentalists there. In short, both friends and foes alike criticized me for different reasons. Only a few critics from both sides of the border took up the book seriously and thought of it as an important book because of the subject and the writer. When in a predominantly Muslim country, a writer who belongs to the majority community sits down to write about the fate of the minority, especially in the charged atmosphere of communal violence, is not that something important? This was their argument.

I do not think that I should apologize to anybody for writing this book. It is the agony of my heart, which I have poured out onto the pages of this little book. I had Hindu classmates in my school and college. We had Hindu neighbors with whom we had very good relations. Personally I have many Hindu friends of both sexes. I knew from my parents that many Hindu families had left our town after the partition. Why should people be compelled to leave their forefathers' land simply for the religion that they practice? I could not but feel sorry for such a situation. I know many Hindu families who stayed back after the partition and fought side by side with the Muslims to make their country free. Why should they be terrorized now, so many years after liberation? Why should they be penalized for a crime with which they were not even remotely connected? These were the questions that tormented me. Tears rolled down my cheeks and, to keep my conscience clear, I could not but write down this testament.

Lajja is the testament of a writer. In this testament I have indicted my country, the ruling clique and the political parties in Bangladesh, and also the intellectuals. In the process I have indicted myself also. *Lajja* means "shame." I felt ashamed to see such human degradation. I felt ashamed for the government of my country, who could not come out to protect the minorities. Protecting them was the government's primary responsibility. I feel ashamed of my fellow writers and intellectuals who, despite their efforts, could do little to save their fellow citizens. Is not this failure a shame for us? Maybe there were similar failures on the other side of the border, maybe there were people who felt ashamed of the happenings in their own country. Maybe nobody felt as outraged as myself. Why should I remain silent because no other writer from the majority community came forward to indict their own government and society like me? Their failure is their own. My conscience is my own. I am not a practicing politician who is careful of the prospective voters' need. I do not believe in compromise when it consists of one's conviction. From a worldly outlook I may be considered a fool. I may be considered a tactless person. I may be considered too dogmatic. I do not care. I know I was honest, I know my sentiments were honest. I knew this little book was a cry of my agonized heart.

Because of my ideals, I was threatened by the fundamentalists. They demanded my execution by hanging.
They attacked me physically, launched hate campaigns
against me. They organized meetings, processions, and
skirmishes. They even manipulated countrywide general
strikes in support of their demand. They have decreed a
fatwa against me and set a price on my head. Not only that,
I was a criminal according to the government of my
country, too. My crime was that I said the religious scriptures are out of place, out of time. I was accused on charges
of hurting the religious feeling of the people. An arrest
warrant was issued against me. I was forced to go underground. I remained confined to a small dark room, which
served as my hiding place for sixty long days. At last the
pressure created by the international human rights movements and the democratic governments of different countries who believe in freedom of expression forced our government to grant me bail and let me leave the country. The
trial is still going on. I have not been able to go back home.
My future remains uncertain.

The disease of religious fundamentalism is not restricted to Bangladesh alone and it must be fought at every
turn. For myself, I am not afraid of any challenge or threat
to my life. I will continue to write and to protest persecution and discrimination. I am convinced that the only way
the fundamentalist forces can be stopped is if all of us who
are secular and humanist join and fight their malignant in-
fluence. I, for one, will not be silenced.

Day One

Suranjan was lying still. Maya, his younger sister, had been nagging him all along to swing into action, "Dada, please do something. If you're late, things may get out of hand." Suranjan knew that "doing something" meant ducking in for some uncertain cover. It was just like a scared rat scurrying for a burrow and waiting for the all-clear signal before venturing out. For them, too, this would be the ordained course: keep watch for the right time in a hideout till the situation outside cooled down. But why should he run away from his own home? Just because of his identity as Suranjan Dutta and his father being known as Sudhamay, his mother Kiranmayee, and his sister Nee-lanjana Dutta? Was that why they would have to run away and find shelter in the house of some sympathetic Kamal, Belal or Hyder as they had done a couple of years ago? At that time, smelling trouble, Kamal had virtually run all the way from his Iskatan residence to their place on October

15

30. He hustled Suranjan out of his bed with the frantic plea, "Hurry up, just pack a few bare necessities. Lock the house up and move out, all of you. Quick, quick." They had, of course, been well looked after at Kamal's house. They had had toast and eggs for breakfast, rice and fish curry at lunch. Their afternoons had floated on the wings of carefree idle talks on the lawn, with nights passing smoothly through undisturbed sleep on soft, thick mattresses; the days, free of anxiety, had indeed danced away on merry steps. But why should he be under compulsion to seek shelter in Kamal's house? True, Kamal had been his longtime friend. Without feeling the least uneasy he could be his guest even with his close relatives for a few days. But the question that ruffled him was: Why, first of all, should such a situation arise to make him look out for a hurried escape from his home? Yet Kamal, a Muslim, was spared this indignity. This country was as much his as it was Kamal's. Both of them were supposed to enjoy the same civil rights. But why couldn't he assume Kamal's in-born defiant attitude? Why wouldn't he be able to say: Look, I'm on the same soil as he is. Why can't I have the same rights of life, breathe the same free air; why the hell do I have to live in haunting fear?

Suranjan remained glued to his bed, showing no signs of getting up. Maya paced restlessly within the confines of their rooms. She still went on hammering at him, trying to impress upon him that no crying over spilled milk would undo the misfortune once it overtook them. CNN was showing the live telecast of the Babri mosque demolition scene by scene. Sitting benumbed in front of the TV screen, Sudhamay and Kiranmayee were watching this macabre play. Their mind, too, ran along the same line as their

16

daughter's. As he had done last time, perhaps this time also, Suranjan would whisk them away to the relative safety of a Muslim household. But Suranjan was thinking nothing like that. If Kamal or, for that matter, anyone came to take them under his protective wing, he would flatly turn down the offer, saying, "Look, I won't leave my home, come what may."

The day was December 7. The previous afternoon an ominous darkness had cast its gloom on the bank of the Saryu river in the city of Ayodhya. Hordes of fanatics and religious zealots called "Kar Sevaks" had already demolished a 450-year-old mosque there. The incident had preceded the organization of bigots, Visva Hindu Parishad's, formal launching of the much-publicized "Kar Seva" voluntary service by twenty-five minutes. The "Kar Sevaks" had frenetically labored for about five hours to raze the triple-domed structure to dust. The top leadership of political parties and outfits with strong religious overtones like the BJP, Visva Hindu Parishad, RSS, and Baj Rang Dal watched this bizarre incident. The contingents of armed security personnel like the Central Reserve Police Force, Provincial Armed Constabulary and Uttar Pradesh police watched the spectacle with idle detachment. At two forty-five one of the domes was destroyed. At two forty-five one of the domes was destroyed. At four, the second was smashed, and by four forty-five the third dome was also broken to pieces. The madness had cost the lives of four frenzied men who lay buried under the rubble. A hundred more, overtaken by the same wild craze, had been injured. Lazing on the bed, Suranjan casually glanced over the screaming headlines of the morning newspaper: "THE BABRI MOSQUE DESTROYED, DEMOLISHED."

17

He had never been to Ayodhya. Nor had he seen the Babri mosque. The reason was simple enough: he had just never had any occasion to step out of his land. Where Rama, the protagonist of the epic *Ramayana*, had been born or how the mosque sprouted or from which point of the soil, concerned him the least. His mind, anyway, glided along the paper's view, conceding: "The destruction of this sixteenth-century architectural movement hadn't hurt the sentiments of the Muslims alone; the Hindus, too, would be equally offended by this senseless act that had dealt a vicious blow to the whole idea of human welfare and to the collective conscience of humanity." He mused over the grim predictions of things to come.

The Babri mosque issue would unleash a tremendous upheaval in Bangladesh, too. The Hindu temples would be demolished, the Hindu houses would be targets of arson, their shops would be looted in the massive retaliatory strike. The fanatics, egged on by the BJP, had in fact given extra muscle to the fundamentalists of this land by demolishing the mosque. Had the BJP, Visva Hindu Parishad and their camp followers thought that the impact of their crazy act would remain confined within the geographical boundaries of India alone? Bloody communal riots had already broken out all over India. The number of deaths had been mounting remorselessly—500, 600, 1,000. The death toll had been going up from hour to hour. Were the standard bearers of Hinduism aware of the existence of two to two and a half score Hindus in this Bangladesh as well? Why Bangladesh alone? Had the Hindu zealots even cared to think of what a catastrophe would strike their brethren in each of the West Asian countries? As a political party, the BJP should realize that India couldn't have an isolated existence like an island. The appearance of a pustule in India would send down waves of agony not only to its own people alone, but its ripples would spread all over the world and the sufferings would smother at least this neighboring country first of all.

Suranjan stayed stretched out on the bed closing his eyes. Giving him a nudge, Maya said, "Just tell me if you're leaving the bed or or not. Baba and Ma are depending solely on you."

Slowly stretching himself, Suranjan said, "Go wherever you like. I'm not going to budge an inch from this house."

"What about Baba and Ma?"

"Can't say."

"If anything happens?"

"Like what?"

"Take, for instance, the house being looted or even set on fire."

"Let 'em do what they like."

"And you intend to sit unmoved even after that?"

"No, I'll prefer lying down as now."

Suranjan lit a cigarette on an empty stomach. He felt like having a cup of tea. Kiranmayee used to give him his morning cup of tea every day; but today was an exception. Who could give him a cup of steaming hot tea at this time? It was pointless to convey the request to Maya. The girl was thinking of nothing else but escaping from here. Asking her at this moment for a cup of tea was to invite a strong retort with a sharp rise in her voice. It was not that he couldn't make tea for himself, but he was feeling too indolent for such an exercise. The TV was on in the next room. The idea of watching the CNN telecasts on the TV with goggle-eyed wonder didn't appeal to him. From that room, Maya kept on announcing every now and then, "Dada is still in bed going through newspapers with a 'couldn't care less' sort of attitude."

It was, however, not true that Suranjan was unaware of the gravity of the situation. He clearly could visualize that any time a horde of people might force their way into their house in a sudden burst. Some of the faces would be familiar, some unknown. They would ransack the house, loot all the movables and, as a grand finale to their retreat, set the house aflame. In the circumstances, if he asked for shelter from Kamal or Hyder, none of the them would elude his request with the plea of a shortage of space. But he felt ashamed to make such a request. He could hear Maya's shout, "If you don't make a move, I'll fend for myself. I'd better take shelter in my friend Parul's house. It doesn't seem Dada will take any initiative. Maybe he has lost the will to live, but I haven't lost mine."

Whatever might have been the reason, Maya had conjectured at any rate that this time Suranjan wouldn't make a move for their protection. That was why she was thinking of her own safety alone. The expression "safety" pained Suranjan.

Nor was there any safety in October of 1990. A crowd of maniacs had burned down the ancient Hindu temple of Dhakeshwari. The police remained inactive, not offering the slightest resistance. The fire destroyed the pivotal temple. The arsonists didn't spare the adjoining structures of the pillar-supported entry hall, the Shiva temple, guest house for the temple visitors, even the ancestral home of Sridam Ghosh located by its side. In the same way they destroyed the central temple of the Goudian monastery, assembly hall and the guest house. Before this orgy of destruction, however, they hadn't forgotten to loot from within the temple whatever could be removed. In the same way they destroyed the temple of another Hindu religious sect, the Maddhwa Goudya monastery. On the other side, the Jaikali temple was smashed up. The room within the boundary wall of the Brahmo Samaj was demolished with bombs. The ornate throne of the deities in the Ram-Sita temple was pulled down. The main hall, too, was devastated. The monastery at Nayabazar, fell in this trail of rage as well. The temple at Banagram was laid waste with the use of pickaxes. Seven Hindu shops at the entry point of Shankharibazar were plundered first, then set ablaze. Nothing from the rows of shops like Shila Bitan, Soma traders, a hairdressing salon, a tire shop, a laundry, Mita Marble, Saha Cabin, a restaurant and so on could escape the sack. This tornado of destruction reached such a level of fury at the crossing of Shankharibazar that later nothing but rubble could be seen as far as the eye could see. The Shani temple at Demra was looted. Several hundred communal fanatics ransacked some twenty-five households. They destroyed everything within the inner sanctum of the Birbhadra temple at Demra after smashing the temple wall. Flames consumed the umbrella and gold shops on Islampur Road. The famous sweetmeat shop of Maranchand on Nababpur Road was completely destroyed together with the one bearing the same name at Purana Paltan. The image of the goddess at the Kali temple at Rayer Bazar was broken to pieces by hurling it on the ground. At Sutrapur, all the Hindu-owned shops were looted and destroyed first and then their signboards were replaced by new ones proclaiming their Muslim ownership. A variation on this pattern occurred at the sweetmeat shop of Ghosh and Sons at Nababpur Road, where after the customary looting, a banner in the name of the Nababpur Youth Union Club was hung outside, announcing the transfer of ownership. The Bat tali temple at Thatari Bazar was plundered. The long list of destruction also included the old shop of Ramadhan Pashari at Nababpur, the sweetmeat shop of Shuklal at Babubazar within a stone's throw of a police outpost, the shop of Jatin and Co. and its adjoining factory, a portion of the historical snake temple, and Ratan Sarkar market at the crossing of Sadar Ghat. One by one all these horrendous scenes of wanton devastation and plunder kept on rushing up in Suranjan's mind. Could it be called a riot? Could this chain of terrible incidents of wanton violence witnessed during October 1990 be identified as such? The riot, as he understood, meant a free-for-all between two sides or between members of two communities. But this couldn't be described as a riot. What he had seen was an unabashed attack by the members of one community on members belonging to another community. Rather a one-way torrent of torment and torture. The sun's rays peeping through the window reached Suranjan's forehead. It was the soft winter sun, its rays couldn't produce the burning sensation on the skin. He again felt the thirst for a cup of tea while lying on the bed.

Sudhamay could still conjure up those scenes. All his uncles and aunts were leaving this land one after the other. The Phulberia-bound train started from Mymensingh Junction station. The coal-fired steam engine, after emitting billowing sooty smoke which shrouded the sky, sent out a long whistleblow followed by a heart-rending, doleful wail from those passengers leaving their ancestral homes for the last time. Neighbors, too, were leaving, re-

22

minding his father, Sukumar, "This country has now turned into a homeland for the Muslims. We have no security in our lives here."

A principled man, Sukumar Dutta replied, giving forceful expression to his conviction: "If I don't feel secure in the place of my birth, then where else on earth can I expect security? Go if you want. I'll never leave my ancestral home. Leaving rows of coconut and betel nut trees, extensive paddy land, the residence sprawling over two-thirds of an acre, I'll never opt to be a penniless refugee on the Sealdah Station. It's a repulsive idea." Sudhamay was just nineteen then. His college pals, too, were leaving for good before his eyes with identical warnings, "You just see, your father will have to repent later for his doggedness." But Sudhamay, too, had, by that time, picked up the same strain of his father's convictions. He said, "Why should I leave for another country, leaving my own land? I'll live or die on this very land." Even in 1947, the college presented a virtually deserted look. Those who hadn't left were also biding their time. Sudhamay went through the college along with some poor Hindu boys still living there and a handful of Muslim boys to pursue his further studies at Lytton Medical College.

In 1952, he was a vibrant youth of twenty-four. The Dhaka roads had become crowded with slogans demanding Bengali as the state language. Excitement was running high all over the country. Voices of protest had been raised by the bold and conscious Bengali youths against Muhammad Ali Jinnah's decision to enforce Urdu as the state language for Pakistan. Holding aloft the demand for the implementation of Bengali as the state language, these youths had straightened their bent spines, defying police firing on them, treading the blood-soaked streets, remaining firm in their resolute assertion. Sudhamay, his spirit bubbling with fervor, had lent his voice to the "We want Bengali" slogan standing at the van of the processions. He was a member of the huge crowd of protest marchers out of which bullets fired by the police killed Rafique, Salam, Barkat and Jabbar. He, too, could have been the target of a bullet. He also could have been one of the immortal martyrs of the country.

Sudhamay hadn't sat idle during the turbulent days of the mass movement of 1969. Ignoring the menace of the trigger-happy policemen of General Ayub Khan, the Bengalis pressed their eleven-point charter of demands; nothing could keep the Bengalis at that time from the protest marches. He had been one of the the pallbearers of the police firing victim, Alamgir Mansur Mintu. The sorrow-benumbed participants of this funeral procession on the streets of Mymensingh had clenched their fists once again in an affirmation of their movement against the military rulers of Pakistan.

The costly mistake of dividing the country on the basis of a "two-nation theory" had been proved repeatedly in the united movement of the two communities in the country during the language movement of 1952, the elections of 1954, the educational stir in 1962, the agitation for the realization of a six-point charter of demands in 1966, the anti-Agartala Conspiracy case movement in 1968, the general election of 1970 and finally the Liberation War of 1971. Indian National Congress leader Moulana Abul Kalam Azad had said: "It is one of the greatest frauds on the people to suggest that religious affinity can unite areas which are geographically, economically, linguistically and culturally different. It is true that Islam sought to establish a society which transcended racial, linguistic, economic, and political frontiers. History, however, proved that after the first few decades or, at most, after the first century, Islam was unable to unite all the Muslim countries on the basis of Islam alone."

Jinnah, too, was aware of the hollowness of his own "two-nation theory." He disagreed with Mountbatten's plan to divide Bengal and Punjab, as he himself said: "A man is a Punjabi or a Bengali before he is Hindu or Muslim. They share a common history, language, culture and economy. You will cause endless bloodshed and trouble."

The Liberation War of 1971 was the climax of all the "bloodshed and trouble" the Bengalis had witnessed between 1947 and then. The freedom earned at the price of three million people's blood had underscored once again that religion could never be the basis of nationhood. Language, culture, and history could be the only pillars for founding a nation. True, the religious affinity between the Punjabi Muslims and Bengali Muslims once led to the creation of Pakistan. Yet the Bengalis of this same land showed up the concept of two separate nations on the basis of the separate religious identity of Hindus and Muslims to demonstrate that they had never compromised with the Muslims of West Pakistan.

In 1971, Sudhamay was a doctor at S.K. Hospital at Mymensingh. He was quite busy whether at home or away. In the afternoons, he was a private medical practitioner in a medicine shop at Swadeshbazar. Kiranmayee had a six-month-old child to nurse; Suranjan, the eldest son, was then twelve. Sudhamay had plenty of responsibilities; he had to look after the hospital almost single-handedly. If time permitted, he would go to the shop of his friend Sharif to talk. It was either March 8 or 9. They had heard the clarion call of Sheikh Mujibur at the massive rally on the Dhaka Race Course grounds on March 7. At midnight the rally participants Sharif, Bablu, Faizul and Nemai knocked at the door of Sudhamay's Brahmo Palli residence. Sheikh Mujibur had declared: "If a single bullet is fired, and if my people are killed, then it's my request to you to convert each of your homes into a fortress and fight back the enemy with whatever is handy. This is the struggle to achieve liberation, this is the struggle for freedom." Their voices were trembling with excitement. Thumping on the table, they said, "Sudha'da, now something will have to be done." Sudhamay, too, realized that merely sitting wouldn't be of any help. Then on that dark night of March 25, when the men of the Pakistani army pounced on the Bengalis, there came another knock on the door of Sudhamay's house. They said in whispers, "Now is the time for going to war. There's no way out." He had his hands full with family responsibilities. Nor was he any longer a fit age for direct combat. Still, he couldn't concentrate on his hospital duties. He paced up and down the corridor. Off and on, he was overcome by a strong impulse to go to war. He said to Kiranmayee, "Would you be able to run the household, do you think, if I went somewhere else?" Kiranmayee turned cold with fear and replied, "Let's go to India; many from our neighborhood are going away." Sudhamay, too, had noticed the exodus of 1947 being repeated as Sukanta Chatterjee, Nirmalendu Bhowmik, Ranjan Chakravarty, all were leaving. He considered them to be cowards. Nemai told Sudhamay one day, "Pakistani army men are moving around the town. They're arresting only the Hindus. Come, let's also escape." The strength of confidence that his father had in 1947 surged into Sudhamay's voice. He told Nemai, "Go if you want to. Anyway, I'm not fleeing. We'll free the country after eliminating the Pakistani curse." It was decided that leaving his family members in the house of Faizul in Phulpur village, he would set out in the direction of Nalitabari along with Sharif, Bablu and Faizul. But he was entrapped by the Pakistani army men. He had gone out to buy a lock at Chaarpara crossing. That was to move out his family members on a buffalo cart under the cover of darkness after locking up the house. His chest was heaving in excitement and emotion. The town had the stillness of the graveyard, roads presenting a deserted look. A few shops had lowered their shutters just halfway. Suddenly they intercepted him, shouting, "Halt." There were three of them. Pulling the collar of his shirt from behind with a sudden jerk, they asked in their language, "What's your name—"

Sudhamay was at a loss what to say. In a flash he remembered their neighbors' suggestion to his wife about changing their identity with Muslim-sounding names like Fatima or Akhtar. Sudhamay thought his Hindu name was sure to spell disaster at this moment. Besides forcing his own name into oblivion, he did the same to his father Sukumar Dutta and grandfather Jyotirmay Dutta's names. He was startled by his own voice when he revealed his name as Sirajuddin Hussain. Hearing the name, one of the interceptors commanded in a gruff voice, "Drop your *lungi*." Sudhamay did not, but they pulled down his *lungi*. Only then did it dawn on him what prompted his friend Nemai, Sudhangshu and Ranjan to flee from their homes.

27

Many Hindus had left the country immediately after the partition of India. The border on the other side was then open for the escaping Hindus after the land was split up for the emergence of two countries, India and Pakistan, on a communal basis. The rich and educated middle class left in droves. The census report of 1981 gave the number of Hindus in the country as over 10.5 million, which came to about 12.1 percent of the country's total population. Twelve years after that, the figure must have been at least 20 million or even more. The official figures, however, always played down the number of Hindus. Sudhamay's guess was that about 20 percent of the population in this country consisted of Hindus. In 1901, the percentage of Hindus in East Bengal was 33. The number dropped to 31.5 in 1911 and in the continuing process of decline went further down to 30.6 in 1921, 29.4 in 1931 and 28 in 1941. Within forty-one years before the partition of India, the percentage of Hindus was reduced by five. But the decade following the partition, the percentage of Hindus went down from 28 percent to 22 percent. In ten years there had been a greater reduction in the number of Hindus than there had been in the previous forty years. During the Pakistani regime, the migration of Hindus from the country continued unabated. In 1961, their percentage fell to 18.5 and in 1974, 13.5. Only after Bangladesh achieved independence was the hemorrhaging of Hindus from the country somewhat stanched, with the rate of decline coming close to that of the prepartition period. If they were 13.5 percent of the population in 1974 and 12.1 in 1981, then it must be conceded that the number of Hindus leaving their homes had declined. But which year did this figure remain at the low level? How long could this be expected to continue, especially after the troubles in the years leading to the 1990 riots and now this in 1992?

Sudhamay felt a sharp pain on the left side of his chest. It was the return of the pain that he had suffered earlier. The back of his head was throbbing. Perhaps, his blood pressure had shot up. The telecast was being switched off when CNN referred to the Babri mosque. Sudhamay guessed that the government was being gracious to spare the Hindus from being pounced upon by the excited mobs. But the people, who were used to attacking the Hindus on the slightest pretext, would they wait for the CNN telecast scenes? Sudhamay lay down clasping the left side of his chest. Maya was still moving restlessly through the rooms and the verandah. She was frantically seeking to get away from the house. She could not do that unless Suranjan made a move. Sudhamay gazed helplessly at the sun-washed verandah. Maya's shadow was getting longer. Kiranmayee sat still as if the distressed look in her eyes were silently seeking to leave the place in order to survive. But where would Sudhamay go, abandoning his home? Age had consumed much of the earlier physical fitness that sent him running to take part in any protest rally or place him in the front rank of any movement launched against the Pakistani rulers. He couldn't be restricted by his family commitments. But he lacked that strength now. He believed that in the secular Bangladesh, the Hindus would be enjoying political, economic, social and religious freedoms. But slowly, the thin veneer of secularism fell off the state structure. The state religion of the country was now Islam. The fundamentalists who had opposed the Liberation War in 1971 and ducked underground after the country was free, were now emerging from their hideouts. It was they who moved about with unconcealed hauteur, and organized meetings and processions openly. They were the people who ransacked, looted and burned down the Hindu temples, houses, shops and establishments. Sudhamay lay down and closed his eyes. He didn't know what would happen this time. The demented Hindu fanatics had pulled down the Babri mosque. The Hindus of Bangladesh would now have to expiate their sins. The minorities like Sudhamay in Bangladesh couldn't avoid the vengeful claws of the fundamentalist Muslims in 1990. How would they be able to dodge the same murderous attacks this time also? Again people like Sudhamay would have to find a rat hole sort of shelter. But why? Only because they were Hindus? For the demolition of the Babri mosque by some other Hindus in another country? Why should that onus of destruction devolve on Sudhamay? He again looked at Maya and her constantly moving shadow, flitting to and fro, disappearing as soon as Maya entered the room.The shadow of fear had darkened her otherwise soft, lovely face. Her voice suddenly rang out, with rather emphatic loudness, "Then you rot here. I am leaving."

Kiranmayee retorted in a voice just as loud, "Where will you go?"

Maya combed her hair very fast. She said, "To Parul's house. If you've lost your will to live, I've got nothing to do with that. It seems Dada, too, won't go anywhere."

"And what are you going to do with your name Neelanjana?" asked Sudhamay, raising his head. The memory of once identifying himself as Sirajuddin flashed across his mind.

Maya said without faltering, "One can become a Muslim by chanting *La Ilaha Illallahu Muhammadur Rasul-*

ullah. I'll do that. From now on, I'll be known as Fatima Begem."

"Maya," Kiranmayee warned to put an end to her out-pourings.

Maya tilted her neck, looking straight at Kiranmayee, as if she had said nothing improper, and giving the impression instead of doing only what was natural. Her mother's sad face left Maya unmoved. Heaving a long sigh, Sudhamay looked first at Maya, then at Kiranmayee. Maya was fidgeting. A vibrant girl of twenty-one, she hadn't seen the country's partition in 1947. Nor had she been a witness to the communal riots of 1950 or '64 or the Liberation War of 1971. Since she had grown up, she had known Islam as the state religion and the way the members of the minority community, which included her family, tried to compromise with the society for their survival. She had seen the leaping flames of the 1990 disturbance. She was prepared to face any challenge to save her life. She didn't want to sacrifice herself in the fire of blind rage. The vacuousness of Sudhamay's gaze swept over Maya, making her invisible. No one called Maya stood before him. A sharp pain slowly spread waves of agony in his chest.

Suranjan couldn't give up his craving for tea; he eventually ambled to the toilet. It would have been better if he could have a cup of tea even before brushing his teeth. No sound of Maya's movement could be heard. Did the girl go away on her own? Suranjan brushed his teeth, taking a long time. A strange dreadful silence, felt only prior to a death in the family, had gripped the house. It seemed like everyone was awaiting inevitable death from a lightning strike. With the craving for a cup of tea still burning in him, Suranjan moved into Sudhamay's room. Lifting his feet onto the bed, he sat in a comfortable position. "Where is Maya?" Nobody cared to reply to his question. Kiranmayee sat staring blankly near the window. She rose and went to the kitchen suddenly without uttering a single word. Lying on his back, Sudhamay was staring at the roof with utter unconcern. He changed his position to rest on his side. None perhaps felt the need to inform him of the news. Suranjan felt he was failing to discharge his duty at this critical time. He had failed to take his family members to a safe place, which was a must for him at this hour. Or he was not feeling like doing anything like that. Suranjan was aware of a romantic relationship between Maya and a Muslim youth named Jehangir. Given a chance, she would certainly go out on a date with him. Once she was away from home, she needn't look behind. Some Muslims liked to show their superficial concern for the Hindus when the riots broke out. Jehangir wouldn't be an exception to this rule. And Maya would feel obliged. What if Maya's feelings of gratitude led her to marry Jehangir, who was two classes above her? But Suranjan feared Jehangir would never go to that extent. His almost certain marriage with Parvin was foiled at the last moment. It might be like that, he felt. His experience had taught him so. Parvin had asked for his conversion to Islam. But Suranjan's contention that neither of them need change religious identity was unacceptable to Parvin's family. Finally Parvin, through the haze of her tears, had to marry a Muslim businessman.

Suranjan gazed blankly at the strip of verandah. It was a rented house with no courtyard or bare earth to walk or run on. Kiranmayee entered the room with a cup of tea. Accepting the teacup from his mother Suranjan unconcernedly said, "December is nearing its end, yet we don't feel the pinch of winter. When I was a boy, I would drink the juice of date trees at this time."

Emitting a deep sigh, Kiranmayee said, "How could you expect to have that juice in a rented house? We had to come here after selling for a song our house surrounded by plantations we planted ourselves."

Sipping the tea, Suranjan could visualize date tree tappers bringing down pitchers of juice as excitement ran high in him and Maya. Clouds of steam would come out of his mouth if he talked during those winter days. Where could he find that playground, orchards of mango, blackberry, jackfruit, guava, betel nut, coconut? Sudhamay would say, "This is the seat of your ancestors, you will never leave this place."

But finally, Sudhamay was compelled to sell the house. When Maya was a child of six, she failed to return home from her school. She couldn't be traced anywhere in the town, neither in the houses of relatives nor any other who knew her. The whole family suffered from nerve-racking tension. Suranjan guessed that some knife-carrying youths who spent their time in idle talk near the gate of Edward School must have carried her off. Maya came back alone after two days. She couldn't throw any light on who her kidnappers were and from where they had abducted her. She behaved abnormally for two full months afterward. Her sleep was disturbed by sudden spasms of shock. She would feel scared even at the look of any person. During the night, stones were pelted at the house. Anonymous letters came with the threat that kidnappers would have to be paid ransom to stop them from repeating the act. Sudhamay went to the police station to lodge a formal complaint. But the police showed no interest beyond noting down the names of suspects. The mischief-makers would pluck the fruits from the orchard and flowers from the garden, trample the vegetable patches whenever they felt like it. No one could restrain them. Referring the matter to the locals was hardly of any help. They just pleaded their inability to do anything to stop this torment. There had been no change in the situation as the same trend persisted. Suranjan, aided by a few friends, made an attempt to put a stop to these intrusions. But for the disapproval of Sudhamay, they might have succeeded. He decided to seek out a transfer from Mymensingh by selling the house. A protracted litigation also prompted him to go in for the sale. Shaukat Ali, a next-door neighbor, had been constantly trying to dispossess him of his property with faked documents. A prolonged court case to thwart this attempt left Sudhamay totally exhausted and bitter. Suranjan wasn't in favor of selling the house outright. He was then a college student, full of life. He had just been elected a member of the student union; he could have soundly thrashed those ruffians quite easily. But Sudhamay became frantic to sell the property. He would be better leaving this place for Dhaka. His medical practice in this town was said to have taken a downward plunge. He spent his time at the Swadeshy bazar medical stores idle most of the time, examining only an occasional patient who invariably was a poor Hindu and too badly off to pay his consultation charges. Sudhamay's restiveness kept Suranjan from putting pressure on him. He could still recall their sprawling house built over two-thirds of an acre. The day Sudhamay sold his house, which could fetch him at least a million takas, to Raisuddin for one-fifth of its worth, he told Kiranmayee,

"Now, get ready, start packing up things." Kiranmayee cried inconsolably. Suranjan was incredulous, unable to think they were indeed leaving the house for good. He was not inclined to give up the playgrounds familiar from his childhood, the great river Brahamputra, his friends. Maya, whose misfortune had goaded Sudhamay to make this drastic decision, was equally unwilling to bid adieu to the house. In protest, she said, "I won't leave Sufia," her schoolmate who lived nearby. The two of them played with their dolls and toy pots and pans. She, too, became very much involved with Maya. But Sudhamay stayed firm although his roots in the place were the deepest. He said, "I want to live in peace with my children in the remaining days of my life."

But was it secure anywhere? Suranjan knew how illusory his father's hopes for peace were. In the city of Dhaka, where Sudhamay heaved a sigh of relief after his arrival and which was the capital of a free country, he had to change into *pyjamas* from his long-accustomed *dhoti*. Suranjan could understand his father's intense agony even through the wall of his silence. An insurmountable barrier had always been there in front of them which neither he nor his father could get over.

Suranjan was jolted out of reverie, spun around the sunlit verandah by the shouts from an approaching procession. Suranjan trained his ears as Sudhamay and Kiranmayee did the same, to grasp what the processionists were shouting about. Suranjan noticed Kiranmayee closing the windows. But even through the closed window, the message spread by the processionists marching past their house along the road was unmistakable: catch a Hindu or two for your breakfast and dinner. Suranjan found his fa-

35

ther shivering. Kiranmayee stood still with her back to the window. Suranjan recalled identical slogans shouted during the 1990 violence. They wanted Hindus for breakfast, meaning their total extermination. If Suranjan came in their way, they would gobble him up. Who else could these people be other than the local boys like Jabbar, Ramjan, Alamgir, Kabir or Abedin? They were his friends, just like younger brothers. He would talk with them any time, sometimes about local problems, and they would arrive at a solution in a collective decision. Yet the same people, on this beautiful morning of December 7, were keen on having Suranjan for their breakfast.

Reaching Dhaka, Sudhamay came straightaway to Tantibazar where one of his cousins resided. His brother, Asit Ranjan, found a small house for him and said hesitantly, "Sudhamay, you come from an affluent family. Will you be able to stay in a rented house?" Sudhamay replied, "Why not, aren't other people living in such houses?"

"That's true, but you haven't been in need since your birth. And why, first of all, have you sold your house? Maya is just a small girl, not at all an eye-catching woman. I don't think anything would've happened to her. We sent our daughter Utpala to Calcutta. She couldn't go to the college here because of constant kidnapping threats from the local boys. We were really scared. Now she is in her maternal uncle's house in the Tiljala area in Calcutta. We feel scared as our daughters grow up, my brother."

Sudhamay couldn't brush off Asit Ranjan's warnings. Well, there would certainly be anxious moments. But the parents of Muslim girls were not immune from such apprehension. A Muslim girl student of Sudhamay was

36

nearly stripped by some ruffians, who were also Muslims. So Sudhamay sought to comfort himself with the argument that it was not a question of Muslims torturing the Hindus. The powerful people have done almost the same to the weak all along. The women, being weak, were easy targets of torture for the mighty men. Asit Ranjan had sent both his daughters away to Calcutta. He was quite well off from the earnings of his gold shop at Islam Bazar. He had an old double-storeyed house over whose repair he didn't bother much. He didn't feel enthused to construct a new house either. One day he advised Sudhamay, "Brother, better to save money than to spend it. Remit the money that you have received from the sale of your property if you can. My relatives there will find suitable land for you."

Sudhamay asked, "What do you mean by 'there'?"

Asit Ranjan replied softly, "Why, in Calcutta. I have also bought some land."

This time Sudhamay's voice rose in anger: "That means you will earn from this land to spend there. You can easily be branded as a traitor."

Asit Ranjan was taken aback by Sudhamay's outburst. He had never heard any Hindu speak in such a way. Most of them were keen on saving the money they earned instead of recklessly spending it here. The situation was so uncertain, it was difficult to predict what was going to happen next. What guarantee was there that any bid to put down roots here wouldn't be defeated?

Sudhamay occasionally brooded over why he didn't feel any remorse over leaving his Mymensingh home. The trouble over Maya was not altogether unanticipated. Both communities might suffer from such incidents of kidnapping. Did he suffer from insecurity in his own house? He would pose the question to himself without letting anyone know. In the small, cramped house at Tantibazar, Sudhamay thought again and again about why he left his home to stay in an utterly unknown area. Was he trying to hide himself? Why did he feel like a refugee despite having his own home? Or was he overcome by the fear of losing the court case that lingered over the fake document of his neighbor Shaukat? How galling it was, he thought, to lose a case that had to do with one's own home. But if he looked at the whole thing positively, it was obviously wise to have left the place with self-respect intact instead of fleeing after losing the case. Sudhamay had seen his first cousin lose possession of his own house in similar circumstances. The poor man had his house in the Akur Takur area at Tangail. His next-door neighbor, Jamir Munshi, wanted to extend his land by a single yard. The case dragged on in the court for five years, only to be decided in favor of Jamir Munshi at the end. Tarapada Ghosal, after breaking all his ties with this land, had finally migrated to India. Had he sold out his possessions at home because of the fear that his property would ultimately slip from his grasp like Tarapada Ghosal's? That might have been it. It had to be conceded, however, that Sudhamay had lost much of his former stature and importance. His friends were deserting him. Given an opportunity, a Hindu family would rush for it to get out of the country. Quite a few died. Sudhamay had to carry the bodies of the dead along with others every now and then, shouting the funeral chant *Bol hori, hori bol.* The living were always in a depressed state of mind, as if their existence had become totally devoid of any purpose. Talking with them, Sudhamay, too, suffered from the fear of being crushed by a giant in the dead of night very soon.

India was everyone's dream; they schemed secretly to somehow cross the border. Hearing their whispers, Sudhamay had retorted, "When the Liberation War broke out, you bolted for India. When the country became free, you returned, marching like heroes. Now every now and then, you try to rush back there if anyone just gives you a mild poke. All of you are cowards."

Sudhamay's bold stand distanced his friends like Jatin Debnath, Tushar Kar and Khagesh Kiran from him. No more did they speak their minds to him. Sudhamay felt all the more isolated. In his own home town, the rift in his relationship with Muslim friends like Shakur, Faisal, Majid and Guffar, too, was widening. His impromptu visits to their houses were discouraged on some pretext or other. Some would say, "Please wait in the drawing room. Meanwhile, I shall pray my *Namaz*." Others would say, "You have come today. But there is *Milad* in my house today." When the one-time leftists sought refuge in religion, now that they were getting older, Sudhamay felt increasingly lonely. The gradual erosion in the rational sense, intelligence and conscience in his own town hurt him deeply. That was why he wanted to escape from his beloved town, but not from the country, before a gloomy death triumphed over the dreams he still held frantically to.

Suranjan, at the beginning, would argue over this compulsive stay in the tiny rented house after leaving their mansion. Later, he, too, became used to living here. By that time, he had enrolled at the university. He had a new circle of friends. And he, too, learned to love the place. He had become involved in politics. He was called away to attend meetings and processions every now and then. Kiranmayee was opposed to the sale of the house. During the night she shed tears for what had happened to the scaffold covered by the broad bean creepers she had grown. The guavas they grew in their orchards were the largest in the locality. Who knew what was the condition of the coconut trees? Did the present owners apply brine water at their roots any more? Such thoughts brought no less anguish to Sudhamay.

Opting for a transfer to Dhaka, Sudhamay deluded himself into believing that perhaps something could be done to get his long-deserved promotion in the medical service. He had been to the Health Ministry, sometimes waiting there interminably before a petty clerk, or at most an assistant personal secretary, and never receiving any direct reply to his frantic queries regarding the movement of his personal file. Mostly he had to be content with a perfunctory "the matter is being looked into" sort of reply. Some of them would say, "Doctor, I have been feeling pain in my left chest, my daughter has an upset stomach. Why don't you prescribe something for us?" Sudhamay was more than eager to oblige them by readily scribbling prescriptions on his printed pads. But his fervent appeal, "Shall I get what I'm hoping for?" would invariably bring forth replies like "Do you think the matter rests in our hands?"

Sudhamay would later come to know of the promotions being given to his juniors. Before his eyes, in blatant violation of his rightful claim, Dr. Karimuddin and Dr. Yakub Molla were promoted to associate professors and they started functioning in that capacity. Sudhamay succeeded only in wearing out the soles of his shoes with his pointless walking exercises to solicit petty officials. They constantly warded him off with various petty excuses like, "Please come tomorrow, your file will be moved to the secretary's table today"; "not today as there's a meeting, better come tomorrow"; "The minister is out of the country, come next month," and so on. Hearing such excuses again and again, Sudhamay realized that he, in fact, faced a bleak future. Following this wild goose chase after the elusive promotion for a year and a half, he eventually found out that the fortunate ones could make it easily even if they were incompetent. As he was nearing his retirement, he hoped for the post of associate professor, but without actually demanding it, since he was a rightful claimant. Yet his juniors overtook him.

At last, Sudhamay retired as an assistant professor. On his last day, his colleague Madhab Chandra Pal told him, after putting a wreath of marigolds around his neck, "It's futile to hope for better prospects in this land of Muslims. What we're getting is more than we can expect." He then burst into laughter. He, too, was serving as an assistant professor without making any fuss. But as his name came up for promotion, objections cropped up immediately. Another factor against him was that he was said to have visited the Soviet Union. Sudhamay later thought Madhab Chandra had indeed said the right thing. There was nothing discriminatory in the law in Bangladesh about the promotion of Hindus in the high ranks of administration, the police or the army. But the reality was something different: the ministries had no Hindu in the post of secretary or even additional secretary. There were only three joint secretaries and a few more deputy secretaries. Sudhamay was more or less certain even these few officers did not hope for any further promotion. There were only six deputy commissioners in the country. And a single Hindu judge on the high court. They were sometimes taken into the lower ranks of the police force, but how many of them could rise to the level of superintendent of police? Sud-

41

hamay realized rather late he had not been promoted to the post of associate professor only because he was a Hindu. There would be no such impediment were he a Mohammad Ali or Salimullah Chowdhury. Hindu businessmen, unless they had Muslim partners, were denied trade licenses. Nor did they get loans from state-regulated banks, the industrial financing outfits in particular.

Sudhamay Dutta arranged things in a manner befitting his style of living in his Tantibazar house. Although he had forsaken his home town, he found he could not forsake his country. He would say, "Why Mymensingh alone? All of Bangladesh is my country."

Kiranmayee heaved a long sigh and said, "My dreams about releasing fish into the pond, planting a vegetable garden so that my children can get better nourishment, have now turned to dust in this rented house that is eating up the bulk of our meager income." Occasionally she would suggest to her husband as the night advanced, "The money you have from the sale of the house and your retirement benefits make quite a tidy amount between them. Why don't we go to Calcutta? We have plenty of relatives there."

Sudhamay would counter, "Don't even think that your relatives would treat you even to a single meal. If you're thinking of staying with them, you will be disappointed to find that you are unwelcome in their house. They can at most offer you some tea, nothing more than that."

"If we take our money with us, why should we depend on others?"

"I won't go. You can, if you like. I've left my home, but that doesn't mean I'll leave my country," Sudhamay said in a loud voice.

After Tantibazar, Sudhamay lived in Armanitola for the

next six years. He had been living in Tikatuli for the last seven years. By that time, he had developed heart trouble. He couldn't keep up with his appointments at his clinic in a medicine store at Gopibag which he was supposed to attend in the afternoons. Patients now mostly visited him in his house. A table was kept in the drawing room for Sudhamay to examine his patients. The room also had a divan on one side. Cane sofas occupied the other side. There were plenty of books on shelves. Besides medicine, he had collections on literature, sociology, and politics which stood in tightly packed rows. Sudhamay spent most of his time in that room. In the evening, Nishith Babu, with his loose sandals flapping, would stroll in leisurely. So would Akhtaruzzaman, Shahidul Islam, and Haripada frequently. Talks revolved around national politics. Kiranmayee would make tea for them, without sugar, of course, in view of their advanced age. No less worn out by age was Sudhamay himself.

Hearing the approach of the procession, Sudhamay sprang up. Suranjan clenched his jaws. Kiranmayee's chest was heaving up and down like a pigeon's, in anger and fear. Didn't Sudhamay, too, feel any apprehension? Should he not also have any reason to be angry?

Day Two

Most of Suranjan's friends were Muslims. Of course, they couldn't be strictly called Muslims because of their indifference to the religious practices. Even those who were a bit off Hindus never hesitated to accept Suranjan as someone close to their heart. True, Pulak, Kajal, Ashim and Jaidev, too, were friends of Suranjan; but he was more at home with the crowd of Kamal, Belal, Hyder or Raibul. It was his Muslim friends who always rushed to his side at the time of need, not Hindus. Sudhamay once needed hospitalization in Suhrawardy Hospital in the middle of the night. Doctor Haripada suspected he had a myocardial infarction that called for immediate removal to the hospital. When Suranjan asked for Kajal's help, he yawned and said, "How are you going to shift him to hospital at such an unearthly hour of the night. Wait until the morning when some arrangements can be made." But hearing the news, Belal lost no time in speeding to Suranjan's place in his car. He ran from pillar to post to get Sudhamay admitted to the hospital, constantly comforting him, saying, "Uncle, don't feel worried at all. Please treat me as your own son." Suranjan was overwhelmed with gratitude. During Sudhamay's stay in the hospital, Belal regularly inquired after his health, entreated the doctors known to him to take special care of the patient, visited him whenever he could carve out some time and lent his car for the use of his family members to make trips to the hospital. Who would have done so much? Kajal, too, was quite affluent, but would he show that much concern for Suranjan? Rabiul footed the entire hospital bill. He suddenly appeared one day at Suranjan's Tikatuli house. He said, "I heard your father was in the hospital." Before Suranjan could say anything, Rabiul placed an envelope on the table and said, "Don't think of your friends as distant and unconcerned."

Then he stormed out as suddenly as he had entered. Opening the envelope, Suranjan was staggered to find five thousand takas. It was not for such help alone, but Suranjan had greater mental and intellectual affinity with his Muslim friends. His closeness with Rabiul, Kamal and Hyder outweighed that with Ashim, Kajal or Jaidev. Not only that. The intensity of love that he had felt for Parvin would never be the same with a Deepti, Archana, Geeta or Sunanda.

Suranjan never got used to accepting someone as a member of a particular community. In his boyhood, he was not at all aware of his identity as a Hindu. When he was a student in a lower grade at Mymensingh school, one day he got into an animated argument over study matters with a boy called Khaled. At the height of their altercation, Khaled called him names, hurling choice epithets like "son of a dog," "son of a pig" and so on. Suranjan paid him back in kind, trading the abusive "son of a dog" with him. Khaled, in final desperation, called him a "Hindu." Suranjan lost no time on hurling back the identical tribute, being under the impression that the word "Hindu" was simply another form of insult. Much later he realized Hindu was the name of a community of which he was a member. His conception, however, finally turned into a conviction with the passage of time that he, in fact, was a member of the human race and that his national identity was Bengali. No religion nurtured its growth. He was keen on viewing the Bengalis as a noncommunal, all-absorbing nationality. He firmly believed Bengali was an inclusive epithet. Yet the Bengalis themselves had always treated foreign co-religionists as their own and those conforming to other faiths as something different. This wrong conception, awareness and belief had divided the Bengalis into Hindus and Muslims.

Today was December 8. "The committee for the extermination of killers" had called a general strike all over the country. Jamat-i-Islami, however, gave a separate call for a strike in protest against the demolition of the Babri mosque. They were passing through the strike period. Suranjan went through limbering-up motions before leaving bed. He thought of making the rounds of his dear city which he had not seen for the last two days. In the other room, Kiranmayee was scared stiff. Suranjan was not sure whether Sudhamay was gripped by a feeling of insecurity. He had made it known at home he was not going to look for safety elsewhere. Should he become a target of death, he would rather die. If the Muslims were going to kill all of them, let them go ahead. Maya had left on her own. Her atavistic urge for survival had prompted her to take shelter in a Muslim household. She was trying to save her life under the protective umbrella of her friends like Parul Rifat. Poor Maya.

When Suranjan, after a two-day stretch in bed, was getting ready to go out, a startled Kiranmayee asked, "Where are you going?"

"Let me see how the city is going through the strike."

"Please don't go out, Suro, no one can can say what's going to happen."

"Whatever happens, let it happen. One is going to die some day or other. Don't be so afraid. Your fright makes me angry," Suranjan replied, combing his hair.

Kiranmayee shivered. She came rushing to snatch the comb from Suranjan's grip. She implored him, "Suranjan, please listen to me. Be cautious. I've heard even in the midst of the strike, they are ransacking shops, burning down temples. Better stay put at home. There's no need to see what's happening in the city."

Suranjan had been persistently disobedient. Why should he pay attention to Kiranmayee's warnings? He ignored her entreaties and went out. Sudhamay was sitting alone in the outer room. He, too, was watching Suranjan's exit, dumbfounded.

When he stepped out of the house, the overpowering desolation, added to the ghostly stillness, hit Suranjan physically, casting a pall over the otherwise pleasant afternoon. He was seized a bit by a creeping feeling of fear. The fear seemed to be real. Still, he decided to stick to his decision of moving around the city. This time no one turned up for their rescue. Neither Belal nor Kamal, nor anyone else. Even if they had come, he wouldn't have accompanied them. Why should he go? Such troubles would break out intermittently and they would have to rush out with their bags; the idea revolted him. He had committed an asinine blunder by fleeing to Kamal's house last year. Had Kamal come this time, he wouldn't have hesitated to say bluntly right to his face, "Instead of killing us with a simultaneous show of mercy, why not place the entire Hindu population before the firing squads and finish them off? Once all of them are dead, you will get rid of a nagging trouble for good. You'll be spared the problems of killing us and then go in for mercy missions with great fanfare."

As Suranjan came up the road, a group of boys standing nearby shouted, "There goes a Hindu, catch him and kill him." The boys belonged to this locality. Many faces had become familiar to him during his seven-year stay here. There was a boy called Alam, who would turn up every now and then to ask for a donation. They had a club here. Suranjan used to sing at their cultural functions. He thought of teaching some of the boys the songs of D. L. Roy and Hemanga Biswas. Off and on, they would gather at his house asking for some favor or other. Sudhamay had given them medical assistance free of charge for their being residents of the locality. And it was the same chaps who were now mockingly threatening to kill him. Suranjan walked rapidly in the opposite direction, not driven by fear, but feeling shame. He was shamed by the thought of local boys beating him up. He felt the shame not for himself, but for his supposed attackers. Shame gained a new dimension not for the tortured people, but for those rogues inflicting the torture.

Walking gingerly, Suranjan came to the open square Shapla Chattar. The air was charged with tension. Small

48

groups of men stood here and there. The road littered with
brickbats, burned wood, and glass fragments suggested
something terrible must have happened just a little while
ago. An occasional youth was running helter skelter. Some
stray dogs, too, were racing along the middle of the road.
A few rickshaws were plying either this way or that way,
ringing their bells. Suranjan was at a loss to perceive what
had happened and where. Only the street dogs felt no fear
of being members of a particular community. Suranjan
could guess that these dogs were running merrily at the
sheer joy of finding the road empty, giving them greater
freedom of movement. Suranjan, too, was overcome by a
desire to run just for the joy of running. Finding the nor-
mally busy road at Matijhil totally devoid of traffic,
Suranjan felt like playing football as he had done in his
boyhood, using that oversized variant of orange called
Batabi for the ball, or cricket with makeshift strips of firewood. Toying with such idle thoughts, Suranjan suddenly
noticed a burned-out building on his left. Signboard, doors
and windows—everything had turned into heaps of ashes.
It had been the office of Indian Airlines. Some people stood
around the charred ruin, gesticulating and laughing. The
eyebrows of some of them were raised in suspicion upon
seeing Suranjan, who walked straight ahead quite fast. He
sought to give the impression that he was not the least concerned with such cases of arson. He was going to see what
else had been consigned to the flames, perhaps liking the
smell of the burned bricks and woods as he felt pleased at
the smell of gasoline. Walking further, he found a large
crowd outside the office of the Communist Party of
Bangladesh. Brickbats were everywhere on the road. Once
there was a bookstore on the pavement from which he had

bought many books. A partially burned book struck his foot. It was Maxim Gorky's *Mother*. For a moment he thought he was Pavel Vlasov, and he imagined himself setting fire to his mother and later crushing her beneath his feet. The thought sent goosepimples all over his body. He stood nonplused with the book lying in front of him. The area was tense with milling crowds and whispers. What had happened and what more might have happened were the topics talked about. The CPB office couldn't escape the mob fury unleashed by the fundamentalists, although the communists had changed their strategy by using Islam. When Comrade Farhad died, the mourners observed all the Muslim religious formalities and rituals, including a community feast. Even after that the flames of communalism licked the Communist party office. Speechless, Suranjan stared at the burned office. Suddenly he confronted Kaisar with his disheveled hair, unshaven face, and eyes bloodshot like someone suffering from conjunctivitis. He asked Suranjan anxiously, "Why have you come out?"

"Am I debarred from going out?" came the pat retort from Suranjan.

"It's not that. But these beasts can hardly be trusted. These religious fanatics, do they actually observe the religion for which they make such a big noise? The terrorists of the Jamat Youth Commandos did all this vandalism yesterday afternoon. It was they who set fire to the party office, pavement book stall, Indian Airlines office. All the forces against the country's freedom always lie in wait to raise hell over any issue that may come in handy to them. As if shouting the loudest, they'll reach everyone."

They walked toward Topkhana side by side. Suranjan asked, "What are the other places they have set fire to?"

"In Chittagong, Tulshidham, Panchanandham, Kaibal-yadham temples were smashed to smithereens. Malipara, the cremation ground temple, Kalibari, the Chatteshwari temple and the Vishnu temple as well as temples in Hajar-ilane and Fakirpara were sacked before being set on fire. Of course, processions preaching maintenance of communal harmony have also been led to defuse the tension."

Suranjan sighed. Kaisar, while pushing his unruly shock of hair back with his right hand, said, "Not only the temples, they have set fire to the houses of boatmen and fishermen as well at Majhinghet and Jelepara. At least fifty huts have been burned to cinders."

"And?" asked Suranjan utterly unconcerned.

"The Madhab temple and the Durga temple of Jaidev-pur were attacked. The Annapurna temple in the Sherpur agricultural center and Kali temple at Sherighat Ashram have been destroyed. The temples of Ramkrishna Mission at Faridpur have been looted. The head of the mission and his students have been seriously injured."

"And?" Suranjan's voice continued to be disinterested.

"At Narasinghdi, all the houses and temples at Cha-lakchar and Monohardi have been set ablaze. The temple at Marapara in Narayangunj was razed to the ground. The old Abhay Ashram at Comilla was set ablaze. Similar reprehensible incidents have occurred in Noakhali."

"What sort of incidents?"

"Adhar Chand Ashram and seven Hindu houses in the Sudharam police station area have been set on fire. All the Hindu houses in Gangapur village were looted first and then set on fire. Other sites of arson and looting include the Shib-Kali temple and Bindopur Akhra at Sonapur; the Kali temple at Choumohani; the Durgabari temple at Burgapur;

51

temples at Qutobpur and Gopalpur; the drug factory of Dr.
P. K. Sinha; Akhanda Ashram; temples in the Chaiani area;
ten more temples at Choumohani, Babupur, Tetuia,
Mehdipur, Rajgunj Bazar, Tangirpar, Kajirhat, Rasulpur,
Jamidarpur and Porbari as well as eighteen Hindu houses
in these places. A woman, too, was consumed by the flames
along with a car and a shop. Thirteen of seventeen houses
in Bhabardi were set on fire after being looted. Women
were molested. Biplab Bhowmik, a Hindu, was stabbed. All
the houses and temples at Birahimpur were attacked. The
torrent of violence swept over Jagannath temple, three
shops in Charparvati village and a club house, two other
temples at Charkukri and Mucchapur, Jaikali temple. All
the Hindus at Surajpur were beaten up, their houses were
looted before they were consigned to the flames."

"Oh."

Suranjan did not feel like uttering anything more. He
felt as he did in his childhood, kicking a pebble constantly
as he walked. He only half-listened to the grisly inventory
of arson and destruction intoned by Kaisar. He was not at
all inclined to listen. Both of them stood outside the Press
Club. They watched the crowd of journalists, listened to
the drone of their talk. They also heard bits of news,
someone saying that up to now, some two hundred people
had been killed in riots in India. Thousands had been injured. All the fundamentalist organizations like Rashtriya
Swayamsevak Sangh and Shib Sena had been banned. The
leader of the Opposition in the Indian Parliament, L. K.
Advani, had resigned from his post; someone else was
saying how some local Muslims had saved Dipak Ghosh,
an acolyte of Tulsidham at Chittagong, by passing him off
as a Muslim. The fanatic Jamat followers tried to torture

him. The man, however, was not spared the customary beating.

The sight of Suranjan strolling freely shocked the people who knew him. They advised him to go back home, warning him of the impending danger.

Suranjan said nothing to them; he felt extremely embarrassed. Why should he, being Suranjan Dutta, be advised to return home and remain there, while Kaisar, Latif, Belal and Shaheen could move unhindered, discuss the incidents, and join processions against communalism? Was Suranjan not as conscientious, free-thinking, rational as they were? He bought a single cigarette, lit it from the coir rope at the shop's side with one end burning for precisely this purpose and leaned against a wall with utter nonchalance. He felt himself totally isolated, even in the midst of people, many of them known to or even intimate with him, as if he alone had been barred from discussing the Babri mosque demolition, heatedly debating the fallout from the incident in this country. Despite his eagerness to participate in the talk swirling around him, he couldn't. Something was restricting him. Suranjan could realize everyone was keeping him out, pitying him, not accepting him as an equal. He took a long puff on the cigarette and threw out a smoke ring. In the midst of the bubbling excitement around him, he allowed his weight to rest on the wall. Many people were vaguely staring at him. They were surprised at his cheek in coming out when all the Hindus had holed themselves up in fright.

Kaisar melted into a group of people. A procession was being formed. Journalists were running to and fro with their bags and cameras. Suranjan found Lutfar among them, yet didn't feel like calling to him. But noticing him,

Lutfar himself came forward. In wide-eyed surprise, he asked, "Dada, you are here?"

"Why? Shouldn't I be?"

Anxiety was writ large on Lutfar's face. He again asked, "I hope there wasn't any problem at your home?" Lutfar's way of talk had an avuncular shade. This Suranjan could guess. Previously he had been rather the shy type. He had always been quite humble and excessively polite while talking with Suranjan without looking at his eyes. He got a job at the newspaper *Ekata* (Unity) on the recommendation of Suranjan to the paper's editor. Lutfar lit up an imported expensive cigarette. Coming close to him, he said, "Suranjanda, have you experienced any inconvenience?"

"What sort of inconvenience?" Suranjan asked, smiling.

Lutfar was visibly shocked at Suranjan's casualness. He said, "You know how it is, Dada. I mean, the state of the country." Suranjan crushed the cigarette under his foot. Lutfar's voice, generally low, sounded unusually loud to him. Blowing out cigarette smoke, Lutfar said, frowning at him, "Dada, you better stay in some other house today. Staying at your home won't be the right thing for the present. Can't you make arrangements to stay for two nights in some Muslim house in your neighborhood?"

Suranjan stared at the coir rope with a fiery tail and said "No" in a detached voice.

"No, you say?" Lutfar appeared to be worried. Suranjan could sense Lutfar was trying to be his custodian. Anyone now could emerge as his guardian angel and give him unsolicited advice: "Better hide yourself elsewhere rather than stay at home. Don't venture out of your house for a few days. Never give out your real identity. Come out only when the situation begins to return to normal."

Suranjan wanted to light another cigarette. But the urge died then and there at Lutfar's grave didactic tone. He could feel the pinch of cold. Folding his arms across his chest, he observed the green and deeper green colors of trees. He had always enjoyed the wintertime. Homemade cakes in the morning, the warmth of the sun-baked quilt at night, ghost stories told by his mother—this chain of thoughts gave a thrilling feeling to Suranjan.

Standing in front of Lutfar, a bearded youth with a bag hanging from his shoulder started giving a grisly commentary on the extent of devastation: Crowds of people marching in procession were throwing brickbats, looting Dhakeshwari temple, Siddeshwari Kali temple, Ramkrishna Mission, Mahaprakash monastery, Narinda Goudiya monastery, the hermitage of the saint Bholagiri. Swamibag hermitage has been plundered. Twenty-five houses in Shanir Akhra had been looted and subsequently burned down. Rishipara at Narinda and Jelepara at Narinda had not been spared either. Maranchand's sweetmeat shops at Farmgate, Paltan and Nababpur, the Deshbandhu sweet shop at Tikatuli, too, had been looted, smashed and set on fire in this dance of violence. The temple at Thataribazar was in flames.

Emitting a deep sigh of regret, Lutfar said, "Oh."

Suranjan listened with his ears open to the deep sigh of Lutfar. He had no idea what he should do now. Should he stay planted where he was, take part in the procession now being formed or just escape? Sit alone in a deep jungle, bereft of friends and relatives? The youth with the bag disappeared in a group. Lutfar, too, was almost making a move the same way. He was unnerved by Suranjan's expressionless features.

Everywhere muffled tension could be felt. He wanted to participate in the talks about destruction of houses and temples, about arson and looting. He wished he could speak out spontaneously: "These religionists should be whipped to put an end to their insanity. They are, in fact, the greatest frauds and deceivers." But he couldn't do that. Everybody was looking at him with sidewise glances, pitying him. They were giving the impression that it was not at all safe for him to stay here any longer, as if he were not fit to stay here, or get worked up like them, or take part in their procession. Till the other day, he had been an artful speaker on the stage or talking circles around everyone on the topics of language, culture; yet an invincible power had kept him tongue-tied. Nor was anyone asking him to say anything or lodge a strong protest.

Detaching himself from the crowd, Kaisar came forward forward and whispered to Suranjan, "People are gathering at Baitul Mokarram where a meeting against the demolition of the Babri mosque is about to begin. It's better for you to go home."

"Won't you go?" asked Suranjan.

Kaisar said, "Well, no. Won't I have to make arrangements for taking out a procession for the communal harmony?"

Two other youths, Lyton and Mahatab, were behind Kaisar. They, too, said, "Speaking frankly, we are asking you to leave this place for your safety. We have heard that the sweet shop 'Jal Khabar' has been set on fire. Incidents have occurred in nearby areas. Can you think what'll happen if they spot you? Mobs armed with daggers, clubs and large choppers are openly roaming around."

Kaisar called a rickshaw with the idea of sending him

away. But Lutfar intervened, pulling his hand, saying, "Come, Dada, go home straightaway. I wonder what made you come out at this time."

Many others were equally eager to force Suranjan back home. Even those who didn't know him came rushing to know what the matter was. His friends explained that being a Hindu, he was not safe here. Everyone nodded affirmatively. Yes, he should leave immediately. But Suranjan hadn't come out to be forced to go home. Suranjan pulled himself away as soon as they were coaxing him toward the rickshaw. He wrenched his hand free from their grip.

Sudhamay wanted to stretch himself fully, yet he couldn't. He was restless. The thought that Suranjan had gone out at this time troubled him. After he had left, there were cautious knocks on the door. Sudhamay jumped out of his bed thinking Suranjan had come back. Not, it was not him, but Akhtaruzzaman, a retired professor over sixty years old, their neighbor. Entering the room, the professor put the latch on himself. He asked in a muffled voice, "I hope nothing is wrong?"

"No, what will happen?" Sudhamay said nodding his head, casting his glance over the bed at the table and the books lying on top.

Akhtaruzzaman pulled up a chair. Suffering from cervical spondilitis, he said, moving his eyeballs back and forth but keeping his neck straight, "Don't you know what's happened to the Babri mosque? Nothing is left. What a shame!"

Sudhamay emitted an indistinct sound.

"Why don't you say anything? Are you supporting this?"

"Why should I support it?"

"Then why are you keeping mum?"

"Evil people have done evil work. All I can do is feel very sorry about the whole thing."

"If such things are allowed to happen in a secular state, what a shame! The entire national ethos, all those political announcements, Supreme Court, Parliament, democratic tradition—all bunkum. Whatever you may say, Sudhababu, compared to the spate of riots in India, virtually nothing like that has happened in this country."

"Yes, since 1964, this is the first large-scale riot here."

"It is better to say 1950, rather than '64. The most positive feature of the '64 riot was the spontaneous resistance of the people to communalism. The day the riots began, all the dailies under the initiative of Manik Mia, Jahur Hussain Chowdhury and Abdus Salam carried the headline, 'EAST PAKISTAN, RESIST THIS MADNESS.' In his bid to save a neighboring Hindu family, 55-year-old Amir Hussain Chowdhury sacrificed his own life. Oh ho."

Sudhamay felt the intensity of the pain in his chest all the more. He leaned on the divan. He would have felt somewhat better with a cup of hot tea. But who would serve it? Kiranmayee was worried to the breaking point for Suranjan. Why did he have to go out alone? It would have been better to take Hyder with him. Her worries infected Sudhamay. Suranjan had always been highly emotional; he could never be held back at home. Sudhamay was quite aware of the nature of his son, but his worries could hardly be comforted by such thoughts.

He returned to the topic raised by Akhtaruzzaman: "It is said that peace is the basic tenet of all religion Yet it is in the name of religion that there has been so much disturbance, bloodshed and persecution. It is indeed a pity that even at the close of the twentieth century we've had to witness such atrocities because of religion. Flying the flag of religion has always proved the easiest way to crush to nothingness human beings as well as the spirit of humanity."

Akhtaruzzaman replied with a noncommittal muffled sound.

Kiranmayee came in with two cups of tea. "Has your chest pain increased or will you have sedatives?" she asked, placing the cups on the divan.

Akhtaruzzaman said to her, "Boudi, you don't wear sanka and sindur, do you?"

Kiranmayee looked down and answered, "Not since 1975."

"Thank God! At least you can be sure of your safety. It's better to be safe than sorry."

Kiranmayee smiled a wan smile. Simultaneously, a similar smile appeared on Sudhamay's lips. Akhtaruzzaman drank his tea in quick gulps. Sudhamay's chest pain remained. He said, "I gave up my *dhoti*, too, quite some time back. For the sake of dear life, my friend."

Akhtaruzzaman put down his cup and said, "I'll be off now. I think I will check up on Binod-babu before I get back"

After the professor had gone, Sudhamay lay back on his bed. His tea, which he had not touched, cooled on the table. Kiranmayee shut the door and sat down. Her back was to the light and her face was covered in shadow. There was a time when Kiranmayee sang devotional songs. She was the daughter of a well-known police officer in Brahmanharia and had been married at sixteen. After they were married, Sudhamay had encouraged her to learn Rabindra

Sangeet. And she had, in fact, taken lessons for a while, from Mithun Dey. Soon she had become such a good singer that she was often asked to sing in public, in Mymensingh, for there was only a handful of talented singers in town. Sudhamay recalled one incident, when she was to sing at the town hall. Suranjan was only three or four years old. Sudhamay had begun to sweat with nervousness as Kiranmayee's turn to take the stage came after Samir Chandra Dey sang. Kiranmayee sang a Tagore song, *Anandoloke Mongolalake Birajo Satya Sundara* (O beautiful truth, take your piece forever in the land of bliss). The audience shouted, "One more, one more!" Kiranmayee next sang: *Bhubaneshwar hey Mochon Koro* . . . (O Lord of this World, remove all shackles. Oh remove, O Lord, remove all fear, eradicate all weakness, make my ever fickle, restless mind free of all doubts). She had put so much feeling into her rendition of the song that tears welled up in the eyes even of an atheist like Sudhamay. Kiranmayee, however, was averse to singing publicly after independence. Suranjan would sometimes implore his mother to sing, exhorting her by dropping the names of other singers in the same function, like Sumita Naha or Mitali Mukherjee. Kiranmayee would laugh away all his importunities on the pretext of her lack of practice and loss of confidence. But Sudhamay would keep at her: "What keeps you from going? You had once been known as a good singer, received plenty of applause."

"That's true. But the very people who clapped in appreciation would denounce the Hindu girls as shameless for singing in public, showing their uncovered arms and face to unknown menfolk."

"But don't the Muslim girls sing, too?" Sudhamay

would try to counter. "They sing now. But when they didn't, all the jeering comments were aimed at us. Minatidi sang so well, yet a horde of youths accused her of spoiling the Muslim girls by giving them music lessons."

"But there's nothing wrong in teaching music," Sudhamay had sought to argue.

"But those chaps said it was highly indecent for the Muslim girls to learn music. Singing, so they said, was a sin, extremely harmful to their girls."

"Oh." Sudhamay could add nothing more.

Kiranmayee didn't put her heart into music any more. Mithun Dey would often lament, "You had such a good voice, Kiran, yet you gave up singing."

Kiranmayee would say, sighing deeply, "Dada, nothing appeals to me any more. What is the point in pursuing music? The people don't like the songs and dances, they call them evil."

Her tenuous link with music was totally snapped eventually. And Sudhamay didn't insist on her continuing. Occasionally he would reproach her mildly, "If you are unwilling to sing in public, you can at least sing at home." But that was hardly feasible. On sleepless nights, both of them would climb the stairs to the roof and shed tears for Brahmaputra, for their house near the river Brahmaputra left far behind. They would stare at distant stars. Kiranmayee would hum the tune of the song *Puran osei diner katha* . . . (The memories of those old days). Even a tough-hearted man like Sudhamay felt a jab of nostalgic pain. He, too, would want to have back the pleasant scenes of childhood, boyhood, the school courtyard, overflowing river, the joy of walking along the bridle paths, through the dense shrubberies on the riverside in the quest of his dreamland. On some nights his

naturally strong mind would crack; he would sob inconsolably, hugging his wife. His mental agony knew no end. In
1971, he had suffered the trauma of seeing friends like Ja-
ganmoy Ghosal, Prafulla Sarkar and Netai Sen killed before
his eyes. The Pakistani army would catch hold of Hindus,
shoot all of them and then dump truckloads of their bodies
on the killing fields. Whenever they found Hindus, they
would first torture them by kicking them with hobnailed
army boots, stab them with bayonets, even gouge their eyes
out or break their bones. All those various forms of torture
were aimed at creating an illusion of eventual release for the
entrapped people. But death was their sole rescuer. Sudhamay had seen Muslims being released after a severe
thrashing, but not a single Hindu had ever come out alive
after his capture. A well in the Metharpatti area choked with
the bodies of both Hindus and Muslims, all victims of the
Pakistani army's savagery, was discovered after the
country's independence. Stacks of bones were all that was
left. The relatives of Majed, Rahim, Idris and others killed by
the Pakistani army hurled themselves on thousands of
bones lifted from the well and wailed in grief. Those were
just piles of bones; no one could distinguish the bones of
Muslim Majed from those of Hindu Anil. Sudhamay's
broken leg and three fractured ribs were mended. Similarly
healed was the wound from his mutilated penis, but not the
festering sore within caused by this emotional shock; nor
did it ever dry up his invisible tears. Was survival of this
holocaust a great thing? That he had happened to come out
alive from the concentration camp didn't elate him with
such a feeling. For seven long months he continued his existence with his identity as Abdus Salam in a thatched hut in
Arjunkhila village in Fulpur, passing Suranjan off as Saber

and suffering the indignity of his wife Kiranmayee being known as Fatima by the people around. This pain of calling Kiranmayee Fatima was much more excruciating than the sufferings caused by the still unhealed fractures in his chest. When in December, the freedom fighters finally liberated Fulpur amidst the people's full-throated cheers of *Jai Bangla* (Victory to Bengal), Sudhamay, after the long lapse of seven months, could call his wife by her name, so dear to him, "Kiran, Kiran, Kiranmayee." All the flames of agony burning in his heart so long were extinguished at last. That he now had the freedom to call Kiranmayee by her own home in the midst of so many people was Sudhamay's own idea of having achieved *Jai Bangla*.

Both Sudhamay and Kiranmayee were suddenly jolted by the noise of sharp pounding on the door. The visitor was Haripada Bhattacharya. The pain in his chest had abated a little after the use of Niphicard tablets and stretching out on the bed with eyes closed. Haripada was almost like a family member. Seeing him, Sudhamay got up.

"Are you feeling sick? You are looking very pale," said Haripada.

"You are right, Haripada, not keeping well for the last few days. Haven't checked my blood pressure for quite some time."

"Had I known earlier, I would have brought the blood pressure gauge."

Kiranmayee said, "On top of this, Suranjan has gone out. Now you can guess what it's like. But how did you manage to come here?"

"Made a shortcut. Did not come by the main road."

None of them said a word for some time. Haripada removed his shawl and said, "Protests are being raised all over Dhaka today against the demolition of the Babri mosque. At the same time processions for the communal harmony are also being taken out. Different political parties and organizations have given calls for preserving communal amity. A cabinet meeting communique has given an identical call for observing restraint and showing tolerance. Awami League leader Sheikh Hasina, too, has asked for the maintenance of communal amity at any cost. In India riots have claimed 223 lives, curfew has been imposed on forty towns and cities, all the communal parties have been banned and Prime Minister Narasimpa Rao has given assurance about reconstruction of the Babri mosque."

Haripada paused, grimfaced. Then he said, "Have you decided on doing something? Will you stay here? I don't think it'll be the right thing to do. I was thinking of moving to my father-in-law's place at Manikgunj. But my elder brother-in-law arrived here this evening with alarming news: about a hundred houses in Manikgunj and Gheor police station areas have been looted and then set aflame. Twenty-five temples have received the same treatment. In Bakjhuri village, the Hindu houses were set on fire. Eight or ten youths forcibly abducted a girl, Saraswati, the daughter of Deben Shor, at midnight, and gang raped her."

"What are you saying?" said Sudhamay in panic.

"Where is your daughter?"

"Maya has gone to a girlfriend's."

"Is that a Muslim house?"

"Yes."

"Then it's all right." Haripada heaved a sigh of relief.

Kiranmayee also felt some comfort. Cleaning his glasses, Sudhamay said, "In fact, most of the riots occur in this area. I have witnessed nothing like this in Mymen-

64

singh. Well, have you heard any news from Mymensingh, Haripada?"

"I've heard two temples, one prayer hall in Bathuadi village in Phulpur police station area and the Kali temple at Trishal were destroyed last night."

"But the town must have been spared. Nothing like this happens in the northern part of the country. What do you say, Kiranmayee? Have you ever heard of such temple-burning incidents in our area?"

Before Kiranmayee could reply, Haripada said: "The community puja office on Northbrook Hall Road, the Kali image and temple at Jamidarbari have all been destroyed. Today, a sweetmeat shop called 'Jalkhabar' and Shatarupa Stores at Shantinaghar were smashed and set on fire. The fanatic Jamat Shibir gang members destroyed six temples at Kusthia last night. The news coming from Chittagong, Sylhet, Bhola, Sherpur, Coxbazar, Noakhali are harrowing enough. I'm indeed feeling very scared."

"Scared of what?"

"A mass exodus."

"No, no, the riots in this country will never reach that level to cause such an exodus."

"Have you forgotten what happened in 1990, Dada? Or didn't you consider those incidents that serious?"

"Those were cooked up by General Ershad's government."

"What are you saying, Dada? Why don't you have a look at the report of the Statistical Bureau of Bangladesh Government? The exodus will be of tremendous magnitude this time. No one leaves his home and hearth at the outbreak of cooked-up incidents. After all, the soil of one's own country is not like the soil in a flower pot, which can be watered every day and changed occasionally. Dada, I'm really frightened. My son studies in Calcutta, but I've two grown-up girls. It's their safety and well-being that keeps me awake during the night. I'm thinking of quitting this land."

Sudhamay shuddered. With a jerk he took out his spectacles and said, "Have you gone mad, Haripada? Don't ever utter such words of bad omen."

"I know what you are going to say. I've a good practice here. I'm earning well, have my own house, isn't that it?

"No, Haripada, not for that reason. The question is not that you cannot because you have facilities here. Isn't this your country as well? I'm just a retired person earning hardly anything save for what trickles in from the fees paid by the few patients that I attend to and their number, too, is going down. My son doesn't do anything gainful. Shall I, therefore, leave my country? Do you consider them to be human beings who can leave their own country? Whatever might happen, however many riots there may be, Bengalis are, after all, not uncivilized. There has been some trouble which will end ultimately. There are two countries side by side. The fire burning in one cannot but set pieces of cinders burning in another. Mind you, Haripada, Bengali Muslims did not participate in the 1964 riots. It was Biharis who instigated it."

Haripada covered his nose and mouth with his shawl and said: "That I come out with my mouth covered by my shawl is out of fear not of Biharis, but of your Bengali brothers."

Haripada opened the door with a slight touch of his fingers, and with measured steps entered the lane on the left side and disappeared. Kiranmayee kept the door slightly ajar, restlessly waiting for Suranjan. Processions were passing by intermittently shouting slogans: "*Naraye Takbir Allah-hoo Akbar*"—The Government of India must re-

construct the Babri mosque, or else they won't spare anyone—they threatened.

Suranjan returned quite late at night. He was unsteady
on his feet. He informed Kiranmayee that he had no ap-
petite. He wouldn't take any food.

Suranjan switched off the light and went to sleep. But
sleep eluded him. He passed the night restlessly tossing
from one side of the bed to the other. Failing to get a wink
of sleep, Suranjan returned to the past, step by step. There
were four fundamental principles of the state: nationalism, secularism, democracy and socialism. Commu-
nalist and religious fanatic forces were defeated through
the language movement of 1952 and the long-drawn democratic movement, culminating in the liberation war of
1971. But the reactionary forces opposed to the consciousness of the liberation struggle captured power and completely altered the character of the constitution to facilitate
the rehabilitation of the rejected and defeated commu-
nalist and fundamentalist forces. The activities of the com-
munalist and fundamentalist forces gained momentum
after Islam was made the state religion in an illegal and
unconstitutional manner through the use of religion as a
political weapon.

On February 8, 1979, in the early morning, about four
hundred people suddenly attacked the Hindu Rishi community in Sabahal village, the Daudkandi subdistrict of
Comilla. They loudly proclaimed: "The government has
declared Islam as the state religion. So in order to reside in
an Islamic state, everyone must become a Muslim. If you
do not adopt Islam, you will have to leave this country."
These rowdies plundered every house of those belonging

to the Rishi community and set them on fire, demolished temples, and abducted many people who are still missing. The women were brutally raped and many of those injured in the attack never recovered completely.

Nripendra Sengupta and his wife Anima Sengupta of Abirdigha village in Sibpur of Narsingdi were forcibly kept in the house of an advocate and a document was registered under compulsion for eight and a quarter *bighas* of land. On March 27, 1979, Anima complained to the superintendent of police of Narsingdi in a written statement that the accused had threatened her and that the people of the locality were silent out of fear. After this Anima was kept in police lockup and tortured.

On May 27 that year ten or twelve armed men raided the house of the Haldars in Baulakanda village of Firozpur. They plundered whatever they found in the house and, after demolishing the temple, raised the slogan "Kill *malauns*, construct mosque after demolishing temple." They also asked the Hindus to leave this country without any delay.

On May 9 in broad daylight about 100 or 150 Muslims raided the house of the Baidyas of Paschimgram in Raujan of Chittagong and bombed it, setting the house on fire and firing at the people with their guns.

On June 16, ten or twelve policemen captured about fifteen or sixteen Hindus, including Gauranga Mondal, Nagendra Mandal, Amulya Mandal, Sobodh Mandal, Sudhir Mandal, Hirendra Nath Mandal and Jahar Deuri, and beat them after bringing them to the courtyard of Gauranga Mandal. When Gauranga Mandal's wife tried to stop them, they took her to a room and raped her continuously. Other women who tried to protest were also molested. Sanatan Mandal's daughter Rina was also forcibly captured and raped. She was later kidnapped. There is no trace of Rina as yet.

On June 18 at about eleven o'clock at night, three policemen along with the village *Chowkidar* and some armed persons raided Chandkathi village in Nazirpur subdistrict of Perozpur and launched a search operation. During the search they asked the Hindus to leave this country. They arrested four or five Hindus, including Dulal Krishna Mandal, and took them to the police station where they were mercilessly tortured. Later, they were released on payment of eight hundred or a thousand takas. Many Hindus of this locality have left the country.

Minority Hindus of twelve villages in Gazir Hat Union of Dighalia subdistrict of Khulna have been subjected to unimaginable atrocities. Molla Jamluddin, a candidate for the chairman's post, following his defeat in the elections, prevented the Hindus from tilling their land, took away their paddy from the field, snatched their cattle and plundered their shops.

On December 10, 1988, Abdus Subhan Bhuyan and Union Council member Golam Hussain and their armed henchmen raided the house of Rajendranath Das who had filed a case against them for taking illegal lease and forcible occupation of the bestowed property in Durgapur village in Barishal. They threatened to kill Rajendranath, looted golden ornaments and other valuables and set fire to the house. They took away an idol of Radhakrishna made of an alloy of eight types of metal and those who tried to resist them were mercilessly beaten. Before their departure they told Rajendranath Das to leave the country.

At the instigation of some fundamentalists, police stormed the house of eighty-year-old Lakshman Chandra

69

Pal in Talbunia village in Rampal subdistrict of Bagerhat district on the morning of August 26, 1988, severely assaulting the grandson of the old man, Bikash Chandra Pal, besides meting out identical treatment to the eldest son, Pulin Behari Pal, and the second son, Rabindranath Pal. The policemen also gave a thrashing to Pulin's wife when she tried to resist them. The police then dragged Pulin, Rabindranath and Bikash to the police station lockup on false charges. They were yet to be released on bail. The incident had its root in the longterm imprisonment of Hakim Molla, a resident of Sholakura village, for raping a niece of Lakshman Chandra Pal and assaulting other members of the family some time before the partition. After his release from the jail following the creation of Pakistan, this convict, aided by Siraj Mullick, Haroon Mullick and Abdul Jabbar of Talbunia village, decided to settle the score with Lakshman Chandra and punished his family members in this manner with police assistance. After this incident the Hindus began feeling insecure and prepared to leave.

The Hindu residents of Gopalganj, Kotalipara, Kaksudpur, that is, the entire Gopalganj district, were being subjected to thefts in their houses, looting and armed holdups, illegal occupation of their properties through forgery, rape of their women and destruction of their religious places coupled with persecution and torture by the police. The members of the goon squad of Mantu Kaji, chairman of Kotalipara subdistrict, mounted an attack on the Mandra Lakhirpara village in Kushala union in broad daylight and tortured the Hindu women. They were now extorting money and forcibly taking away all valuable movable properties, forcing the Hindus to put their signa-

tures to stamped papers to legalize this plunder. Most of
the Hindus of the area had left the country out of terror.
Mantu Kaji abducted a woman official of Sonali Bank, Mrs.
Bhowmick, and subjected her to beastly torture. Luring the
girls like Mamata, Madhu and others from Kandi village,
under the pretext of giving them jobs, he trapped them in
the subdistrict office and raped all of them.

During the night of July 3, 1988, the police entered the
house of Anil Chandra in Pilmari village in Chilmari subdistrict of Bagerhat during his absence and severely assaulted his wife and young children. The police also looted
the house of the schoolteacher Amulya Babu. They also
raided the house of Khstish Mandal in Suriguri village on
the night of the 4th and, finding the menfolk away, raped
the wife and daughter of the house's owner. Next day, their
target of attack in the same village was Shyamal Biswas's
house where, finding him absent, they raped his daughter
and looted all the valuables. A few days after these incidents, a vandal forced his way into the house of Nirode Behari Roy in Chitalmari village and took up residence there.
The local administration remained silent. Forcibly ejecting
a Hindu from his house in Kalshira village, a Union Council member, Mansur Mullick, illegally occupied the property and started residing there. The homeless Hindu
family was now on the road.

Jahur Ahmed, an official of the district education department, raped some Hindu girls on the pretext of giving
them jobs. Two women of the Biswas family in Demakair
village had been ravished in this way. The man was now
engaged in a flourishing business of extorting money from
the Hindu teachers and lady teachers solely under the
threat of transferring them.

The police and the local rowdies led a combined raid on the house of Jagadish Halder of Alti village in Gopalganj. The entire house was ransacked, residents were beaten up and the valuables looted. Before leaving the place the raiders threatened to kill everyone. On August 12 the same year the rowdies and police together again launched an attack on several other Hindu houses in the same village and demolished several temples. Both Hindu men and women like Ashutosh Ray, Manoranjan Ray, Anjali Ray, Suniti Ray, and Bela Biswas were molested by them. They threatened, before their departure, that they wouldn't allow any temple to remain standing in this country.

The fundamentalists combined with the police attacking the Hindus after the death of Khayer Khan, chairman of Ujani Union in the Maqgdpur subdistrict of Gopalganj district, torturing all the members of the community in the area. The police raped the wife of one Shibu in Basudebpur village and Miss Anjali Biswas in Mahatali village. Twelve people were arrested by the police from Shimulpur village for being members of the Proletariat party. They were subjected to severe torture and released only after large amounts of money were extorted from them.

The police suddenly attacked Bashtukathi village in Swarupkathi subdistrict in Pirozepur district on June 20 for launching an attack, indiscriminately destroying the standing crop of the Hindus on either side of the river. The peasants working in their fields were arrested and released later after coming up with ransom money. Minati Rani, subdistrict health center worker, was proceeding to a friend's house in the company of her sister-in-law and brother. They were forcibly detained in the temporary police camp in the same village and secured their release after paying one thousand takas. A man called Rustam Ali raped a fourteen-year-old girl, Shiuli, daughter of Sudhangsu Kumar Halder, in Purbajala Bari village of Swarupkathi on her way to her maternal uncle's house. When Sudhangsu Halder sought to take the matter to the village leaders, he was bluntly told that they were unable to bear with such incidents, and that he had better leave the country.

The men of a mosque committee keen on building a new mosque in Buriganj bazar in Shibganj subdistrict of Bagura district attacked the house of Dr. Sachindra Kumar Saha near the site of the proposed mosque. They broke all the doors and windows of Saha's house, looted all that they could lay their hands on and set fire to the house. They also demolished a nearby temple. After continuing this plunder for more than two hours, they returned with a booty of more than one million takas. During the raid, Dr. Saha's son managed to slip out unnoticed and informed the police. But when for once the police decided to act, they were attacked by criminals like Altaf Hussain Mandal and members of his gang with clubs, iron rods and brickbats. Eight of the policemen were injured. Later the police official at Shibganj himself lodged a complaint and arrested Altaf Hussain and sixty-five others. But under pressure from the people at the top, all the accused had now been released and they were openly threatening the members of Dr. Saha's family with death. The incident led to a deep sense among the local Hindus who were thinking of leaving the country.

The Hindus of Tikrapara village in Alfadanga subdistrict in Faridpur district, following an attack on them on May 3 and 4, 1979, left their homes to take shelter elsewhere.

An influential man, Nazir Mirdha of Rahatpur village in

Raipur Union of Mohammedpur subdistrict in Magura district, raped the wife, minor daughter and daughter-in-law of Haren Biswas. When a case was filed against the accused, Nazir and his henchmen tortured the complainant so much that he, along with his family, was forced to leave the country.

On the 19th and 20th, the police of Debagram in Kotalipara subdistrict of Gopalganj arrested Anil Kumar Bagchi, Sushil Kumar Pande and Makhanlal Ganguly on the charge of being involved with the Bangabhummi movement and later set them free after extorting money from them. Ramesh Chandra Ojha, a mentally unsound person of Mirakathi village in Jhalakathi subdistrict of Gopulguy district, was forcibly converted to Islam. His wife, Minati Rani, and his elder brother, Nirode Ojha, were pressured to convert. She faced the threat of being raped when she tried to take up the matter with the senior people in the area. Minati Rani was now on the run, fearing for her life.

Sultan, a dismissed police constable, raped the wife of Sudhir Baidya, a resident of Jobai village in Kachua subdistrict of Gopalganj. She now hid herself from the public in sheer shame. Sudhit Baidya himself was facing a threat against his life. A cow belonging to Upendra Malo, of the same village, was killed and a feast was made of its meat by some people in that village. Upendra was humiliated for the crime of seeking justice from the administration.

In his bid to save the paddy of his own land, Kartik Ray of Beltali village in Boultali union in Gopalganj had to pay with his own life. His wife was forced to declare the brutal murder of her husband as a natural death.

One Abdul Rahim, through his henchmen, kidnapped Manju Rani Seal, a student of Class IX and daughter of Premananda Seal of Dekshin Chandpur in Luksum subdistrict of Comilla district, at about eight in the evening on December 4, 1988. Next day a complaint was lodged with the Luksum police station. But the girl was not found. The abductors threatened her father and other members of the family, but the police took no action. The Hindus were frightened to send their daughters to school in this area.

The police arrested sixteen people from Gutia village in Ujirpur subdistrict of Barisal district on April 25 while they were singing religious songs. They were daily wage workers engaged in betel leaf cultivation.

After the State Religion Bill was passed, some people in Siddhirpasha village in Abhay Nagar subdistrict of Jessore district circulated the rumor that the Hindus would no longer be able to sell their lands. The frightened Hindus decided to sell their land at a quarter of the actual value. Madhab Nandy, a sensible Hindu of the village, who sought to assuage the fear of the people and to urge them to ignore the false propaganda about the so-called ban on the land sale, had to pay very dearly for his wise counsel. A few days later, Madhab Babdy's house was raided by twelve or fourteen men armed with long choppers and spears who raped his daughter-in-law, who was seven months pregnant, and his young daughter.

Deben Biswas of Khoksa subdistrict of Kustia was killed by unknown gunmen. The formal complaint did not lead to any arrests.

Armed police along with young thugs led a joint invasion on Gaibpur village in Chtalmari subdistrict of Bagerhat district on August 12 and 16, 1988. They smashed the idol of the local temple and raped the women. More than twenty people were severely beaten up and then released after money was extorted from them. Narayan Bairagi,

Sushanta Dhali, Anukul Baroi, Ranjan Dhali and Jagadish
Bairagi had to stay confined in the police lockup for a long
time. An identical raid was conducted on Charbaliari village and fifteen or sixteen people arrested there were later
released after heavy extortion.

The teenage daughter of Rabindranath Ghosh of Parku-
mira village in Tala subdistrict of Satksheera, Chanda, a student of Class III, was raped by a schoolteacher. The incident
occurred on May 3, 1979. That night Chhanda was asleep
on the verandah of her house along with other family members. In the dead of night her teacher, a Muslim called Nasi-
muddin, and some other men picked her up and then
raped her in a nearby garden. Next day Chhanda was
found unconscious and bloodspattered. Despite the lodg-
ing of a complaint at Tala police station, none of the accused
was arrested. The girl was sent to Satkheera hospital.

The minorities were persecuted like hell in the name of
arresting the members of the Proletariat party in Barisal
district's Jhalakathi, Najirpur and Gouranadi areas. All the
arrested men were released after the police got some
money. Many Hindus in those areas were on the run,
fearing arrests. Kashinath Halder, a resident of Agailjhara
subdistrict, was all but killed as a result of police torture.

A mob of seventy or eighty people led by Sahabuddin
and Alauddin attacked the Hindus of the carpenters'
colony in Charmadhua village in Raipur subdistrict of
Narasingdi district and looted their movables. Nearly 150
people from some twenty families were now living the life
of wandering refugees.

A fundamentalist group raided the house of minority
leader Binay Baishya in Jehangirpur village in Madan subdistrict of Netrokona district. The members of Binay

Babu's family were kept confined for thirty-six hours and all his belongings were looted. When the police were informed of the attack, they arrested his two sons instead. They were later released, however.

A mob of nearly one hundred, under the leadership of local Union Council member Golam Hussain Pintu, attacked the house of Rajendra Chandra Das in Durgapur village of Chandpur Union of Bakherganj on December 10. They went through the routine of looting the house, beating up the residents and finally setting the house on fire. There was a second arson attack on his house following his complaint to the police along with the threat of killing all members of his family.

Some people had forcibly occupied the property of Dinesh Chandra Das of Miwarishpur village in Begumganj subdistrict of Noakhali district.

Sleep continued to elude Suranjan. He had worked for paper *Ekata* for a couple of years in 1988–89. As a reporter he had to rove a lot all over the country. His bag would invariably be loaded with the sad tales of such persecution of minorities. Some were used, some not. The editor would explain, "Look, Suranjan, this is nothing but oppression of the defenseless weak by the high and mighty. All these are cases of the strong oppressing the weak, the rich oppressing the poor. If you are rich, it does not matter much if you are Hindu or Muslim. Unfortunately, that is the rule of a capitalist society. If you go and look for yourself, you'll find that poor Muslims also are being persecuted. This is because the rich always torture the poor—they don't care whether their victims are Hindu or Muslim."

Day Three

Did the winter lack its expected nip this year? Suranjan pushed the quilt away from him. He didn't feel like leaving bed. He had roamed around the city last night, but he had not felt like visiting anyone or talking to anybody. Not that he hadn't felt for his worrying parents. Still, he wasn't keen on returning home. He himself felt scared seeing Kiranmayee's fear-stricken face. Sudhamay's eyes were becoming expressionless. Suranjan felt like having a drink somewhere else. If only the haze of drink could erase from his mind the dreamy eyes of Maya exuding a fear that prompted her to repeatedly seek his help. How rapidly she had grown up. Just the other day she would go to the riverside holding on to his fingers. The beautiful brown girl would invariably nag him for new clothes before Durga Puja. Suranjan would try to dissuade her, saying, "Why don't you rid yourself of all those trashy rituals like Puja? Those uncouth boys dance in front of that clay image and

78

you enjoy putting on that new dress. Don't you feel ashamed? It's a pity I couldn't rear you up to my liking."

Maya would still importune him, saying, "I'll go out to see the Puja pandals, won't you escort me?"

Suranjan would scold her: "Be a rational being, be a human being, don't be a Hindu." Maya would burst into giggles and ask, "Don't you consider the Hindus human beings?"

Maya had to be called Farida in 1971 to conceal her Hindu identity. Even in 1972 Suranjan would carelessly call out the same name much to Maya's annoyance. Then she had to be placated with chocolates. The girl was crazy about chocolates which would bring instant happiness to her eyes. During Eid festival, when she saw her Muslim friend playing, she would urge him to buy her balloons, firecrackers and sparklers, whining for Kiranmayee to cook pilau which her friend Nadira would be having in her house. Kiranmayee would oblige her.

Maya hadn't been heard of since she left home the day before yesterday. Her absence made her parents' burden of worry much heavier. Her survival in the shelter of a Muslim house was more or less assured. Even at her age she earned something by coaching two girls. She rarely, if ever, asked for any financial help from her parents to continue her studies in the Eden College. But Suranjan frequently had to ask for money. He couldn't get any job, despite having a master's degree in physics. At the outset, he hoped to land a job, and had had several interviews. He was a brilliant student in the university. Yet the very students whom he coached voluntarily scored better marks than he in the final exam. The same trend persisted in his job-hunting forays. The teaching jobs went to those with far inferior grades. This happened despite his standing up well to the grilling by the members of the interview boards before whom he appeared. Yet the boys who lamented over their poor performance at such interviews or cut sorry figures in the oral examination would, much to Suranjan's surprise, invariably receive the appointment letters. Complaints about him were heard in some interviews that he hadn't been properly respectful to the board members. But the real matter was that he never thought the Muslim way of paying respect by saying *"Assalammu Alaikum"* or, for that matter, the Hindu manner of doing so by saying *"Namaskar"* to be the only acknowledged method of showing reverence to the elders. Yet the boys who, while being obsequious and courteous to the examiners with *"Assalammu Alaikum"* and all, called them "swine" just after coming out of the hall, eventually were successful in the interview. But Suranjan did neither. Yet he had been branded discourteous, or rather had earned a bad reputation for improper behavior. That might have been the reason or it might have been his being Hindu, but no government jobs came his way. He got a job in a private concern. But he didn't like it and gave it up after three months. On the contrary, Maya had somehow adjusted herself to the situation and got private coaching assignments quite easily. She might even have gotten a job in a nongovernment organization. Suranjan suspected that Maya was getting these facilities because of the manipulation by her boyfriend Jehangir. Could Maya go to the extent of marrying that boy out of her gratitude to him, Suranjan wondered. Such a suspicion took a definitive shape of apprehension in his mind.

Kiranmayee came with a cup of tea. Swollen pouches

under her eyes showed that she, too, had missed her night's sleep. But Suranjan didn't like to expose his lack of sleep. He yawned and said, "I couldn't guess I would be so late getting up in the morning." As if he had slept too deeply during the night. Otherwise, he would have gone out for his early walk or jogging.

Kiranmayee still stood with the cup of tea in her hand. She didn't make any move to put the cup on the table and leave the room. Suranjan could feel that Kiranmayee was about to tell him something. But she remained silent as if she were waiting for her son to take the cup of tea from her hand. Suranjan realized that the distance between them had widened so much that both preferred silence. Suranjan took the initiative to say, "Hasn't Maya returned even today?"

"No," as if Kiranmayee were awaiting for this question from him. She sat silently on his bed. Within his easy reach. Such closeness, Suranjan could feel, was indicative of her restlessness caused by the sense of insecurity. He took his eyes off Kiranmayee's sleepless eyes, uncombed hair and none-too-clean sari. Lifting himself partially, he sipped his tea. "Why is she not coming back? Are the Muslims keeping her safe? Doesn't she have any trust in us? She is so unconcerned about us. Does she think that her own survival is enough?"

Kiranmayee still kept mum. Suranjan lit up a cigarette after his tea. He was suddenly oblivious of his own rule of never smoking before his mother. It didn't occur to him even when he struck the match and blew out the smoke from his mouth and nostrils. But it was a different day, which brought them much closer, removing the thin wall between them. He hadn't placed a hand, though craving a mother's affection, on Kiranmayee's lap for a long time.

Did grown-up children move away from their mother's touch in this way? Suranjan had an irresistible desire to lie with his head on his mother's lap like an innocent child and talk of kite flying. There was a maternal uncle, Nabin Mama, who would come to their place from Sylhet and make kites with his own hands. He was a champion kite flier whose kite would rule the sky.

Suranjan just looked at his mother's lap with craving eyes. He asked, after having his last puff at the cigarette, "Did Kamal or Belal or anyone like them call on us yesterday?"

Kiranmayee dully answered, "No."

He was amazed at his friends' lack of interest in his survival. Did they think that he was dead, or weren't they feeling any urge to save him?

Kiranmayee's voice became choked as she said, "Where did you go yesterday? We were left alone in the house. Don't you think about us? If anything happened to you? Gautam, a boy from a nearby house, went out to buy some eggs. The Muslim boys beat him up so severely that he lost two front teeth and possibly had his foot broken."

"Oh," came the brief reply.

"Do you remember a couple of years ago, our maid called Geeta's mother, who would come to work from Shanir Akhra, had her house burned down? She rebuilt her hut by saving money by working in different households. Again her hut turned into a heap of ashes. She came yesterday with her children moving about on the roads. She asked, 'Can you tell me where I can buy poison?' I think she's gone mad."

"Oh," said Suranjan, keeping the empty cup by the side of the pillow.

"When Maya comes, don't you think she will be a greater source of worry?"

"Does that mean she will have to stay all her life under the protective umbrella of a Muslim household?"

Suranjan's voice sounded hard. He didn't feel disgrace for once taking shelter in the house of his Muslim friend Kamal. He once thought the situation created by the mischief of some rogues, who invariable figured in every country, would be normalized. Nothing like that would happen again. Now it didn't seem like the pranks of a handful of mischief-makers. His suspicion deepened, leading him to believe that none of his friends, Kamal, Belal, Kaisar or Lutfar, was really noncommunal. In 1978, Zia-ur-Rahman introduced *Bismilla her Rahman er Rahim* (I am beginning with the name of Allah) into the constitution, not out of deference to any popular mandate. Nor did President Ershad declare Islam as the state religion in conformity with the people's wish. But why did he do that? The Bengali Muslims were said to be great believers in secularism, particularly those who supported the Liberation War. But wasn't it surprising that they didn't raise any voice of protest when the seeds of communalism were being sowed through these actions? Were they not aggrieved? These very people, who became so hot-headed as to declare a war of liberation, now seemed to be cold-blooded as reptiles. Why weren't they feeling the need for this sapling of communalism then? How could they dare nurture such an absurd thought as ushering in democracy in a country rejecting secularism? It was truly ironic that those who had joined hands to strengthen the fight for independence were now the same people who were allowing the nonsecular state, which was the good ground of communalism.

"Have you heard about the destruction of the Soraighat Temple yesterday? And the Shyampur temple, too?" Kiranmayee said in a plaintive voice.

Suranjan twisted himself in a limbering exercise. He said, "Did you ever visit a temple? So why are you moved over temple demolition? Let all these buildings dedicated to religion be ground to bits."

"They feel offended if a mosque is destroyed; don't they ever feel that the Hindus, too, are equally hurt in the case of temples? Or rather, they don't want to understand. And for the destruction of a single mosque, they are plundering hundreds of temples. Isn't Islam called a religion of peace?"

"The Muslims in this country know quite well that the Hindus' anger can't cause any harm to them. That's why they are acting this way. They know not a single mosque can be touched. Since its destruction a couple of years ago, the Nayabazar temple is still a heap of rubble. The children play on it, even urinate on it. Is there a single Hindu who dares strike a blow or two against the polished walls of a mosque with bare hands?"

Kiranmayee went out silently. Suranjan could understand that even a woman like Kiranmayee, who seldom bothered about the outside world, had in her inner thoughts put a Parvin and an Archana on the same footing; she, too, had reached a precarious stage. She, too, was being ruffled by questions like: Do the Muslims have the monopoly on pride and anger?

It was not the first attack on the Babri mosque in October 1990 that marked the beginning of Hindu persecution in this country. He could remember, on the morning of April

21, 1979, how a man named Ayub Ali smashed with his own hands the image of Kali in the historic temple in Rajsahi town. After that, Hindu-owned shops were subjected to similar attacks.

On April 16 of the same year, the famous image of Ramgopal was stolen from the temple at Ramgopalpara in Shailakupa subdistrict in Jhanaidaha. Later, the image was recovered, although considerably damaged, next to the local cremation ground. But the image's gold and silver ornaments were never found. Jaigopalhat Kali temple in Purana Lalanagar village in Seetakunda was set on fire. The image of Durga at Kuraisha Chandgaon Durgabari in North Chandgaon was broken to bits.

After two months of legislation declaring Islam the state religion, the black touchstone image of the old Kalachand temple, along with its ornaments, was stolen from near Dakshindihi village in Pultala subdistrict of Khulna. When the secretary of the temple committee went to the police station to lodge a complaint, he was put behind bars and physically tortured. Arrest warrants were issued against all members of the temple committee. The Additional Superintendent of Police, who went to the spot to investigate, threatened the Hindus and charged them with stealing the image. In the single night of December 8 the white marble Shiva, the images of Radha-Gavinda and Annapurna and the sacred Salgram stone disappeared from the old temple in Dwimukha village in Kalihati subdistrict of Tangail district. The police inquiries revealed the identity of the idol thief as one Nur Mahammad Talukdar. Yet no action was taken against him. An organization known as "World Islam" sent threatening letters to the Hindus in Mainamati Union in Burichang subdistrict in Comilla telling them to leave the country at once. They were warned that unless their worship was stopped, they would be at the receiving end of riots. On April 14, the banyan tree beside the temple was doused with gasoline and then set on fire. A man called Ali Ahmed openly declared in the Mainamati market that the Hindus would have to be evicted through riots. While devotional chanting was going on in Sri Sri Madanmahan Akhra in Lalmohan sub-district in Bhola on March 11, more than a hundred people attacked the pandal. They forced their way into the temple, smashed the image and beat up the assembled devotees. They then started a game of sack and fire that left a trail of devastation on Hindu temples in Baratia village in Gheor subdistrict in Manikgunj district, with a local advocate, Zia-ur-Rahman, taking the initiative to set up a Muslim graveyard and mosque in the land adjoining the Kali temple that was more than a century old. The long-worshiped Hindu temple at Kalihat in Mahammadpur Union in Chatkhil subdistrict of Noakhali district was converted into a place for business transactions due to a conspiracy by local Muslims. The image in the Lakshmi temple in Phaukal village in Gazipur Municipality was broken first and then its head carried away.

A mob pounced on the assembly during the ritual of Charak in the monastery building in Kashtasagara village in the headquarter subdistrict in Jhinaidaha. They severely assaulted the priest, threw away the offerings for worship and snatched the drum from the drummer. Muslims attacked the Kali temple at Nijra Purbapara in Gopalgunj headquarter subdistrict at about nine at night on October 17, 1988, causing extensive damage. The lock of the Ulpur Shiva temple was broken to storm the inner sanctum. The

Phallic Shiva image also was carried away with many other valuables.

A similar fate of image destruction befell the Durga temple at Thanapara in Kushthia on October 17, 1988, and later, all the idols in the temple at Paler Bazar in Khulna district, even before the evening worship could begin; Durga temple at Gobra in Jessore district; another famous Durga temple at the hermitage of Sri Sri Pranabanandaji Maharaj in Khulna; and some time earlier, the Durga idol near Kaligunj bus stand at Kaligunj in Satkhseera district.

The Imam of the Jama mosque at Madhugram in Dumuria subdistrict in Khulna sent letters before the Durga Puja festival to all the organizers of different community pujas in the areas, that they would have to interrupt their rituals every time a call for *Namaz* was given from the mosque. In early October, all the communal elements in Khulna came out in a procession shouting slogans, "No idol worship is allowed. Break them, smash them."

The image-breaking spree also engulfed Kali temple in Mahishkola village in Kumarkhali subdistrict of Kustia. The image of Kali under construction at Kaligunj Bazar in Kaligunj subdistrict in Gazipur was destroyed and the idol destroyed before Puja in Haritala temple in Nakipur village in Shyamnagar subdistrict of Satkhseera. The boundary wall of the Kali temple in Bhandaria subdistrict in Pirozepur was being pulled down to dig a drain. On the day of the immersion of the Durga image of a community puja in Phuljhuri bazar of Barguna district, it was the target of attack by the fundamentalists. Just a few days before the Puja festival, the Durga image in Bukalunia union of Bamna subdistrict was smashed. None of these iconoclasts was ever tried.

It is said that Bangladesh is a country of communal

amity. Suranjan suddenly burst out laughing. He was alone in the room. A cat was lying by the door. Stirred by Suranjan's laughter, the cat looked at him. Hadn't the cat been to Dhakeshwari temple today? Well, what could the communal identity of this cat be? Was it a Hindu? Possibly so, since it resided in a Hindu household. Was this black-and-white cat looking at him with its blue eyes sparkling compassion? It must be a Muslim then. It must be a liberal Muslim who viewed the Hindus with pity. The cat eventually ambled out. The cooking stove in this household was mostly unlit. Might be the cat would have a try in the kitchen of the Muslim next door. Then cats couldn't be branded as members of any particular community. Only men could be marked by such a distinction. All the mosques and temples were meant for human beings.

Suranjan saw the sun creeping up the stairs. The day was advancing. It was December 9. If only he could become a free-moving cat. He never offered prayers in his life, nor did he ever visit a temple. He made a pledge to usher in socialism in the country, roamed about the streets for this cause, took part in processions, gave fiery speeches at meetings, and thought of peasants and workers, but never found any time to look after his own or his family's interests, thinking constantly about the socio-economic up-lift of the country. And against this same Suranjan accusing fingers were raised, pointing to his Hindu identity. Yesterday, the local boys had chased him, shouting "Catch that one." Till now, he had been spared physical assault; tomorrow he might not be that lucky. Gautam had been beaten up for venturing out to buy eggs. In his case, a cigarette-buying mission to Mati's shop at the street crossing might invite showers of blows on his back, making the cigarette drop from his lips. Turning around, he would recognize his attackers as Kuddus, Rahman, Bilayet, and Sobhan carrying clubs and daggers, encircling him menacingly. Suranjan closed his eyes as he conjured up the scene. His body hairs stood on end. Was he frightened then? He was not one to be easily frightened. Leaving the bed, he looked for the cat. How silent the house was! As if no one had stayed here for a long time. When they returned from their hideout in 1971 to their Brahmo Palli house, they were greeted with an eerie silence, overgrown grasses and the house totally denuded of everything, even his spinning top, marbles, kites, carom board, chessboard, books and magazines. Nothing was there. Suranjan had an uncanny feeling in his heart as he surveyed this desolate house. He again had a similar feeling. Would Sudhamay remain stretched out on the bed all day? If his blood pressure suddenly rose alarmingly, who would call the doctor? Household tasks like shopping, buying medicine, calling a mason or a plumber, ordering newspapers, he had never done. He took his meals twice or three times every day, returned home at night; if he was too late and the front door was locked, he would let himself in through a door that opened into his own room. If he needed money, the supplier was either Kiranmayee or Sudhamay. Of course, he felt ashamed to ask for money. He didn't earn anything although he was thirty-three. Sudhamay once said, "I'll soon retire from service, you had better do something." He had avoided all his responsibilities by saying, "Routine work doesn't suit my temperament." Sudhamay was now footing the household expenses by attending to patients in his makeshift clinic in the outer room of the house. Suranjan sometimes returned home late at night after going through his circuit of the party office, the canteen operated by Madhu, the office of the Committee for the Extermination of Killers and Informers, Press Club and 32 Dhanmadi Road, thoroughly exhausted. His dinner was kept warm. Some nights, he would go right to bed. Thus a distance was building up between him and his family. But when Kiranmayee sat on his bed with the teacup this morning, Suranjan could realize that his parents depended a lot even on their reckless, unconcerned, irresponsible son. But what had been his contribution to this family? Sudhamay, who was once quite affluent, now was quite satisfied with his frugal meals. Suranjan, too. But he remembered during his childhood, he was forcibly fed milk and he would be licked for his refusal to take butter. But if he now insisted to Kiranmayee that he wanted that pure milk of the old days, butter and cottage cheese together with fish, mutton and breads fried in melted butter during lunch, would she be in a position to oblige him? Anyway, Suranjan had never been drawn toward abundance or luxury. This was because of Sudhamay's attitude to life. When his friends were crazy about clothes of the latest fashion, he would bring his son books on the lives of Einstein, Newton and Galileo, the history of the French Revolution, stories of the Second World War, Tolstoy and Gorky. Sudhamay would always want his son to be someone. This morning, looking for the cat, Suranjan wondered whether he had really become someone his father would have liked him to be. He was not greedy, nor did he have any craving for affluence or accumulation of property; he treated other people's interests far above his own. Were these enough for his becoming someone? Suranjan walked along the verandah without paying any particular attention to his surroundings. Sudhamay was reading the morning newspaper. As his attention turned to his son, he said, "Suranjan, listen to me."

"Yes," Suranjan said, leaning against the railing.

"Eight Indian leaders, including BJP stalwarts like Murali Manohar and L. K. Advani, have been arrested. The death toll in that country exceeds four hundred. Kalyan Singh, chief minister of Uttar Pradesh, would face trial. The United States, in fact the entire world, has condemned the Babri mosque demolition. In our country, a curfew has been imposed on Bhola. The Bangladesh National Party, the Awami League and some other parties are launching campaigns for the preservation of communal harmony, besides issuing statements." Sudhamay's eyes appeared to be kindled with the same sort of softness as the cat's eyes.

"Do you realize the fact that those who are indulging in riots are not motivated by any religious zeal? They are basically hooligans with looting as their sole objective. All these ruffians are behind the mischief; otherwise, there would be no conflict here between one community and another. From the rise in the number of peace processions, it seems something positive will certainly emerge. It is this very issue which brought about the downfall of President Ershad. Well, Suro, Ershad said the Hindus would be given compensation for their losses. But have they been given compensation?"

"Are you in your right mind, Baba?"

"I'm not sure, there's a lot I can't remember. Those accused in the Nidarabad murder case will be hanged, do you know?"

Suranjan realized Sudhamay was trying to convince him that the Hindus would still get justice in this country.

The Nidarabad murders meant the grisly killings of Mrs. Birajabala Debnath in Nidarabad village of Brahmanbaria, and her five sons and daughters who were hacked to death. Their dismembered bodies were packed into several empty drums with their openings sealed with salt and lime and dropped into the marshy area of Dhopajhuri. The drums eventually floated to the surface. The murders were done with the aim of hushing up the earlier killing of Birajabala's husband, Shashanka, and the forcible occupation of nearly three and a half acres of land. The death sentence for the principal accused in the case, Tajul Islam and "Thief" Badsah, was confirmed by the Supreme Court about four months ago. Was Sudhamay repeating this known fact just to seek solace from this single incident that went in favor of a butchered Hindu family? He was trying to convince himself that justice was still not being denied to the Hindus in this country. The Hindus and Muslims were treated as equals. The Hindus were not second-class citizens after all.

"Did you take part in the procession for preaching communal amity? How many people participated in it?"

"Can't say."

"All the parties, barring the fundamentalist Jamat supporters, came out on the streets in these processions, didn't they?"

"I don't know."

"Isn't the government giving police protection?"

"Don't know."

"Didn't you notice that truckloads of policemen had take positions on either side of Shankharibazar?"

"Don't know."

"They say the situation at Bhola is bad. Is it that bad or are the incidents there being unnecessarily played up?"

"Don't know."

"Gautam was beaten up for personal reasons. He was said to be a pot addict."

Suranjan's detached attitude dampened Sudhamay's ebullience. Spreading the pages of the paper before him, he said in an offended voice, "It seems you don't read papers."

"What do you gain from it?"

"Well, you can know how resistance is growing, protests are being raised everywhere. Are the Jamat supporters that powerful so as to force their way into temples through the police cordon?"

"What is your interest in temples? Are you feeling any urge to offer prayers near the end of your life? Let them demolish all the temples, I'll at least be happy."

Sudhamay felt embarrassed. Suranjan deliberately hurt the feelings of his good-natured father. What was there to make a big fuss about? To feel like a first-class citizen of the country, oblivious of one's actual second-class status, was nothing but sheer foolishness. What did Sudhamay gain, or, for that matter, Suranjan himself by not observing any religious rites and treating the Muslims as brothers and friends for so long? After all this, everyone still branded them as Hindus. What did this family achieve by always remaining atheist and professing humanism and humanitarianism? They couldn't save themselves from stones on their house. They were still scared stiff. Still they had to cringe in fear in anticipation of being consumed by the flames of communalism.

Suranjan could remember that when he was in Class VII, his classmate Farookh took him aside. Farookh gave him a kebab from his tiffin box. They ate the kebabs, talking all the time. He asked Farookh, "Who prepared these? I think it's your mother. I, too, shall bring food prepared by my mother for you."

But unexpectedly, Farookh, the tiffin over, sped down the stairs to merrily inform the whole class that Suranjan had taken beef. All the boys started dancing around Suranjan in frenzied glee. Besides the noisy jeers, someone pinched him, another slapped him on the top of his head, some tugged at his shirt, some wanted to pull down his shorts, some stuck out their tongues at him; another, bubbling with mirth, thrust a dead cockroach in his pocket. Tears rolled down his cheeks as Suranjan hung his head in shame. He was not feeling any guilt for taking beef; it was the beastly revelry swirling around him that made him feel small. He felt a deep sense of isolation. The idea that he was one kind of human being and they another crossed his mind for the first time. Returning home, he cried inconsolably. He told Sudhamay, "They tricked me into eating beef."

Sudhamay laughed it away, saying "Is this any reason for you to cry? Beef is a delicacy. Tomorrow I'll buy some beef from the market, and all of us will eat it together. Just see if I can do it."

Sudhamay did exactly what he had said. Kiranmayee cooked that beef. She didn't do it easily. Sudhamay had to persuade her till late at night that these superstitions made no sense. Lots of great men violated this taboo. After all, the meat was indeed tasty. She could just as well prepare spicy fried beef. Slowly Suranjan was able to emerge from the shame, fear, regret and prejudice of his childhood. Sudhamay was indeed a teacher to the family. Suranjan believed his father to be a sort of superman. No one of such calmness and sensibility; with so much honesty, simplicity, purity of thought and deed; with such a deep sense of secularism and love for everyone and noncommunal feeling, could survive these days.

Suranjan didn't care to touch the newspaper. He found no reason to lean over the paper to read the statements made by members of the intelligentsia against the communal riots, and to look at photographs of peace processions. These would hardly be able to inspire confidence in his wounded heart. Rather, he found it more useful to look for that elusive cat, which had no caste, no religion or communal identity. If only he could be a cat.

How many days had Sudhamay remained a prisoner in the Pakistani army camp? Six days? Seven? He hadn't been able to tell for sure. All he knew was that he had been extremely thirsty. So overpowering was this craving for water that, although blindfolded and trussed up, he was rolling in search of an earthen pitcher full of water. But where would he find such a vessel in the camp? The river Brahmaputra gurgled far in the distance, and there was no water container. Sudhamay's parched tongue and throat felt like dried wood. When he whimpered for water, the armymen would only laugh derisively at him. One day, however, his tormentors obliged him in a perverted way. They removed his blindfold and pissed into a small metal pot in his full view. When they tried to force the urine down his throat, he turned his face away in revulsion. But one of them forced his jaws open while another poured the contents into his mouth to the lusty cheers of other military personnel in the camp. He would have preferred poison as the salty warm water trickled down his throat. They suspended him from the beam across the roof and beat him.

They insisted that he convert to Islam, while showering blows on him, reciting the customary *Qualma*. He resisted with the doggedness of the black boy Kunta Kinte in Alex Haley's *Roots*, who, despite being repeatedly whipped for not accepting his new name ,Toby, stuck stubbornly to his original name.

When Sudhamay stubbornly refused to be a Muslim, one day they lifted his *lungi* and mutilated his penis, saying, "Since you are so persistently refusing to be a Muslim, let's make you one." Their action was accompanied by the same peal of wild cheers as on the day they forced urine down his throat. Sudhamay possibly lost consciousness immediately. He had no hope of coming out alive. He saw the Hindus trussed up like him, who, although willing to become Muslims in deference to their captors' command and to save their lives, couldn't escape death. Perhaps moved by kindness resulting from completely mutilating his penis, they let Sudhamay go. But his emerging alive from this death trap spoiled his plans to go to Nalitabari to train himself for war as a freedom fighter.

When he regained his senses by the side of a drain running along Dak Bunglow, he found himself alive but bleeding from his serious wounds. He was still amazed at his strength that made him drag his pain-racked, inert body with its broken leg and several fractured ribs up to Brahma Palli. Perhaps it was the same inner strength that kept him alive. Returning home, he fell face down before Kiranmayee, who shuddered seeing him in that condition. It was Kiranmayee who guided him to leave his house and cross the Brahmaputra by a ferry boat, dragging two weeping children. But she didn't shed any tears. Faizul's mother would suggest, "Let me call a *maulavi*, better become Mus-

lims for your safety. You try to convince your husband."
Kiran still didn't cry. She hid deep inside her all her pains.
After all the members of the household had fallen asleep,
she would tear strips from her sari to bandage Sudhamay's
wounds, keeping her eyes dry. She released all her pent-up
pains during this harrowing period when, following the
country's liberation, the entire village celebrated amidst
shouts of *Jai Bangla*. Unconcerned about what other villagers would say, she cried, resting her head on Sudhamay's chest. And she cried unrestrainedly like a child.

Now looking at Kiranmayee, Sudhamay got the impression that, like during those cursed months in 1971, she
had again started to gather her agonies. Suddenly one day,
there would be an outburst breaking all her silence. Like
dark clouds, sorrow was being heaped up inside. One day
it would turn into a torrential rain when good tidings akin
to those Jai Bangla days would arrive. But when would
that freedom arrive, that freedom for her to wear conch
shell bangles and display the vermilion mark on her forehead and for him to put on a *dhoti* without fear? When
would it end, this long, suffocating, stormy night like the
ones witnessed during 1971? Sudhamay had noticed that
patients were no longer coming to him. Even in the time of
torrential rain, he would treat at least six to seven patients
a day. He felt the drudgery of sitting idly at home listening
to the processions passing and intermittently shouting slogans like, "*Naraye Taquebir, Allahu Akbar*" (Hindus, if you
want to survive, quit this country at once). At any time
bombs might be hurled at his house, fundamentalists
might set it on fire; they might loot it any moment they
liked or kill anyone. But were the Hindus leaving the
country en masse? Sudhamay knew many of them had

done so after the 1990 riots. In the latest census, the Hindus and Muslims were not counted separately; otherwise, the number of Hindu evacuees would become apparent.

Dust had accumulated on the bookshelves. Sudhamay tried to blow away the dust. But the attempt seemed futile. As he started to remove the dust with the loose end of his *punjabi*, the title of one book arrested his attention: *Yearbook of Bangladesh Statistical Bureau*. It gave the figures of 1986. There were details on 1974 and 1981. In '74, the total population of Chittagong Hill Tracts was five hundred and eight thousand, which increased to five hundred and eighty thousand in 1981. The number of Muslims within this time period rose from ninety-six thousand to one hundred and eighty-eight thousand. The number of Hindus rose during the same period from fifty-three thousand to sixty-six thousand. The growth rate of Muslims was 95.83 percent, while that of Hindus was 24.53 percent. In Comilla, the Muslim population showed a growth rate of 20.13 percent, rising from five million, two hundred fifty thousand to six million, six hundred thousand, contrasting with the meager 0.18 percent for the slender one-thousand increase in the Hindu population from 5,064,000 in 1974 to 5,065,000 in 1981. The population in Faridpur went up by 17.34 percent. Meanwhile, Muslims went from 3,100,000 to over 3,852,000, recording a 24.26 percent growth rate. On the other hand, the number of Hindus dropped from a little more than nine hundred thousand to a bit less than that, which meant a decline of 5.30 percent. In Pabna the population had increased by 21.13 percent between 1974 and 1981. There were 2,546,000 Muslims in 1974, and in 1981 the figure had gone up to 3,167,000. The rate of increase among Muslims was 24.39 percent. On the other hand, there were 2,060,000 Hindus in 1974 and in 1981 their number had decreased to 2,051,000. The rate of increase was –3.46 percent. The same decline in Hindus persisted in Rajsahi, where their population had increased 23.78 percent, while the Muslims had increased by 27.20 percent. In 1974 Hindus numbered 5,058,000 and in 1981 they numbered 5,003,000. The rate of increase among Hindus was –9.68 percent. On page 112 of the book, Sudhamay noticed the following fact: In 1974, the Hindus constituted 13.5 percent of the country's total population, while it was 12.1 percent in 1981. Where were the Hindus going? Sudhamay cleaned the lenses of his spectacles on the sleeve of his *punjabi*. Are they going away? Why? Did real freedom lie in this sort of escape? Shouldn't they have offered resistance by staying in the country? Sudhamay again felt the urge to call the fleeing Hindus cowards.

He was not feeling well. After taking down the statistical yearbook, he felt weakness in his right arm. In his effort to replace the book, he felt the same weakness. He called Kiranmayee, but noticed that his tongue, too, felt heavy. Terror, hard and unyielding, enveloped him. He tried to walk, but his right leg appeared to have very little strength. Still, he called: "Kiran, Kiran."

Kiranmayee had just put a vessel full of lentil soup on the stove. Silently she stood in front of him. Sudhamay wanted to offer his right arm to her, but he couldn't raise it. "Kiran, please put me to bed," he said haltingly.

Kiranmayee, too, was at a loss to understand what had happened. Why was he shaking like this? Why was his speech again slurred? Somehow, she put Sudhamay to bed and asked, "What has happened to you?"

"Where is Suranjan?"

"He just went out. Didn't listen to my warning."

"I'm not feeling well, Kiran. Just do something."

"Why is your speech becoming slurred? What has happened?"

"I'm feeling no strength in my right arm and leg. Am I becoming paralyzed, Kiranmayee?"

Kiranmayee grasped Sudhamay's two arms with hers and said, "Let no evil touch you. It's all because of weakness. You can't sleep during the night, you're not eating well either. Perhaps that's why."

Sudhamay was restless. Uneasiness was creeping in all over his body. He said, "Kiran, do you think that I am dying? I feel that I am."

"Whom shall I call? Will Haripadababu do?"

Sudhamay clasped Kiranmayee with his left arm. He said, "Please don't leave me. Where's Maya?"

"You know she's gone to Parul's house. Hasn't returned from there."

"Where is my son, Kiran, where is my son?"

"Are you all right?"

"Kiran, please open the doors and windows."

"Let me call Haripadababu. You please keep still for a while."

"Those Hindus have escaped from their homes. You won't find them. Better call Maya."

"Who will I give the message to? There's no one in the house."

"Don't move even a bit from here, Kiran. Please call Suranjan."

Sudhamay then mumbled something which couldn't be understood. Kiranmayee shivered. Should she cry out for help from the people of the neighborhood? Or some

100

neighbor with whom they had been living for many years? Her heart sank at the thought that there was hardly anyone who would come to her rescue. Should she call someone from the houses of Hyder, Gautam or Shafique Sahab? Kiranmayee felt quite helpless. The smell and smoke of burned lentils filled the room.

Suranjan had no particular plans to go anywhere even today. Once he thought of going to Belal's place. After crossing Kakrail, he found the ransacked remains of a sweetmeat shop. The shop chairs and tables had been brought out to the road for a bonfire. Burned wood and ashes lay in heaps. Suranjan stared at this scene of destruction as long as he could. Pulak, too, lived in nearby Chamelibag. But he suddenly changed his mind. He decided to go to Pulak's house, instructing the rickshaw puller to turn on a lane at the left. He hadn't seen him for a long time. Pulak lived in a rented flat. He worked in a nongovernment organization. Suranjan had gone to Belal's house quite often just for idle talk. Yet he never felt any urge to meet his college friend Pulak.

He pressed the bell. But no sound came from inside. He went on pressing the bell. A very feeble voice asked from inside, "Who's that—"

"This is Suranjan."

"Which Suranjan?"

"Suranjan Dutta."

The sound of the lock could be heard. Pulak himself opened the door. He said in a hushed voice, "Get inside, quick."

"What's the matter, why such an arrangement for protection? You could have easily installed a peephole."

Pulak relocked the door. Then he pulled the lock to check if it had been properly fastened. Pulak again asked in an undertone, "Strange, you've come out quite casually."

"Feeling like that."

"What do you mean? Don't you have any fear? Are you hell-bent to die just to display your courage? Or is it just an adventure for you?"

Reclining on the sofa, Suranjan said, "Whatever you think."

Fear shone in Pulak's eyes. He sat by Suranjan's side on the sofa. Heaving up a long sigh, he said, "Are you aware of what is happening around?"

"Nope."

"The situation at Bhola is extremely alarming. About fifty thousand Hindus belonging to ten thousand families in places like Tajmuddin, Golokpur in Borhanuddin police station, Chhoto Dauri, Shambhupur, Daser Haat, Darirampur, Padmaman and Maniram villages have been robbed of all their possessions and turned into paupers. Everything they could call their own has been plundered and later set on fire. The extent of losses would be to the tune of five hundred million takas. The people have neither any clothes to cover themselves nor any food to eat. They didn't leave a single house untouched by fire. Hundreds of shops have been looted. Not a single Hindu shop in Daser Haat market has survived this orgy of violence. These shelterless people are spending their winter nights under the open sky. In Bhola town, Madanmohan Thakurbari temple, Lakshmi-Govinda Thakurbari, its temple, the *akhra* of Mahaprabhu, all of them have been looted first and then burned down. Not a single temple or *akhra* stands now in the areas of Daultkhan, Charfashion, Tajmuddin and Lalmohan police station. All the Hindu houses in a two-mile stretch at a place called Ghuinyar Haat have been set ablaze. On the seventh night, the large *akhra* in Daulatkhan police station area was burned down. The *akhra* at Borhanuddin Bazar has gone the same way. Fifty houses in Qutuba village met with the same fate. All the Hindu houses in the Charfashion police station area have been looted. A Hindu called Arabinda Dey has been stabbed." Pulak's chronology of violence came to an end.

"Where is Neela?"

"She is shivering with fear. How do you feel?"

Suranjan relaxed comfortably on the sofa, closing his eyes. He was wondering why, instead of going to Belal's place, which was just next door, he sauntered into Pulak's flat. Had he turned a communal in his heart or had the situation made him so?

"I'm alive, this much I can say."

Pulak's six-year-old son was crying and rolling on the floor. Rather, he was sobbing in fits. Pulak explained the reason for his crying: his next-door playmates were not allowing him to take part in games with them. They said he wouldn't be accepted in their circles, as the huzoor had forbidden them to keep contact with the Hindus.

"Who is this huzoor?"

"Huzoor is that *maulavi* who comes in the morning to teach them Arabic."

"Isn't Anis Ahmed, who is a member of the Communist party, your neighbor in the next flat? He, too, allows his children to be taught Arabic by this blessed huzoor?"

"Yes," affirmed Pulak.

Suranjan again closed his eyes. He tried to fathom Pulak's feelings. He could feel the wails of Pulak's little

103

son as if he, too, had been forcibly kept out of the play-ground. The people with whom he had played so long or whom he thought of playing with, were not accepting him in their circle. The huzoors had issued a religious order. The Hindus must not be accepted as playmates. He re-membered Maya once returning from school crying. She said the teacher had turned her out of the class. The reality was that religion was a compulsory subject in her class cur-riculum. And she was invariably forced out of the Is-lamiaat class. She was the lone Hindu girl in the school. That was why no Hindu teacher was provided specially for her. Standing alone close to the verandah railing, she would feel companionless, utterly isolated.

Sudhamay asked, "Why were you turned out of the class?"

"Everyone joins the class. They leave me out for being a Hindu, that's the reason."

Sudhamay held Maya close to his chest. Humiliation, pain kept him speechless for a long time. The same day, he visited the house of the religion teacher and requested that he not keep her out of class so that she wouldn't feel she was someone different. Maya became much happier, but she came under the spell of her newly learned alphabet: Alif, Be, Te and so on. While playing at home alone, she would blurt out suddenly, *"Alhaamdulillah he rabbil al amin, ar rahmanir rahim."* Hearing this outlandish expression, Ki-ranmayee would ask Sudhamay, "What is all this she is doing? Will she be able to pursue her school studies only by giving up her own religion and communal identity?" Sudhamay, too, was worried. If the girl became an addict to Islam in an effort to maintain her peace of mind, a new problem would then arise. Within a week, he wrote to the school headmaster, pointing out that religion was a matter of individual conviction, hence not a requirement to be included in the academic curriculum. Besides, if he didn't feel the need for his daughter to be taught a particular religion, then the school authorities couldn't take that same responsibility upon themselves. And the teaching of religion could be replaced by inclusion in the syllabus teaching about outstanding people, great men's lives. This would benefit the students of all communities alike and not give the minorities an inferiority complex. The school authorities didn't pay any heed to Sudhamay's pleading. What was going on was allowed to continue.

Meanwhile Neela came into the sitting room. She was a beautiful, slim woman, who was usually well turned out. But today her dress was grossly unkempt. There were dark patches under her anxious eyes. She asked as she entered, "Suranjanda, how long has it been since you've visited us? You don't care to know if we are alive or not. Yet we hear you visit the house next door." She burst into tears as she said this.

But why should Neela cry over his not coming around? Was it her concern for the helplessness of her community since she had to bear its pain, or her awareness of the same agony and lack of security that affected Suranjan as well? Perhaps this made her realize that Pulak, Alak and Suranjan were co-sharers of her own helplessness. The family appeared to be very close to Suranjan. He never felt the urge to visit them, even when he had taken part in animated discussion in Belal's next-door residence even four or five days ago. This awareness of the closeness of this family was a new experience for him.

"Why are you getting so nervous? They won't be able to cause much harm in Dhaka. There are strong police guards at Shankharibazar, Islampur, Tantibazar," Suranjan said as he sought to allay her fear.

"The police were there during the last riots. They just idly watched as the mischief-makers plundered and set fire to Dhakeshwari temple. Did they lift even a finger?" countered Neela.

"Hum," Suranjan replied, unable to add anything more.

"Why did you take the risk of coming out on the streets? The Muslims can't be trusted. Someone you consider to be a friend can easily slit your throat without any compunction."

Suranjan again closed his eyes. Could he reduce the agony within by keeping his eyes closed? The noise of some argument was coming from outside, perhaps a shop belonging to some Hindu was being set on fire. If he closed his eyes, he could inhale the smell of burning; he could also visualize the fundamentalists armed with long choppers, axes and shovels dancing wildly. He went to see the injured Gautam last night. He found him lying with nasty livid bruises under his eyes and all over his body. Suranjan sat by the bedside, keeping his hand on Gautam's chest. He didn't ask him anything; rather, his touch spoke for him. Gautam said on his own, "Dada, I did nothing. They were returning after offering noon prayers at the mosque. I was asked by my mother to buy some eggs, as we had nothing to eat at home. I thought there was hardly any risk in buying from the local shop since I wasn't going anywhere far. After buying the eggs, as I was taking the change, suddenly someone kicked me heavily on my back. What could I do on my own, as the attackers were six or seven in number? The egg-seller, other passersby just watched them beat me with amused detachment, never trying to interrupt. For no reason, they assaulted me and continued to hit me even when I fell to the ground. Please believe me, I never said anything to them. They were shouting, "You bloody Hindu, son of an infidel, we'll finish you off. You think you can get away after smashing our mosque? We'll hound you out of the country."

Suranjan just listened, he had nothing to say. He could feel the furious thumping of Gautam's heart. Had he ever heard his own heart beat so hard? Maybe once or twice he had had such an experience.

Neela brought tea. Conversation over the tea touched on Maya.

"I'm very worried about Maya," said Suranjan. "Who knows if she will marry Jehangir on a sudden impulse?"

"What are you saying, Suranjanda? Try to make her see reason. In bad times, anyone is prone to make sudden decisions."

"Let me see. I'll try to pick her up from Parul's house on my way back. Maya is getting spoiled. Just for the tremendous craze for keeping alive, she might become a Farida Begum or something like that. Selfish!" Suranjan concluded.

Neela's eyes were restless with anxiety. Alak, her son, fell asleep as his cries trailed off, leaving tear marks on his cheeks. Pulak kept on pacing to and fro, with his fretfulness working its way into Suranjan. The tea was left unsipped and turned cold. Suranjan craved a cup, but his desire had somehow disappeared. Closing his eyes, he tried to think that this country belonged to him, to his father, grandfather, great-grandfather and so on. Still, he was feeling isolated. Why could he have no rights in this land?

He had no right to move freely, to speak out about whatever he liked, to put on clothing of his choice and to think freely. He would have to cringe in fear, hide himself, he wouldn't be able to go where he liked or talk. Suranjan felt suffocated like a man being strangled. He suddenly held his throat firmly with his hands. Unconcerned about his loss of breath, Suranjan impulsively blurted out, "Pulak, I'm finding no interest in anything."

Beads of sweat were gathering on Pulak's forehead. Why was he perspiring during the winter? Suranjan touched his own forehead. He was surprised to find it sticky. Was it fear? But no one was beating them up. Or killing them. Why, then, did they feel scared with their hearts beating rapidly?

Suranjan dialed the telephone. Dilip Dey, a spirited student leader of the past, suddenly came to his mind. Dilip Dey was at home.

"How are you, Dada? Are you suffering any inconvenience? I hope nothing untoward has happened."

"There's no problem except not having peace of mind. And why should it happen to me only? The entire country is going this way."

"That's true."

"How are you? Must have heard of the situation at Chittagong."

"Three temples at Bauria at Sandeep police station, two at Kalapania, three at Magdhara, three at Teuria, one at Harishpur, one at Rahmatpur, one at West Sarikai, and one more at Mitebhanga have been destroyed. At West Sarikai, a man called Sucharu Das was beaten up and then robbed of fifteen thousand takas. Two houses at Tokatuli have been looted and two men stabbed. One house at Kachua in Patia police station area, one temple at Bhatikain . . ."

"Where did you get such precise, accurate reports?"

108

"You are forgetting that I am from Chittagong. Even if I don't go looking, reports reach me anyway." Then he resumed his bizarre litany of looting, arson, and destruction of Hindu houses and temples in numerous places that included Bailchari, East Chumbul, Sarafbhita, Paira union, Shilk union, Badamtoli, Joava, Boalgao, and Tegota of Bashkholi, Rangunia, Chandnaish, and Anwara, making a total of thirty-five houses, seven temples and one hermitage.

Suranjan added his token to this grisly list: ten Kali temples including those at Kaibalyadham, Tulshidham hermitage, Abhay Mitra cremation ground, and Panchanandham.

Dilip Dey was irrepressible about pouring out the gory details of destruction and continued to rattle out names of places and numbers of houses, shops, temples, and cremation grounds as well as other religious places put to sack and fire: Sadarghat Kalibari, Golpahar cremation ground temple, shops on Jamalkhan Road and Sirajuddaula Road, Enayet bazar, K. C. Dey Road, Kaibalyadham Malipara, Sadarghat fishermen's colony, the same in Idgaon Agrabad, Manager colony at Bahaddarghat, Meerer Sarai, Seetakunda, Saberia, Masdia, Hadinagar, Besharat, Odeyapur, Khujuria, Jafarabad, Muradpur union, Mahalanka, Baharpur, Baraipara, Bansbaria, Barabkunda, Farhadpur, which brought the total number of affected and uprooted families to several hundred, not to mention other places of religious importance.

"How much more can I take, Dilipda? No more, please," pleaded Suranjan.

"Are you sick, Suranjan? Your voice doesn't appear to be normal."

"I'm not really sure."

❖ ❖ ❖

As Suranjan put down the telephone receiver, Pulak suggested looking up Debabrata. One by one Suranjan rang up Debabrata, Mahadeb Bhattacharyya, Asit Pal, Sajal Dhar, Madhabi Ghosh, Kuntala Chowdhury, Saral Dey, Rabindra Gupta, Nikhil Sanyal and Nirmal Sen Gupta. He wanted to know how they were. Contacts were made with acquaintances following a long break. He also felt a sort of intimacy with them.

The phone rang. The sound of the ring was magnified into the beating of big drums in Suranjan's ears. He felt uneasy. It was a call for Pulak from Cox Bazar. After finishing the call, Pulak said, "The followers of Jamat Islam have set fire to the national flag at Cox Bazar."

Suranjan listened to this revelation silently and was amazed at his own detachment. He should have exploded in anger at this news. But now it seemed it mattered little to him if the national flag was burned down in this manner. This was not his flag. But why was he feeling so? He reproached himself for nurturing such a feeling which made him appear small, mean and selfish in his own eyes. Yet he couldn't get over his nonchalance. He remained unmoved at the report of a flag burning. Pulak came closer to Suranjan. He said, "Don't go home today. Better stay here. No one can say what's going to happen to you once you're out. We shouldn't venture out on the roads at such a time."

Yesterday, Lutfar gave him the same advice. But Suranjan could feel the sincere tone of Pulak's request contrasting with a subtle vanity bordering on insolence in Lutfar's voice.

Neela sighed deeply and said, "Perhaps we won't be

110

able to stay in this country anymore. We have not yet been harmed, but tomorrow or the day after may be different. What terrible uncertainty we all have to live with! I really feel it would be preferable to live a life of poverty than one that is so uncertain."

Suranjan very nearly agreed with Pulak's suggestion. But thinking of Kiranmayee and Sudhamay and their mounting worries in the event of his not returning home prompted him to get up. He said, "If anything happens, let it happen. At the most I'll be a martyr at the hands of Muslims. Just an unclaimed body that will lie under our national flower, Shapla. People will say, it's nothing but an accident. What do you say?" Suranjan asked, laughing. Pulak's and Neela's faces didn't reflect any smile.

Coming out he got a rickshaw. It was just eight in the evening. He was averse to such an early return home. Pulak was a college mate. After marrying, he had nicely organized his family and household. Nothing like that had happened to Suranjan, although he kept getting older. For the last two months, he had come to know a girl named Ratna. Suranjan felt the urge to get married and settle down in life. He had thought of becoming a recluse when Parvin was married off. But Ratna had roused him somewhat from his otherwise listless life. Now he felt like setting his life on a proper course. However, he still couldn't tell Ratna that she was becoming very appealing to him. A few days after they met, Ratna asked "What are you doing now?"

"Nothing," Suranjan replied, pouting.

"No sort of job, business or any professional career, nothing?"

"That's right."

"Didn't you engage in politics? What about that?"

111

"Gave it up."

"I knew you were a member of the Communist Youth Union."

"I don't like those things anymore."

"Then what do you like?"

"Just to move about, to study human nature."

"Don't you like the trees, the river, such things?"

"I do. But still I find man singularly absorbing. I like to unravel the knots of inherent mystery in man."

"Do you write poems?"

"Oh no. But I have plenty of poet friends."

"Do you drink?"

"Quite infrequently."

"But you smoke cigarettes quite heavily!"

"You may say so. But I don't have enough money to smoke as I like."

"Smoking is injurious to the health, do you agree?"

"I'm aware of it, but nothing can be done."

"Why are you not married as yet?"

"No girl liked me."

"Absolutely no one?"

"One, in fact, did. But she didn't take the risk ultimately."

"Why?"

"She was a Muslim and I'm called a Hindu. To marry a Hindu, one doesn't have to become a Hindu. But if I went ahead, then my name would have changed to an Abdus, Saber or something like that."

Ratna laughed at the way Suranjan put it casually. She said, "It's better not to marry; life is short, so it's better to pass through it without any ties or commitments!"

"That's perhaps why you're not going in that direction."

"Exactly so."

"In one sense, it's the right decision."

"If you also think the same way, then you and I shall make good friends."

"But friendship has a far deeper meaning for me. Mere chance similarity between a decision or two doesn't make good friends."

"Shall I try very hard to be your friend?"

"Does one have to pray to earn your friendship?" Suranjan asked, laughing aloud. "Shall I be that fortunate?"

"Do you lack confidence?"

"No. It's not that. I have confidence in myself, but having confidence in others is a different matter."

"Why don't you try to rely on me?"

Suranjan was in a buoyant mood all that day. He was trying to think about Ratna again today, perhaps to drive away the gloom from his mind. That had become his practice, a sort of panacea to do away with the mental depression. How was Ratna doing now? Should he go to Azimpur to look her up? He would ask, "How are you, Ratna Mitra?" Would Ratna feel embarrassed to see him? Suranjan was undecided as to what he should do now. He could guess that Hindus were getting in touch with each other as fellow sufferers of the same terror of communalism. And certainly Ratna wouldn't be surprised. She was more likely to think that at this critical time, when Hindus were inquiring about the well-being of other Hindus and coming to each other's aid, it wouldn't be unlikely for Suranjan to go to her without the usual formalities.

He instructed the rickshaw puller to turn in the direction of Azimpur. Ratna was not very tall; She didn't even come to Suranjan's shoulders. She had a fair round face and her eyes revealed an unfathomable sadness. Suranjan failed to comprehend this. He brought out the address written in the telephone index and searched for the house. He could not fail to trace the house.

Ratna was not at home. Keeping the door slightly ajar, an old man asked his name.

"Suranjan," he said.

"But she has left Dhaka."

"When? Where?" Suranjan felt ashamed at being so distraught and emotionally charged in making these queries.

"Sylhet."

"Do you have any idea when she'll be returning?"

"No."

What had made Ratna go to Sylhet? Official work, a sudden urge to travel, or was she running away? But the informant, sure of his Hindu identity since his name was Suranjan, certainly would not mislead him. With these thoughts swirling in his mind, Suranjan walked down Azimpur's streets. Here he was not recognized. Pedestrians wearing caps, groups of animatedly talking youths, the street teenagers, none could spot him. But if they could know who he was, if they wanted to lift him physically and deposit him in the graveyard, would he be in a position to resist them? He could hear the thumping of his heart again. Walking fast, he found he was perspiring. He wore no woolens, a chilly wind wind was piercing him through his light cotton shirt; yet his forehead was awash with beads of perspiration. He reached Palashi, walking all the way. When he arrived in Palashi he would find out how Nirmalendu Goon was passing the days. He had rented the gardener's room in the colony of the Class IV employees of the Engineer's University. Suranjan had deep respect for this ever-truthful man. As he lightly knocked on the door, it was opened widely by a girl aged about ten or twelve. With his feet on the bed, Nirmalendu Goon was intently watching TV. Seeing Suranjan, he sang a line of a Tagore song to greet his arrival, *Eso eso amar ghare eso amar ghare.*

"What's there to see on the TV?" asked Suranjan. "Why, advertisements. Sunlight battery, Zia silk sari, Peps Zel toothpaste. Hear renditions of Muslim religious songs like Hamd and Naat, see the quotations of the Koran."

The reply sent Suranjan into peals of laughter. He said, "You spend your time in this manner? Certainly you've not gone out?"

"A four-year-old Muslim boy lives with me. I am solely dependent on him for my survival. Yesterday I went to Ashim's place. But all along, he walked ahead of me."

Suranjan laughed again. He asked, "You opened the door without checking who had come. What if it had been someone else?"

Goon said, smiling, "At about two last night, some boys were planning a procession standing on the pavement outside. They were discussing what sort of slogans could be raised to denigrate the Hindus. I shouted, 'What are you doing there? Get out.' They moved away. Seeing my long mane and beard, they think I'm a Muslim, most likely a *maulavi.*"

"Don't you write poems?"

"No, what's the point in writing? I've given up writing."

"And I hear you go to a gambling den in Azimpur market at night."

"Yes, I pass my time that way. But I haven't gone there for the last few days."

115

"Why?"

"I don't get off the bed from sheer fright. It seems if I get off, they'll catch hold of me."

"Has the TV said anything? Have they shown the temple destruction?"

"Nothing of it. TV would rather give you the impression that this is a land of perpetual communal harmony, nothing like riots happening here. All this mischief occurs only in India."

"Someone told me that till now, there had been some four thousand riots in India. But still, Indian Muslims are not leaving that country. But Hindus in this country have one foot in Bangladesh and the other in India. That is, Muslims in India are fighting, while the Hindus in Bangladesh are fleeing the country."

Goon spoke gravely: "Muslims there can fight because India is a secular state. Here the fundamentalists are in power. What sort of struggle can be expected here? Here the Hindus are second-class citizens. Can second-class citizens have the guts to fight?"

"Why don't you write about this?"

"I feel like writing. But if I do, they will brand me as an Indian agent. I feel like writing so many things, but restrain myself from doing so. What's the point in writing?"

Goon unmindfully watched the toy box called the television. Geeta left a cup of tea on the table. But Suranjan hardly felt any urge to drink. He was touched by the inner agony of the poet.

Suddenly laughing, the poet said, "You are inquiring about the well-being of others. What about your own security?"

"Well, Goonda, you often go gambling, but have you ever won?"

116

"No."

"Then why do you play?"

"If I don't play, they start abusing me in the names of my parents, that's why I have to play."

Suranjan burst into resounding laughter. Goon joined him. This man really could crack jokes. He could gamble in a casino in Las Vegas and suffer mosquito bites in a slum in Palashi with the same equanimity. He found nothing objectionable or irritable. He was spending his time quite merrily in this twelve-foot-by-twelve-foot room. Suranjan wondered how he could enjoy such undefiled mirth and merriment. Did he actually enjoy real happiness or did he secretly nurture a sense of grief behind his jovial façade? Or did he pass this unbearable time in laughter since he could hardly go against the tide?

Suranjan got up. The waves of his inner sorrow were on the rise. Was this sorrow something infectious? He started walking toward Tikatuli. He wouldn't take a rickshaw. He had just five takas left. He bought cigarettes at the Palashi crossing. The shop owner looked at him as he asked for Bangla Fives. The way the man glanced at him sent Suranjan's heart pounding again. Was the man aware that he was a Hindu who could be beaten up with impunity for the demolition of the Babri mosque? Suranjan moved away quickly after buying his cigarettes. But why were such things happening to him? He came away from the shop without lighting the cigarette. Was it the fear that asking for a light might expose him as a Hindu? No one can be spotted as a Hindu from looks alone. Still, he suspected something in his gait, use of language and way of glancing that might give him away. He was startled as a dog barked at the Tikatuli crossing. He heard some boys shouting "Catch him,

117

catch him" from behind. He looked no more in that direction. He started to run for his life. Soaked all over with perspiration, the buttons of his shirt flying open with the exertion, still he kept on running and running.

After running to the point of exhaustion, he looked behind to find no one at his back. Had he then run for nothing? Were the shouts not actually aimed at him? Or was it just a hallucination?

When he returned late at night, instead of calling from outside the main door, he unlocked his door and walked into his own room. Entering the room, he could hear a pathetic wail of "Oh God, oh God." He wondered for a while whether by chance some Hindu relative or guest had arrived in his house. It might be like that. Still thinking this, as he was about to enter Sudhamay's room, he was amazed to see Kiranmayee in front of a clay idol installed on a small wooden stool. Putting the loose end of her sari around her neck in the typical ritualistic manner, she was in a kneeling position crying, "Bhagaran, Bhagaran."

Such a scene had never been witnessed in this house. This strange, unfamiliar sight so astounded Suranjan for some time that he lost all capacity to think of doing anything. He couldn't decide if he would smash the clay idol on the ground or pull up Kiranmayee's bowed head. He felt revulsion at the sight of bowed heads. Coming near, he made Kiranmayee stand on her feet. He asked, "Why are you sitting with that idol? Is the idol going to save you?"

Kiranmayee shook with the spasms of a muffled cry. She said, "Your father's limbs are becoming paralyzed. His speech has become slurred."

Immediately, he turned his attention to Sudhamay, who was lying on the bed. He was mumbling something which couldn't be followed. Sitting close to his father, Suranjan moved Sudhamay's arm. It was inert, devoid of strength. Suranjan felt as if his heart had been struck by the blow of an axe. One side of his grandfather's body became paralyzed in the same manner. The doctor diagnosed the condition as a cerebral stroke. He had to be given lots of medicines. A physiotherapist would exercise his inactive arms and legs. Sudhamay's eyes traveled blankly between Kiranmayee and Suranjan.

They had no relative nearby. To whom should he go for help? They had no close relatives. All of them, one after another, had left the country. Suranjan felt absolutely alone, hard up and helpless. As the son, the entire responsibility would now devolve on him. He was the worthless son of the family. Even now, he just aimlessly roamed around with no job. His business attempts had foundered. If Sudhamay became disabled, they would have to take shelter in the streets.

"Did Kamal or anyone look in?" He asked Kiranmayee.

"No," said Kiranmayee, shaking her head.

No one had cared to look up Suranjan. But he had gone around the city. Everybody was all right, barring him. No family possibly faced this much financial hardship and uncertainty. Suranjan, holding the dead arm of his father, felt deep compassion for him. Who knew whether he had deliberately decided to become dead in this hostile world?

"Hasn't Maya returned?" Suranjan asked, jerking himself up all of a sudden.

"No."

"But why?" Suranjan shouted in a sudden fit of anger.

Kiranmayee was taken aback at his vehemence. Suranjan had always been too gentle to behave like a hothead. But why had he raised his voice today? Maya's departure for

119

Parul's place couldn't be faulted. Rather, it gave some sort of comfort. If the mob targeted this Hindu house for looting, the only treasure in it would be Maya. They treated the women as valuable commodities, gold or similar objects.

Suranjan paced restlessly all about the room and said, "Why does she have so much faith in the Muslims? How long are they going to protect her?"

Kiranmayee couldn't understand why her son, instead of calling the doctor for the gravely ill Sudhamay, was making such a fuss over Maya's taking shelter in a Muslim house.

Suranjan muttered, "A doctor will have to be called, but tell me now where the money for treatment is going to come from? At the threat of a couple of urchins you hastily sold a house worth one million takas for a paltry two hundred thousand. Now don't you feel ashamed to live like a beggar?"

"It wasn't the fear of local youths alone; there were lots of legal troubles over the house," Kiranmayee replied feebly.

Suranjan kicked aside a chair on the verandah that stood in his way.

"And your daughter has gone out to marry a Muslim. She thinks Muslims will keep on feeding her. She wants to be rich."

He stormed out of the house. Two doctors were there in the vicinity. Haripada Sarkar lived near Tikatuli crossing, and two houses down lived Amjad Hussain. Whom would he call? Suranjan kept on walking aimlessly. The fuss he made over Maya's not coming back—was it really born out of his concern for her, or was he angry at her dependence on the Muslims? Was he starting to turn communal-minded? He was not sure himself. He moved in the direction of Tikatuli crossing.

Day Four

Hyder had come to Suranjan's house not to inquire about his well being, but just for *adda*, idle talk. Hyder was associated with Awami League politics. At one time, Suranjan had thought of joining him as a partner in business, but its bleak prospects forced him to give up the plan. Hyder liked politics. So had Suranjan once, but these days he was totally averse to anything concerning the subject. He didn't want to bother himself with what Ershad had done, what Khaleda was presently doing, or what Hasina was going to do. Lying quietly on the bed had more appeal to him. Hyder continued his monologue. He went on with a peroration on the state religion of Islam.

"Well, Hyder," Suranjan said, propping himself up in bed, "does your state have the right to create a rift among people conforming to different religious faiths?"

Lifting his feet onto the table, Hyder, who was turning the pages of Suranjan's red-covered books, guffawed. He said, "What do you mean, 'your state'? Don't you think the state is yours, too?"

Suranjan smirked. He said, "I'll put some questions to you. And I expect some answers."

Hyder sat up straight and said, "The reply to your question is no, which means the state has no right to create bad blood among different communities."

Taking a long drag on his cigarette, Suranjan asked, "Does the state have any right to prefer one religion to another?"

There came Hyder's pat reply, "No."

Suranjan fired the third question: "Does the state have any right to show partiality?"

Hyder shook his head.

"Does the parliament have the right to change the policy of secularism enshrined in the People's Republic of Bangladesh's constitution as a fundamental principle?"

Hyder listened to him attentively. Then he said, "Certainly not."

Suranjan let out another salvo: "The country's sovereignty is based on the equal rights of all people. In the name of amending the constitution, isn't the very basis of the constitution being destroyed?"

Hyder, this time, narrowed his eyes and looked at Suranjan. Was he joking? Why raise all these old issues over again?

Suranjan fired his sixth question: "Isn't the declaration of Islam as the state religion going to deprive other religious communities of patronage and acknowledgement?"

Wrinkling his forehead, Hyder admitted that it would. The answers to all these questions were as well known to Suranjan as they were to Hyder. Suranjan was well aware of Hyder's identical views on these points. Hyder wondered what had prompted Suranjan to put these questions to him. Was it a test to find out if Hyder was even remotely communal at a time when the constitution was facing its eighth amendment?

Suranjan stubbed out his cigarette in the ashtray and said, "My last question is why Bangladesh is being sucked into the whirlpool of a two-nation controversy which was the motivating factor behind the creation of two separate states out of British India? And in whose interest is this attempt being made?"

Hyder this time lit a cigarette and did not make any reply; breathing a puff of smoke, he said, "Please remember, even Jinna rejected the two-nation question by announcing that from now on there would be no separate religious identity for the Muslims, Hindus, Christians and Buddhists. Irrespective of their caste and religion they would be citizens of a single country, Pakistan, and they would be identified solely as Pakistanis."

Suranjan sat up straight and said, "We were better off as Pakistanis, don't you think?"

Hyder jumped to his feet in excitement. He said, "In fact, Pakistan was not good at all. Nor did you have anything to look forward to from Pakistan. When the nation of Bangladesh emerged, you thought you would be getting all your rights because this is a secular country. You were hurt badly when this country became an impediment to the fulfillment of your dream."

Suranjan laughed out loud. He said through his laughter, "So finally you, too, said 'your hope,' 'your dream.' Whom do you mean by this 'you'? The Hindus, certainly. You didn't hesitate to link me with the Hindus. So I've gained this at last after being an atheist all my life."

Suranjan restlessly paced from one end of the room to the other. The death toll in India had exceeded six hundred and fifty. The police had arrested eight fundamentalist leaders, including Murali Manohar Joshi and Lalkrishna Advani. All India had observed a massive strike in protest against the demolition of the Babri mosque. People were dying in riots that had broken out in Bombay, Ranchi, Karnatak, and Maharashtra. Suranjan clenched his fist in abhorrence to the Hindu fundamentalists. If he had the power he would line up all the fundamentalists in the world and shoot them. The communalists of Bangladesh were publicly saying that the Indian government was alone responsible for the Babri mosque demolition. The Hindus in Bangladesh could not be blamed for the Indian government's action. Communal harmony would have to be maintained in keeping with the tenets of Islam. This statement was being publicized in the media.

But all these niceties sounded hollow if the waves of violence and terror that swept over this country on the day of the *hartal* against the Babri mosque demolition were taken into account. On the pretext of protest against the mosque's demolition the offices of anti-fundamentalist organizations like the Committee for the Extermination of Killers and Informers and the Communist party of Bangladesh were plundered and set on fire by the killers of 1971. Why? A delegation of the Muslim fundamentalists, Jamate Islami, had met with the leaders of its Hindu counterpart, the BJP. What had transpired at that meeting? Suranjan could sense the nature of their discussion and conspiracy. Suranjan, as a member of the minority community, could realize how harrowing could be the extent of minority-baiting and the flames of riots stoked by religious sentiments engulfing the entire subcontinent. No Christian in Bangladesh could be held responsible for what was happening in Bosnia-Herzegovina. Similarly the Hindus in Bangladesh could not be blamed for any mishap in India. But whom would Suranjan convince of the reasonableness of this way of thinking?

Hyder said, "Let's move, we'll have to take part in forming the human chain." The National Coordination Committee had given this call to form human chains all over the country as a symbol of national unity against the murderers and war criminals of 1971, against all the communal forces with strong fascist leanings and to preserve the national unity and the country's sovereignty as a realization of the ideals of the Liberation War. At the same time it aimed at the goal of world peace through regional amity.

"What have I got to do with that?" Suranjan asked.

"What do you mean? Don't you feel any concern?" Hyder really was puzzled. Suranjan was gentle but firm. He said, "No."

Hyder was so surprised at Suranjan's cool rejection that he slumped down on the chair instead of standing. He lit another cigarette. He said, "Could you get me a cup of tea?"

Suranjan stretched himself fully on the bed and calmly replied, "We have no sugar in the house."

Hyder was elaborating on the plan of the human chain stretching from Bahadur Shah Park to the National Parliament House, which meant a two-hour rerouting of traffic in the area; but Suranjan intervened to ask, "What did Hasina say at yesterday's meeting?"

"At the peace rally?"

"That's right."

"She gave a call for setting up peace brigades in every

locality comprising representatives, irrespective of their caste, creed or religion, for the preservation of communal amity."

"Will it save us, the Hindus? I mean, will it safeguard our lives?"

Hyder turned to Suranjan without replying. Suranjan's face was unshaven, his hair uncombed. Suddenly, he changed the course of discussion. He said, "Where is Maya?"

"She has gone to *Zahannam*."

Hyder was taken aback by Suranjan's use of the word *Zahannam*. He laughingly said, "What sort of *Zahannam*? Let me hear about it."

"Snakes bite, scorpions sting, the body is enveloped in flames and is gradually burned to cinders, but you don't die."

"Great! You seem to know much more about *Zahannam* than I do."

"I am bound to. After all, it is we who are engulfed by the flames."

"Why is the house so silent? Have you sent your parents away somewhere?"

"No."

"Well, Suranjan, have you noticed how the Jamati fundamentalists on the pretext of protest against the Babri mosque demolition are making the demand for the trial of the notorious Pakistani collaborationist Golam Azam?"

"That's perhaps what they are doing. But I don't share your feelings on Golam Azam. Whether he is hanged or jailed matters little to me."

"You seem to have changed a lot."

"Hyder, Khaleda Zia Begum, too, has demanded reconstruction of the Babri mosque. What deters her from making an identical demand for rebuilding the destroyed temples?"

"Are you in favor of temple reconstruction?"

"You know quite well that I want neither temples nor mosques. But if there is a demand for reconstruction, why should it be mosques alone?"

Hyder lit another cigarette. He found no reason why Suranjan should prefer to remain at home on the day of forming the human chain. The day people's court was formed on March 26 this year, it was Suranjan who whisked away a sleeping Hyder who was enjoying the sound of rain outside while covered with a *kantha*. Reluctant to move out in this weather, he suggested, "Let's stay at home and eat *muri*." But a determined Suranjan said, You must go, get ready. If we lag behind now, how will the others feel?" They had gone out braving the thunderstorm. Yet the same Suranjan was expressing his disgust for the meetings and rallies. The human chain formation was just a farce to him. Even after two hours of attempts at persuasion, Hyder failed to make Suranjan take part in the human chain.

Kiranmayee had brought Maya home from Parul's house. Coming back, Maya threw herself on her father's chest, weeping piteously. Suranjan couldn't stand the sound of wailing. Could tears change anything in the world? Rather, the task at hand was now his father's treatment. Suranjan had bought medicine prescribed by Doctor Haripada that would last only three days. How much money would Kiranmayee be able to find in her cupboard? Was there anything at all?

He had never earned anything from a steady job. In fact, all the jobs looked like various forms of slavery, which was repugnant to him. Musing over whether he would renew his business venture with Hyder, he felt quite hungry. But to whom should he reveal his hunger at such an odd time? Neither Maya nor Kiranmayee was expected to come to his room immediately. Nobody was counting on him, as he was unemployed and worthless. He didn't like to inquire about the kitchen. He had not gone to see Sudhamay today. The outer doors of his room, the usual entry point of his friends, were open. He had shut the door facing inside the house. Was it for that reason no one was caring to knock at his door, presuming he was engrossed in conversation with his friends? Why should Suranjan expect so much? What had been his contribution to the family? He had only roamed about with his friends, and when at home he had made a fuss over trivial matters or had remained totally aloof. He had only taken part in one agitation after another. He had followed the party directives just like an obedient servant. Returning home late one night, he had studied hard the writings of Marx and Lenin. What had he gained from all this? Of what benefit had this been to his family?

Hyder had gone away, let him. Suranjan wouldn't go. Why should he take part in the human chain demonstration? Would it free him from his feelings of isolation? He couldn't believe it. Suranjan these days was losing his faith in everything. This Hyder had been his longtime friend. For days together, they had sharpened their power of reasoning, intelligence, and conscience. They had called upon the people of this country to unite on the basis of the consciousness of the Liberation War. How many years had they spent in the struggle to preserve civilization and hold aloft the ideals of human values? All these now appeared to Suranjan as futile exercises. He could have lived much better with little suffering if, just like other mortals, he would drink to his heart's content, watch movies or blue films on the VCR, indulge in teasing the girls; or if he could have pursued the conventional rut of married life, keeping accounts on the consumption of onions and potatoes, and buying fish after being sure of its freshness by pressing its belly. Suranjan picked up a slender book from the table and browsed its pages. The book dealt with the extent of terrible incidents during the 1990 riots. He had never cared to open it earlier. He just didn't feel any urge. But today he applied his full attention to its contents.

At one in the morning of October 30, the residents of the Panchanandham hermitage suddenly were jolted out of their sleep by the roar of an approaching procession. The processionists broke open the gate and boundary walls, abused the residents in filthy language, and set fire to the adjoining sheds by sprinkling kerosene. The residents fled wherever they could. One by one, they smashed all the idols, the dome of the memorial temple of Sadhubaba and finally made a bonfire of religious books. They also set fire to the library books of the Sanskrit institution outside the hermitage and looted whatever money they could lay their hands on. On the same day at around midnight, a mob of two and a half thousand attacked the Sadarghat Kalibari. Using crowbars, they demolished the image in the main temple as part of their macabre plundering mission. The rows of shops and houses on either side of the temple of Mother Chatteshwari were sacked first, then set on fire. The cremation ground at Golpahar was plundered and set on fire. Then they destroyed the image of the presiding deity of the cremation ground.

Agitated over a Voice of America broadcast the night of

October 30, a communal group launched an aggressive campaign against the Kaibalyadham hermitage. After smashing each and every idol in the hermitage, they set fire to all the things within. The residents of the hermitage were forced to take refuge in the adoining hills. Thousands made repeated attacks. The raiders disfigured the structure by striking it with crowbars and pickaxes. In the Hara-gouri temple, after hurling down the images, they looted whatever cash and other valuables were there. All the religious books were consigned to the flames. The residents of the entire area around the temple, the families living in the Malipara, were forced to live under the open sky. They had no means of sustenance. At around nine at night, armed mobs attacked the Krishna Gopalji temple on Chatteshwari Road. They carried away two thousand grams of silver and two hundred fifty grams of gold ornaments besides many other valuables from the temple. They demolished the image of the sacred cow atop the decorated entrance arch. They even uprooted the pine trees in the temple compound. The idols made for the coming *Rash* festival were not spared from this maniacal fury either. The attackers looted and ransacked each and every Hindu house in the Ilias Colony and physically tortured all the men and women. They even twisted the blades of the ceiling fans to make them inoperable.

The Dashbhuja Durgabari on the College Road in Chittagong, Baradeshwari, the Kali temple of Quorbanigung, the Paramhansa Mahatma Saharinha temple of Chakbazar, the Kali temple of Dewanbari, the Barsha Kalibari of North Changaon, Durga Kalibari, the Siddeshwari Kali temple of Sadar ghat, the Uttar Patenga cremation ground, Kalibari of Katghar, the Magadeshwari image of Purva Madarbari, the Rakshakali temple, the Milan Parishad temple of Mogaltuli, the Durga temple of Tiger Pass, the Shib Bari and Hari temple, Rajrajeshwari Thakurbari of Sadarghat, the Kali temple of Jalalabad, Durgabari, the cremation ground temple at Napitpara of Kulgaon, the Karunamayee Kali temple of Katalgunj, the Jaikali temple of Nathpara, the Dayamayee Kali temple of Nazirpara, the Magadheshwari Kali temple, Kalibari of Paschim Baklia, Brahmamayee Kalibari of Katalgunj, the Bara Bajar Srikrishna temple of Pashchim Bakalia, Brahmamayee Kalibari of Katalgunj, the Bara Bajar Srikrishna temple of Pashchim Bakalia, the Shiva temples of Himangshu Das, Satindra Das, Ram Mohan Das and Chandi Charan Das, the Krishna temple of Manomohan Das, the Tulshidham temple of Nandan Kanan, the Dakshin Halisahar temple of the port area, Golpahar's great cremation ground and Kalibari of Panchlais, the Jelepara Kali temple on Aman Ali Road, and Anandamayee Kali temple on the Medical College Road were looted and set on fire in the blazing trail of violence.

Bura Kalibari at Nalua in Satkania, the community Kalibari and Durga Mandap in Jagaria, Chandimandap of Dakshin Kanchan, the Magadeshashwari temple, Madhyapara Kalibari of Dakshin Charati, the community Kalibari of Madhyanalua, the temple of Charati, the Rup Kalibari and Dhar temple at Banikpaara in Dakshin Charati, the Jwalakumari temple of Paschim Matiapara, the Krishnahari temple of Badona Deputi Haat, the Buddhist monastery Mahabodhi at Durnigar, the tradition-rich Milanmandir of Boal Khali Kadhurkhil and its adjoining Krishna temple, the Jagadananda Mission of Aburdandi, the community Magadeshshawari temple of Pashchim Shakpur, Mohinibabu's hermitage of Madhya Shakpura,

the Kali temple of Dhorla Kaliahaat, the community Ja-
haddhatri temple of Kadhurkil, Kok Dandiya Rishidham
Adhipati, Shashwata Chowdhury's family deity temple at
Kadhurkil, Magadehshwari of Dhanpota, Sevakhola, the
community Kali temple of Patia, the Hari temple and Ja-
gannathbari of Dwijendra Das at Nalua of Satkania, the
Dakshinbari community Kali temple at Charati in Satkania, the community Kalibari at Dakshin Kali temple—all
these Hindu and some Buddhist religious places, too, were
also destroyed in that fiery whirlwind of destruction.

About one hundred communalists raided Mirzapur Jagannath hermitage in Hathajari subdistrict at about eleven
on the night of October 31. The raiders hurled all the images to the ground, smashing them, and looted all the ornaments of the main image of Jagannath. Next day another
hundred came to set the hermitage on fire with the help of
an inflammable powder. A police guard, which had been
posted there for protection, simply moved away to facilitate the marauders' objectives. Later, when complaints over
lack of security were lodged, the police pleaded their inability due to limited resources. The same night, more than
forty armed persons attacked the cowering inhabitants of
Mekhal village. Like commandos, they first frightened the
Hindus by exploding fire-belching Molotov cocktails. As
the people ran away in terror, the attackers broke into their
homes, plundered everything in sight, and smashed all the
family deities. All the idols of Madannath's temple and Magadeshwari bari were subjected to identical treatment. The
image of the Hari temple at Dhairhaat in Chandanaish subdistrict, the chariot of Jagannath were broken in the same
manner. Matri Mandir in Pathandandi village under Bara
Kal union and Radha Govinda temple were attacked.

At about midnight, some four hundred people from Boalkhali destroyed the Milan Mandir Temple and temples in the houses of Himanshu Chowdhuri, Paresh Biswas, Bhupal Chowdhuri, Phanindra Chowdhury and Anukul Chowdhuri of Kadhurkhil Union. They destroyed the old Hrishi Dham Ashram in Banskhali subdistrict. They set on fire all the houses and burned all books.

On the night of October 31 Muslim fundamentalists armed with sticks and spades attacked the Jagannath Ashram at Seetakunda. They destroyed the head of the image of Kali after entering the Shri Shri Kali temple of Battala established around two hundred years ago and looted the silver crown of the image and its gold ornaments. Charsarat is a Hindu-majority village. On November 1 around two to three hundred people arrived and literally looted the whole area. They set on fire whatever they could not carry with them. They left behind heaps of ashes of burned houses and half-burned trees. While leaving the village, they warned that if the villagers did not leave by November 10, all of them would be beaten to death.

The goats and cows which resisted their attempt to lead them out were slaughtered. Paddy stocks were burned. Nearly four thousand Hindus suffered losses. Seventy-five percent of the houses have been burned, one person died and innumerable cows and goats were also burned to ashes. Many women were raped. The losses amounted to over twenty-five million takas. About two hundred people armed with sticks and iron rods attacked the Jagannath temple of Satberia village at 9:15 P.M. and smashed all the temple idols. All the people living nearby fled for their lives when they heard about the attack and passed the night in the forest or in paddy fields. All the houses were looted. No trace remained of the community Durgabari of Satbaria. They set on fire the temple and the houses of Khejuria village. The peasant families lost everything. They tried to burn alive the wife of Sailendra Kumar. She was badly injured. While the devotees were engaged in prayer at the Shiva temple, some people abused them with coarse language, destroyed the idol and its seat and urinated on them.

Suranjan's eyes became full of tears and he felt as if he had been bathed in their urine. He threw the book aside.

Haripada the doctor had taught them the ways Sudhamay's inert limbs were to be exercised for the return of his strength. Both Maya and Kiranmayee meticulously followed his instructions, exercising Sudhamay's arms and feet and giving him medicines. Maya's natural ebullience diminished. She had always seen her father as a very lively person. The same man was now lying still. When he called out, "Maya, Maya" in a slurred voice, she had a feeling of something snapping within her. Sudhamay's helpless, dull eyes seemed to tell her something. Her father would always ask her to grow up to be an ideal person. He himself was honest and courageous. He would invariably resist Kiranmayee's occasional plea to marry her off when she had grown up. His set reply was: She would now pursue her studies, would then get a job, and only after that should she marry, if she wanted to. Kiranmayee would heave a sigh and say, "Or should we send her to my brother in Calcutta. All the girls of her age group, Anjali, Neelima, Abha, Shibani, have left for Calcutta to continue their studies there." Sudhamay would retort: "So what? Is there anything to stop her here? Or have studies been abolished?"

"She is a grown-up girl now. I feel so concerned that I

can't sleep in peace during the night. Wasn't Bijaya harassed just the other day by some Muslim boys on her way to college?"

"The Muslim girls aren't spared either. Are the Muslim girls immune from rape and kidnapping?"

"That's true, still . . ."

Kiranmayee came to realize that Sudhamay would never accept her suggestions. His consolation was that if he lost his ancestral home, he at least had the soil of his own country beneath his feet. Maya, of course, never felt any urge to go to Calcutta. She had visited her maternal aunt in Calcutta on one occasion. But she didn't like the place. All her cousin were snobs and never took her into their intimate circles. Sitting all alone throughout the day, she would muse over her own country. She had gone there to spend the Puja festival vacation; before the end of her stay, she requested her uncle to make arrangements for her return home.

Surprised at her request, her aunt exclaimed, "What are you saying? Your mother has sent you to stay at least ten days."

"I'm feeling homesick," Maya replied unhesitatingly. Tears indeed had welled up in her eyes as she revealed herself. She didn't like the supercharged exuberance of the Puja in Calcutta. In the midst of the city glittering during the festive period, she was feeling utterly alone. Otherwise, she wouldn't have returned within a week instead of her scheduled stay of ten days. Kiranmayee had a vague idea Maya would stay there if she liked the place.

Sitting near her father's head, Maya was thinking of Jehangir. She had talked with him over the telephone from Parul's place. But Jehangir's voice was devoid of earlier emotion. He said that he was planning to go to the United

135

States. One of his uncles, who lived in the country, had asked him to come. Hearing of his intention, Maya nearly had let out an anguished scream, "Will you go away?"

"Bah, it's a land like America, why should I miss the chance?"

"What will you do there?"

"For the time being I'll have to get some odd jobs; then in due course, I'll get citizenship."

"When are you going to return home?"

"What's the point in coming back? Can a sensible man survive in this rotten country?"

"When have you decided to go?"

"Next month, my uncle is nagging me. He thinks I'm spoiling myself by getting involved in politics here."

"Oh!" That was all she could say.

Not even once did Jehangir mention what was going to happen to Maya if he left the country. Nor did he ask about Maya's plans, whether she would prefer to accompany him to the States or wait for him in this country. How could his craze for America make him forget their love affair of four years, his promise to marry her while sitting in a restaurant by the side of the Crescent Lake. Was his craving for the abundance and splendor so strong as to totally ignore Maya, leaving her for good! As she sat at Sudhamay's bedside, her thoughts would reach out for Jehangir every now and then. Even her best attempts couldn't make her forget him. At the same time she shared Sudhamay's agony of lying inert. Kiranmayee showed no emotion. Yet she would cry out all of a sudden at midnight. She never said why or for whom she cried. She went about her household chores silently throughout the day. Without troubling anyone, she cooked and kept Sudhamay clean.

Kiranmayee didn't put vermilion at the parting of her hair like other married Hindu women. Nor were there other visible signs of marriage, like the iron and conch shell bangles. Sudhamay, during their period of hiding in 1971, had asked her to take off those signs of her married status. After 1975, she gave them up herself. Sudhamay, too, discarded his *dhoti* after 1975. The day he had given his measurements to a Muslim tailor to make *pyjamas* from white longcloth, he told Kiranmayee after returning home, "Would you please see if I have a fever. I feel as if I do."

Kiranmayee didn't say anything. She knew that Sudhamay always felt feverish when he was upset.

Maya was surprised at Suranjan's aloofness at such a crucial time. He had holed himself up and remained in isolation, putting on a glum face, never even saying if he felt like taking his meals. Didn't he ever think of asking if his father was alive or dead? His friends came to his room and with them he spent his time in endless cycles of idle talk. He went out of his room, locking it from the outside without telling anyone that he was leaving or the time of his return. Didn't he have any responsibility? No demand had been made of him to contribute to the family's needs. But he could at least perform the minimum filial duties such as calling the doctor, inquiring about his father's condition, buying medicines, and spending a little while by the sick man's bedside. Sudhamay could certainly expect his son to come to him and touch his left arm, which was not quite paralyzed, as a sign of assurance.

Sudhamay was coming round slowly with the medicines prescribed by Doctor Haripada. His speech had become a little more distinct. But he had no sensation on his right side. The doctor had assured them that this condition would improve if the exercises were continued. Maya had all her time free. She didn't have to coach her student. A girl called Minati was one whom she coached. But her mother had said that there wouldn't be any more need to coach her since the family was migrating to India.

"Why India?" Maya had asked.

Minati's mother had only smiled sadly without offering any reply.

Minati was a student at Vhikarunnesa School. One day, while teaching her mathematics, Maya noticed Minati was fiddling with her pencil and chanting *Alhamdulillahir Rahmanir Rhahim Ar Rahmanir Rahim.*

Rather taken aback, Maya asked her, "What are you saying?"

Minati immediately replied, "We recite from the Koran at the time of prayer assembly in our school."

"Is that so? You have to recite these *suras* from the Vhikarunnesa school?"

"We recite two *suras* followed by the National Anthem."

"What do you do when *sura* is recited?"

"I recite, too, covering my head like other Muslim girls."

"Is there no separate arrangement for the prayers of Hindu, Buddhist or Christian students?"

"No."

Maya was jolted on hearing this. In one of the largest schools in the country, Muslim prayers were offered during assembly. And the Hindu girls were also to take part in that prayer silently — this must be one sort of persecution.

Maya coached another girl, Sumaia, who was a relative of Parul. She told her one day, "Didi, I won't take coachings from you anymore."

"Why?"

138

"Father has said he will engage a Muslim tutor for me."

"Well, if you want it that way."

Maya informed no one of her loss of these two coaching jobs. Suranjan took his pocket money from the family. Now, if Maya also made the same demand, how would Kiranmayee manage the family budget? After such an accident in the family, she felt hesitant about revealing her own financial problem.

Kiranmayee had of late turned unusually calm. She quietly cooked the simple *dal* and rice. She should have made fruit juice and soup for Sudhamay. But who would bring the fruits for him? Suranjan preferred to stay stretched out on the bed. He could stay in that position for incredibly long periods. Maya, too, nurtured a grudge against her brother. He ignored her persistent pleas to seek shelter on the seventh. But was the danger over now? Seeing the nonchalance of other family members, Maya also became somewhat detached. She, too, began to think: let things take their own course; she was not at all concerned. If Suranjan could stay aloof, what could Maya do by brooding? She had no intimate friend to whose house the whole family could move. Even during her stay at Parul's house, she felt quite uneasy, even though Parul was one of her close friends. Her presence at Parul's place on several occasions did not raise any questions. But that day when Maya went to the house, all the people who knew her there looked at her strangely. Although she had been a frequent visitor, her presence that day evoked silent questions in the eyes of Parul's relatives. Only Parul said it was unsafe for Maya to stay in her own house at this time.

The question of security arose only in the case of Maya, not Parul. Would Parul ever face such a situation when she would be forced to take refuge at Maya's place? Maya was hesitant and somewhat cringing, yet she latched on to Parul's house like an unwanted guest. Parul didn't hold back her hospitality. Yet Maya had to face awkward situations when Parul's visiting relatives asked her name.

She replied, "Maya."

"What's your full name?" the questioner insisted.

Intervening before she could say anything, Parul said, "Her name is Zakia Sultana."

Maya had been startled at the dropping of a Muslim name. Later, after the relatives' departure, Parul had explained, "These people are religious. I was forced to tell a lie. Otherwise they will be circulating the news everywhere that we are offering shelter to Hindus."

"Oh."

The point was driven home. But Maya felt the agony of humiliation. Was it wrong to offer shelter to the Hindus? Another question that had disturbed her sleep at night was, Why should Hindus be forced to seek protection outside their homes? In the undergraduate exam, Maya had scored very high first-division marks against Parul's mere second division. Yet she got the impression that Parul was pitying her.

"Baba, try to flex your fingers; just try to raise your hand a little."

Sudhamay raised his hand just like an obedient boy. Maya thought Sudhamay was slowly gaining back his strength in his fingers.

"Will Dada not have his meal?" asked Maya.

"Who knows? I found him sleeping," said Kiranmayee gloomily.

Kiranmayee didn't take any food. She served a meal for

140

Maya. In the room with its closed doors and windows, darkness reigned. Maya, too, felt sleepy. As she was dozing off, she was suddenly alarmed at the noise of an approaching procession. The procession passed, shouting, "Hindus, if you want to live, leave this country!" Sudhamay also heard. The hand held by Maya sent out tremors which she could also feel.

Suranjan's stomach was cramped with hunger pangs. Earlier, whether he ate or not, his food was kept under a cover on the table. But he wouldn't tell anyone today of his hunger. Going to the tap on the side of the cemented courtyard, he washed his face and wiped it clean with a towel. He changed his clothes on coming back to his room and went out again. Once out of the house, he couldn't decide which way he should go. Should he go to Hyder's? But he would not be home at this hour. Then where could he go? To Kamal's or Belal's? But they might think that he had come to seek shelter with them in sheer desperation. Or to crave their sympathy. No, he wouldn't go. He would roam around the city on his own. After all, it was his own city. At one time, he hadn't wanted to leave Mymensingh. He had plenty of friends at Ananda Mohan College. Why should he depart from them to move to a new city? But Sudhamay sold his house in the dead of night to Raisuddin. Even the next morning, Suranjan was not aware that their ancestral home, known as "Dutta House," along with its fragrance of white kamini flowers and memories of swimming merrily in the clear waters of its adjoining pond, was theirs no more. When Suranhan came to know that they would have to vacate the house within seven days, he was so distraught that he didn't return home for the next two days.

141

Suranjan couldn't understand why he felt so offended. He had no less a grievance against himself than against members of the family. He felt a regret tinged with sorrow also for Parvin. This girl loved him. Often she would come running to his room to say, "Come, let's run away."

"Where to?"

"Far away, to the mountains."

"Where will you find hills. You'll have to go to either Sylhet or Chittagong to find them."

"Then we'll go there and build a house to live in."

"What will you eat? Creepers and leaves?"

Parvin would roll with laughter and lean against Suranjan. She said, "I'll die without you."

"Girls say such things, but they actually never die."

Suranjan proved to be correct. Parvin didn't die. Rather, like an obedient girl, she married the man chosen by her family. Just two days before her marriage, she revealed to Suranjan that her family was insisting on his conversion to the Muslim faith to marry her. Suranjan laughingly said, "You know quite well, I don't believe in religion."

"No, you must become a Muslim."

"But I don't want to be a Muslim."

"That means you don't want me."

"Of course I want you. But why must I become a Muslim for that reason? What's this nonsense?"

In a moment Parvin's fair face had reddened with anger. Suranjan knew that she had been under constant pressure from her family to sever her relationship with him. He, too, was keen on knowing which side Hyder supported. Hyder was Parvin's brother, but he was Suranjan's friend, too. However, he had maintained a deliberate silence about their affair. His aloofness was not at all to

142

Suranjan's liking. He should have taken one side or the other. During his long talks with Hyder in those days, no reference was ever made to Parvin. Since Hyder was reluctant to raise the issue, Suranjan didn't either.

One day Parvin was married off to a Muslim businessman. Suranjan's refusal to convert possibly made Parvin give up her dream of living in the mountains with him. Could the dream be immersed in water the way an image was at the end of merry festival days? But Parvin did exactly that. Parvin's family was not resigned to Suranjan's religion.

This morning Hyder told him Parvin was perhaps going to divorce her husband.

Divorce after only two years of marriage? But Suranjan preferred to remain silent. He had almost forgotten Parvin, yet the mention of her name acted as a shock to his heart. Had he kept the name of Parvin gently, ever so carefully, wrapped in the safety of mothballs in the vault of his heart? Perhaps. How long it had been since he had seen Parvin? He felt a wrenching agony within him. He tried to smother it by recalling Ratna's face. Ratna Mitra. She was a fine girl. She would be a good match for Suranjan. How could it concern Suranjan even if Parvin divorced her husband? She had married a Muslim, someone her family approved of. And everyone had expected everything to take off smoothly from there, almost as it it were guaranteed that if marriages were matched in terms of religion and caste, they would last. Why, then, was she planning to leave that marriage? Didn't her husband take her to the mountains? Hadn't her dreams been fulfilled? Suranjan was an unemployed Hindu boy. He just wandered about here and there. Could he be considered a good bridegroom?

Suranjan hired a rickshaw at Tikatuli crossing. But Parvin's face kept on flashing in his mind. Parvin would kiss him and he would hold her in a firm embrace and say, "You're a bird, just a small sparrow."

Parvin would roll down in laughter and retort: "You are a monkey."

Well, was he really a monkey? But of course he was. Why else would he be stagnating for five years? His age had flowed downstream like bunches of water hyacinth; he did not get anything. No one had come forward to say, like Parvin: "I like you very much." The day Parvin made this revelation to him, he asked, "Have you made a wager with someone?"

"What does that mean?"

"Just to test if you are capable of telling me this?"

"Not at all."

"Do you really mean what you say?"

"I always mean what I say."

And to think that the same girl who had spoken with so much confidence had begun to crumble the moment her family broached the topic of marriage. All her fantastic dreams and her will to carve out her own way also evaporated. When she was forced to marry, not once did she say, "I will only marry the monkey living in that house." His house was only two doors from hers. Yet Suranjan hadn't attended the marriage, which Kiranmayee and Maya had done.

He instructed the rickshaw puller to go in the direction of Chamelibag. Dusk had fallen over the city. His stomach was churning with hunger. He suffered from acidity that resulted in sour belching. Sudhamay had advised him to take antacid tablets, but he was averse to taking them. Besides, he invariably forgot to carry the tablets in his pocket.

He would have to eat something at Pulak's place. Pulak could be found at his home where he had been under voluntary confinement for the last five days. He always kept the door locked. Entering the room, Suranjan said, "Please give me something to eat. Maybe nothing was cooked at my house today."

"Why?"

"Doctor Sudhamay Dutta has had a stroke. His wife and daughter are nursing him. Sudhamay, son of the affluent Sukumar Dutta, is now unable to foot the bills for his own treatment."

"But you should have done something constructive like taking up a job."

"It's very difficult to find a job in this land of Muslims. Besides, who wants to work under these illiterates?"

Pulak was surprised. Coming closer to Suranjan, Pulak asked, "Are you abusing the Muslims?"

"Who are you frightened of? I'm abusing them all right, but only to you. Is this possible in their presence? Will my head still stand on my shoulders?"

Gritting his teeth, Suranjan gripped the arm of the sofa. Pulak looked somewhat dumbfounded. Neela warmed up rice and curry and served them on the table. In a pain-racked voice, she asked, "Have you eaten nothing at all today, Suranjanda?"

Suranjan smiled wanly. He said, "What am I to eat. Who bothers about my eating?"

"Better get married."

"Marriage!" Suranjan choked on the food, then said, clearing his throat, "Who's going to marry me?"

"You lost interest in marriage because of Parvin? That's not fair."

145

"No, no. Why should it be like that? In fact, I forgot that one was supposed to marry."

Even in the midst of their current worries, Pulak and Neela laughed. Suranjan had no taste for the food. Yet he ate just to smother his hunger.

"Could you lend me some money, Pulak," Suranjan said while eating.

"How much?"

"As much as you can. No one at home tells me how much is needed. But I guess that my mother has nothing to meet the expenses."

"Well, I'll do what I can. Do you have any idea about what is happening in the country? Sylhet, Cox Bazar, Pirozepur?"

"I know what you're going to tell me. You'll say all the Hindu temples have been violated and the women raped. If there is anything else, you can tell me."

"Do these incidents appear to be normal to you?"

"Certainly. What do you expect of this country? You'll just offer your back to be struck with blows and if they do that, you will feel offended. What's the point of it?"

Pulak was seated opposite Suranjan at the dining table. After keeping silent for some time he said, "The ancestral home of the great saint Chaitanyadev at Sylhet was burned down. The old library wasn't spared either. My elder brother has arrived from Sylhet with the latest news. Kalighat Kalibari, Shibbari, Jagannath Akhra, Chali Bandar Bhairabbari, Chali Bander cremation ground, Jatarpur Akhra of Mahaprabhu, Meera Bazar Ramkrishna Mission, Balaram Akhra in the same place, the Nirmalabala students' hostel, the Balaram temple of Bander Bazar, Jagannath Akhra of Jinderbazar, Govindaji's Akhra, Narasinha's

146

Akhra at Lama Bazar, Naya Sarak Akhra, Biani Bazar Kalibari, Mahaprabhu's house at Dhaka Dakshin, Shib bari of Gotatikar, Mahalakshmi Bari Mahapeeth, Durgabai fertilizer factory in Fenehuganj, Sajibari of Bishwanath, Bairagi Bazar akhra, the Shiva temple at Chandgram, Akilpur akhra, Jibanpur Kalibari at Companigunj, Jogipur Kalibari at Balagunj, the Amalshi Kali temple of Jakigunj, Barhata akhra, Gazipur akhra, and Birashree akhra have all been sacked and set on fire. Three men, Benu Bhushan Das, Sunil Kumar Das and Kanu Bhushan Das, have been burned alive."

"Is that so?"

"The way such violent incidents are breaking out all around, Suranjan, to be quite frank, I don't know how we are going to survive in this country. In Chittagong, the Jamat and the BNP supporters have joined hands in perpetrating this violence. The Hindus are being robbed of their utensils. They are even looting the fish from the ponds owned by Hindus. All the Hindus of the area have been going without any food for the last seven or eight days. The people of the Jamat Shibir have demanded at gunpoint from Kanubihari Nath and his son Arjun Bihari Nath of Khajuria village at Seetakunda twenty thousand takas in exchange for permission to stay in their homes. They have left their houses. Utpala Rani Bhawmick, daughter of a professor at Meerer Sarai College, was forcibly abducted on Thursday midnight and returned in the early morning after you know what. Now tell me, should we not protest against these atrocities?"

"Do you know what happens if we raise our voice in protest? You must know that poem of D. L. Roy, 'If in a fit of anger I kick on your back, must you have the temerity to cry out in pain?' " Suranjan said, leaning against the sofa with eyes closed. "Several thousand houses have been looted at Bhola, several thousand more have been burned down. A curfew was imposed for twelve hours today. The police stood as silent onlookers while the Lakshmi Narayan akhra was attacked for the third time by a mob of two or three hundred people with iron spikes and axes. More than fifteen hundred houses at Borhanuddin have been reduced to ashes and another two thousand damaged. At Tajmuddin, two thousand two hundred houses were totally destroyed with another two thousand partially damaged. Two hundred sixty temples have been demolished at Bhola alone."

Suranjan, amused, said with a smile, "You narrated the list of destruction just like a reporter. Are you shocked by these incidents?"

Pulak looked at Suranjan with wide-eyed wonder. He said, "Aren't you feeling the same?"

Suranjan's laughter shook the room. He said, "Not in the least. Why should I feel any shock or pain?"

Pulak appeared to be somewhat worried. He said, "To speak frankly, I have lots of relatives in those areas. I'm really concerned over what has happened to them."

"Muslims are doing what Muslims are expected to do. They have set Hindu houses on fire. Will it be proper for Hindus to set fire to Muslim houses? No, Pulak, I don't have any comforting words for you."

Going inside the house, Pulak came back to hand over two thousand takas to Suranjan. Pocketing the money, Suranjan said, "What about your son, Alak? Have his Muslim friends allowed him to play with them?"

"No, he stays at home all day suffering from depression. There's nothing for him to do but watch through the window his friends playing in the field. He fidgets alone in his room."

"Listen, Pulak, the people whom we consider to be noncommunal and treat as our own people and friends are all basically communal elements. We have tried to assimilate ourselves with the Muslims in this country to the extent of naturally greeting them with *Assalamu Alaikum*, bidding them farewell with *Khoda Hafez*; we call water *paani* as the Muslims do, bath *gosol* the same way. During the observance of their month of Ramjan, we refrain from smoking and we can't even eat in hotels and restaurants during the day out of deference to their religious sentiments. But how close are these people to us? For whom do we make this tremendous sacrifice? Just tell me. How many days' holiday do we enjoy during the puja? And during both the occasions of Eid, the Muslims enjoy the holidays while the Hindus are forced to slave in the public hospitals. The eighth amendment to the constitution declaring the country an Islamic state was passed by parliament. The Awami League went through the motions of protest for just a few days. Now, all's quiet. The party chief Hasina herself, supposed to be a champion of secularism, is now covering her head like an orthodox Muslim. After returning from the Haj, she covered her head in such a manner that even her hair was not visible. All of them are the same, Pulak, all of them. Now we'll either have to commit mass suicide or leave the country."

Pulak was leaning against the wall. Suranjan made a move toward the outer door. Kiranmayee had recently asked him to go and meet Raisuddin in Mymensingh. He had bought their house for such a paltry sum of money that perhaps he would help them out of their financial difficulty. Suranjan usually didn't borrow money from anyone. The bill at the grocer's shop was due at the end of the month. But he could take the loan from Pulak easily. Once he had helped him. That might be the reason. Or it could be that Pulak, being a Hindu, was expected to fathom the plight of minorities better than others. Others might help, if approached, but not out of a genuine feeling. Suranjan decided that he would never ask for financial help from any Muslim. No one was assigning him any responsibility at home. They were taking him for a patriot always engrossed in thoughts of the country's welfare. Hence, why bother him with trivial matters? He would give the money collected from Pulak to Kiranmayee. No one knew how she was holding this tottering household together without bearing any grudge against anyone, not even this good-for-nothing son of hers. Even slogging through grinding poverty, she never showed any sign of annoyance.

Coming out of Pulak's house, Suranjan started walking briskly toward Tikatuli. Suddenly he thought, What point is there in staying alive? Take Sudhamay, for instance, who was hanging between life and death. He had to be helped by others in taking his food, requiring assistance even for basic functions like urinating and defecating. What was the point of living like this? Why, then, was Suranjan still alive? Presently he toyed with the idea of buying several ampoules of pethedine with the money he had and injecting the contents into his vein. He would surely enjoy the experience of dying. He wondered about what it would be like if he were lying dead on his bed. Everybody would assume that he was sleeping. So he must not be disturbed. Maya would come to him and say, "Dada, please get up. Please think of doing something for Baba, for us." Her Dada would give no reply.

While he was musing on all this, he noticed a procession preaching messages of communal harmony at the Vijay Nagar crossing with slogans like "Hindus and Muslims are brothers." A sarcastic smile appeared on Suranjan's lips.

Before going home, he dropped in at Gautam's house. Gautam was lying in bed. He was somewhat better than when Suranjan had seen him earlier. But his eyes still held traces of terror. He would start at any sudden sound. He was a plain and simple boy, a medical student uninitiated in politics, who had no axe to grind with anyone; yet he was at the receiving end of merciless beating, as if he were responsible for the demolition of the Babri mosque in India.

His mother was seated nearby. She said in a low voice, as if afraid of being overheard, "My son, we are going away."

"Going away!" Suranjan was shocked.

"Yes, we're trying to sell the house."

Suranjan didn't want to hear where they were planning to go. Nor did he ask. But were they leaving the country forever? Fearing that he would have to listen to this shocking news if he stayed there, he suddenly pushed the chair away and stood up. He said, "I'm going."

Gautam's mother said, "Please stay for a while, my son. I don't know if we will meet before we leave. Let's talk." Her voice sounded distorted with muffled cries.

"No, Auntie, I've work at home, let me go today. I'll try to come on some other day."

Suranjan let the room with downcast eyes, looking at neither Gautam nor his mother. He walked out, failing, as he did so, to conceal a sigh of despair.

Day Five

Birupaksha was a worker in Suranjan's party. A new-comer, quite intelligent. He entered the room before Suranjan had got up from his bed.

"It's ten in the morning and you were still sleeping?"

"How could you say I was sleeping? I was just lying down. One has to remain so if there's nothing to do. After all, we lacked the courage to destroy the mosques. There is nothing else than to stay in bed."

"You're right. They are destroying hundreds of temples; but if we even throw a single pebble at a mosque, what consequences we'll have to face! The Pakistanis just reduced the four-hundred-year-old temple of Ramna Kalibari to dust, but there was no assurance from any government that it would be rebuilt."

"Hasina has repeatedly demanded the reconstruction of the Babri mosque. But in Bangladesh, even if there is some hope of compensation for the Hindus, nothing is ever men-

152

tioned about the rebuilding of temples. They do not seem to realize that Hindus have not drifted into Bangladesh with the floodwaters. We are as much citizens of this country as anyone else. We have the right to live, as well as the right to protect our own lives, property and places of worship."

"Do they indulge in this sort of vandalism only on the issue of the Babri mosque demolition? On the morning of March 21, in the village of Bagerhat, the daughter of Kalindra Haldar, Putul Rani, was kidnapped by Makhlesur Rahman and Chand Mian Talukdar, who lived in the same area. The Mani and Kanailal families were forced to flee their homes following the persistent persecution by Union Parishad Chairman of Baga in Patuakhali, Iunus Mian, and Union Parishad member, Nabi Ali. For the forcible occupation of his land, one Biren in Rajnagar village was whisked away by the miscreants, never to be heard of again. In the same way, they tortured another man called Sudhir to grab his land as well. He fled. Another victim of the Union Parishad chairman's persecution, Chandan Seal of Sabupur village, too, has vanished without a trace. Another victim of the land-grabbing spree was Dinesh of Bamankathi village who was forced to put his signature on a blank stamped paper. The paddy from the field of another Hindu of Baga village, Chittaranjan Chakravarty, was forcibly harvested. As Chittababu filed a case seeking justice in the court of law, he was first pressured to withdraw the case and then was threatened with death."

Suranjan lit a cigarette. He didn't want to take part in the topic raised by Birupaksha. Nevertheless, he found he was getting slowly involved in the incidents. With the cigarette dangling from his lips, he said, "On April 1, seven or eight people demanded a twenty-thousand-taka subscription at gunpoint from the sweetmeat shop of Swapan Chandra Ghosh called 'New Jalkhabar.' They started to beat up the shop employees indiscriminately, when unable to realize their demand. Later they broke open the cash box and forcibly carried away what they wanted. Of course, Muslim shop owners were also not spared by these hooligans. The torture by these subscription hunters has been steadily on the rise.

"Then there is the example of Lal Dhupi of Sidduque Bazar. Several Muslims like Sahabuddin, Siraj, Parvez and Salauddin forcibly occupied half of his personal property. Now they were trying to grab it all."

After a short pause, Suranjan said with a sigh, "The forcible harvesting of paddy, the abduction and rape of Hindu girls, land grabbing, threats of death, forcing Hindus to leave their homes by beating them up, even sometimes making them leave the country—all these are no longer isolated incidents. This sort of thing is happening all over the country. Can we say how many cases of such torture and exile actually come to our notice?"

"At Senbag in Noakhali, several Muslims, including Abul Kalam Munshi and Abul Kashem, kidnapped Swarnabala, the wife of Krishna Lal Das, and then left her unconscious in the paddy field near her house after raping her," said Birupaksha.

Suranjan, leaving his bed, went to the water tap. While sprinkling water on his eyes and face, he asked Kiranmayee for two cups of tea. He had given two thousand takas to Kiranmayee last night. So she wouldn't call him totally irresponsible. She, too, was looking somewhat fresh compared to earlier days. Possibly she had at least been for the time being spared from fear of a financial crunch. Biru-

154

paksha was in a depressed mood. Entering the room, Suranjan said, "Cheer up, cheer up."

Birupaksha smiled wanly. Suranjan, too, was feeling physically quite enlivened. He thought of going to Sudhamay's room. Meanwhile, tea arrived. Maya brought the cups.

"Hey, you seem to have grown thinner in the last few days. Didn't they feed you properly at Parul's house?" Maya went out of the room without any reply. She was unconcerned with Suranjan's joke. Sudhamay was sick. Perhaps Suranjan was somewhat improper in cracking a joke at this time. Maya's silence made him think.

But Birupaksha diverted his mind. Sipping his tea, he said, "Suranjanda, you don't believe in religion. I know that you don't pray to any god and that you eat beef as well. Why don't you tell them you are not a Hindu, that you are a half Muslim?"

"Their real objection is to my being a real human being. Strangely enough, there is no dispute between Hindu fanatics and Muslim fanatics. Aren't you noticing the closeness of the Jamat leaders to the BJP tophats in India? In both countries, the fundamentalists are trying to capture political power. Najami, a fanatical top brass, himself blamed the Congress party, not BJP, for the riots in India at the meeting at Baitul Makaram."

"One thousand people have been killed in the communal riots in India. Communal parties and organizations like Vishwa Hindu Parishad, RSS, the Bajrang Dal, Jamat-i-Islami and Islam; Sevak Sangha have been banned. On this side, *hartol* is being observed in Sylhet; Pirozepur and Bhola have come under Section 144 and curfew, respectively. Besides, peace processions are being organized here and there. The processionists are raising slogans like

"Nizami-Advani are brothers, they must be hanged with the same rope." Today, an all-party peace meeting is being organized. A temple in faraway Britain is said to have been attacked. Tophael Ahmed, after visiting Bhola, has demanded deployment of a paramilitary force like the Bangladesh Rifles. The situation in that area is really bad."

"What'll BDR do if everything is burned to ashes? Will they gather the heaps of ashes at one point? Where was Tophael on the nights of the 6th and 7th? Why didn't he demand protection for minorities the same night?" Suranjan was gripped by excitement. He said, "The Awami League can hardly assume a holier-than-thou stance now."

"Could it be that the Awami League hadn't gone in for anti-riot measures to bring discredit to the government?"

"I've no idea. Might be it was like that. But all the parties are looking after their own interest for garnering votes in elections. No one cares for ideologies in this country. Politics is limited to the success of the parties in the elections. Their aim is to gather votes by any means—by fraud, by brute force or by tactics. The Awami League has already drawn the conclusion that it is going to corner all the Hindu votes. It is an assured 'vote bank.' In some places even their supporters were among the looters."

"The scenario in some places went something like this: The mob led by the ruling BNP, after looting the Hindu houses and sacking Hindu temples, mockingly asked, 'Where are your saviors now, whom you voted for?' Awami League men have behaved in the same way in the areas which return BNP representatives. In Bhola the offender was BNP, while at Maheskhali, in Ghior and Manikgainj the Awami League has been responsible."

"Politics is certainly there at the root of all these incidents.

But the fundamentalists are everywhere. By the way, is it true that there have been identical editorials in all the newspapers? Apparently they have all appealed for communal harmony," Suranjan said.

"Don't you read newspapers?"

"Don't feel like reading them."

Maya reentered the room at this point. She placed an envelope on the table and said, "Ma asked me to give you this. She said she wouldn't need it."

Before he could ask what Maya had given, she went out. Suranjan opened the envelope and found the two thousand takas that he had given his mother last night. Suranjan's face was burning with insult. What sort of hauteur was Kiranmayee trying to show? Or had she concluded that her unemployed son had collected this money by stealing or robbing? Suranjan was too overwhelmed by shame and shock to talk. Not even with Birupaksha.

Kiranmayee's father was a renowned man at Brahmanbaria. He was a reputed police officer named Akhil Chandra Basu. After marrying off his sixteen-year-old daughter to a doctor, he left for Calcutta with his entire family. At one time, he hoped that his daughter and son-in-law would follow him. Kiranmayee also believed that like all her relatives—parents, uncles, and aunts on both her father's and mother's sides—she, too, would leave the country. But she had landed in a strange family. She had been with her in-laws for six years. During these years she had watched her neighboring families take up their households and leave; yet she had never talked of leaving the country. She would often cry without letting anyone know. Her father's letters from Calcutta would invariably say:

My dear Kiran,

Have you decided not to come? Ask Sudhamay to think over the matter. We, too, never wanted to leave our country, but we have been compelled to make the decision. It's not that we are quite happy here. We indeed feel for the land we have left behind. Still one must accept reality. But I feel concern for your well-being.

Your father.

Kiranmayee would read these letters time and again, wiping away her tears. Frequently at night, she would tell Sudhamay, "Almost all your relatives have left. My relatives, too, have gone away. From now on, we won't find anyone to stand by us even with a glass of water at hours of need like sickness or grief." Sudhamay, with a smile on his face, would say, "Do you care so much for water? I'll see how much water you can consume with the entire Brahmaputra river at your command. Can your relatives provide more water than this river?" The proposal for leaving the country was never accepted by her father-in-law, her husband or, for that matter, her son, Suranjan. Finding no way out, Kiranmayee had to adjust herself to this family. In doing so, Kiranmayee was amazed to find that she had become more involved than Sudhamay in their household matters, forging ahead through joy and sorrow, through days of affluence and poverty.

Kiranmayee had sold her gold bracelets to the wife of Doctor Haripada. She kept the matter a closely guarded secret. And what was there to tell anyone? Gold and jewelry, after all, were not so invaluable that they couldn't be sold in time of need. Kiranmayee couldn't understand how she had so much love for her husband. After that traumatic experience of 1971, she couldn't get intimate with her husband. Occasionally, Sudhamay would lament, "Kiranmayee, I've perhaps cheated you too much, haven't I?" Kiranmayee realized what Sudhamay was referring to. She kept silent. She didn't know how she could say she had lost nothing. Heaving a deep sigh, Sudhamay would say, "Will you leave me, Kiran? I feel so scared."

Kiranmayee could never think of deserting Sudhamay. Did sex come above other relationships for all human beings? Could the rest be left out? Was their thirty-five-year marriage so insignificant? Could living together for such a long time through the vicissitudes of joy and sorrow pale into permanent gloom? No, Kiranmayee realized: There was only one life to live. This life would never come back in unending cycles. Why could she not accept the pangs of strange separation? After 1971, Sudhamay had become incapable of making love. He felt so ashamed of his crippling inability. Off and on, he would wake her up during the dead of night to ask her, "Are you feeling any great agony, Kiran?"

"What agony?" She would give the impression of not understanding the question.

Sudhamay felt embarrassed to speak out frankly. He would press his face to the pillow, driven by the pain of his impotence. And Kiranmayee would spend sleepless nights facing the wall. Occasionally Sudhamay would say, "If you want to start your married life afresh, you are free to do so. I won't mind."

It was not that Kiranmayee didn't feel any physical urge. She indeed had. When Sudhamay's friends came to visit and they sat around talking, their shadows would sometimes fall on her lap. She would be overcome with desire, wishing that such a shadow might turn into flesh and blood, resting its head on her lap. However, she was not troubled by this physical urge for long. She passed her years in restraint. Age never stopped at a particular point. Twenty years fled past in this way. Kiranmayee also thought how it would be if the man she might have chosen in place of Sudhamay suffered from the same disability. Even if was potent, he might not be as large-hearted as Sudhamay.

Every now and then, Kiranmayee thought that Sudhamay loved her too much. He would always be with her at the dining table. He would also drop the largest piece of fish on her plate. If she didn't have any help, he would volunteer for dishwashing, sportingly saying that he was quite adept at it.

If Kiranmayee sat disinterested in the afternoon, he would say, "Your hair has become matted, Kiran. Come, let me comb it to remove the knots. Why not got to Ramna Bhavan and buy a couple of new saris for yourself? You don't have saris fit for household work. Had I enough money, I would have built a large house for you. You would then just walk around the courtyard, plant fruit saplings wherever you liked or have a vegetable patch or flower garden. Broad beans hanging from the creeper, gourds on scaffolds, dense jasmine blossoms on the windowframe; in fact, you would have found yourself more at home in that Brahma Palli house. But you know what my problem is. I never went in for the money-earning spree. It's not that I couldn't have earned well had I wanted to. Your father at the time of your marriage thought that I was someone with both a large house and wealth. Both the house and wealth are now gone: ours is more or less a

hand-to-mouth situation. I don't regret this. But you perhaps feel the hardship."

Kiranmayee was sure of the love of this simple,
straightforward and harmless man for her. What was the
harm if some petty pressures of life, or even some larger interests, could be sacrificed by loving such a good man? Kiranmayee had been nurturing a physical frustration since
she was twenty-eight. But her mind was overflowing with
a sea of love which was enough to keep down all her physical discomforts and other pains and sorrows.

Suranjan had given her money, possibly by borrowing
it. Perhaps he suffered from some sort of inferiority complex for not earning. Still, she had some money remaining
to run the household for some more days. Sudhamay
never kept any money with him. He would hand over
whatever he earned to Kiranmayee. Besides, some gold ornaments were still left.

Suranjan suddenly stormed into the room shouting,
"Do you think I've stolen this money? Or do you feel
ashamed to accept money from an unemployed person
like me? Perhaps I can't do anything. But that doesn't
mean I lack the will. Can't anyone understand this?"

Kiranmayee was motionless. Each of the words pierced
her heart.

Suranjan knocked at Ratna's door. It was Ratna who opened
it. She didn't show any sign of surprise, as if she were expecting Suranjan to turn up. She took him straightaway to
her bedroom. He was treated like an old relative. She was
dressed in a cotton sari. She would have looked much better
with a vermilion dot just above the joining point of her eyebrows. And only if the thin vermilion streak were there at

the parting line of her hair. Suranjan didn't have any regard for the signs of rituals. But the Bengaliness of the married women with conchshell bangles, vermilion mark and the sound of conchshell indeed charmed him. All manner of worship was prohibited in their household. But he was not opposed to going round the Puja pandals with friends, dancing to the drumbeats during the time of special worship of the image, keeping beats with the songs blared by loudspeakers at pandals, eating a few sweets and such things. Ratna went inside to fetch some tea for him. Besides "How are you?" she didn't ask him anything. Suranjan also preferred to stay quiet. Rather, no words came to him. He had come to love her. After a long time, he had put on a well-pressed shirt after shaving, taking a bath and even using some perfume. Ratna's family members were her old parents, elder brother and herself. The married brother had his wife and son and daughter. The children were snooping around, finding no answer to their curious questions about who this new man was and what had brought him to her. They were hanging around the door. Suranjan asked a girl, aged about seven, "What's your name?"

"Mrittika."

"Bah, what a fine name. What's Ratna to you?"

"*Pishi.*"

"Oh."

"Do you work in my aunt's office?"

"No, I don't do any work, just roam around."

The idea of roaming around quite impressed Mrittika. Before she could ask anything else, Ratna emerged, carrying a tray with tea, some salted nuts, biscuits, and two types of sweetmeats.

"What's the matter? Hindus are not supposed to be so

generous with food these days. They can hardly go out of their houses. But here I find quite a lot. So, when did you come back from Sylhet?"

"I didn't go to Sylhet. In fact, I visited Habiganj, Sunamgunj and Maulavibazar. I saw the destruction of three temples in Madhabpur market in Habiganj with my own eyes."

"Who destroyed them?"

"Who else but those bearded Mullahs sporting their caps. Then they targeted the Kali temple of the market. Two temples at Sunamgunj went the same way on the 8th. Four more temples, fifty shops were pillaged and then set on fire on the 9th. They smashed and set fire to four more temples and akhras at Rajnagar and Kulaura in Moulabizbazar. Seven shops at Brahmanbazar, too, were looted."

"Certainly all those shops were owned by Hindus?"

"That goes without saying," Ratna said, bursting into laughter. Offering him tea and salted nuts, she said, "Could you tell me if it will be possible to stay in this country any longer?"

"Why not? Is this country strictly the Muslims' paternal property?"

Ratna laughed, although her face reflected a tinge of sadness. She said, "In Bhola the people are forced to sign blank sale deeds for their properties before leaving. Some of them are getting some paltry amount, the less fortunate are going even without that."

"Who are the people leaving Bhola? Certainly Hindus?"

"Of course."

"Then why are you not mentioning that?" said Suranjan, munching salted nuts.

The mention of the word "Hindu" was superfluous.

But Suranjan wanted Ratna to say clearly that the people whose houses and shops were being looted were not just people of Habiganj or Bhola, but belonged to a species called Hindus.

It was not quite clear what Ratna felt. She just stared at Suranjan with her eyes showing unusual depth. He had decided earlier to bare his heart to Ratna unhesitatingly. He would say, "I like you very much. If you wish, we can get married."

Ratna rose to get water. The end of her sari swept past Suranjan's left arm. The touch thrilled him. Well, Ratna could be his wife if she wanted that. It was not that Suranjan was thinking of marriage just to put down his Bohemian ways and settle into a family life of his own. He dreamed of playing with Ratna's fingers lying by her side, talking of his childhood when he could easily go out wearing no clothes at all. Through this idle yet intimate talk, he would reach a stage when there would be nothing unknown between them. There wouldn't be any barrier, visible or invisible, anymore. Ratna, as he perceived her, would rather be his friend than his wife.

Suranjan felt somewhat embarrassed, not quite sure what the penetrating eyes of Ratna wanted to communicate. He said instead, "I just came to find out if you are unhurt."

"Unhurt? The word has different meanings for men and for women. In which sense had you meant it?"

"Both."

Ratna bent her head, smiling. Her smile was not exactly sparkling, yet she looked quite attractive. Suranjan couldn't take his eyes off her face. Had he aged? Did the men of his age look too old, totally unsuitable for marriage? Absorbed in his thoughts, Suranjan suddenly noticed Ratna had her eyes fixed on him. Her gaze had an aura of fascination.

"Are you still sticking to your resolution about staying unmarried?" Ratna asked with a smile.

After a pause, Suranjan said, "Life is just like a river, I think you know it. Does the river ever get blocked up? So, too, resolve can't remain irreversible. It changes."

Ignoring the grim situation arising out of attacks on Hindus in the world outside, Ratna said, flashing a smile even at this critical hour, "I am indeed relieved to hear that."

Suranjan didn't ask what she meant. He could imagine. Ratna was giving him pure joy. He felt like touching Ratna's fingers and proposing a walk in Salborn Bihar. "Let's lie on the carpet of verdant fields with the moon standing guard over us. We won't ask the moon tonight to conceal its shine." He wished he could say and do all this. Going near the staircase, he thought of telling Ratna, standing with her hands resting on the door, "Let's change our firm decisions and do something together."

But he couldn't say that. Ratna came down a couple of stairs and said, "Please come again. Your coming gave me the assurance of someone standing by my side. I feel I haven't turned into a loner."

Suranjan could feel clearly the stirring of the spring that the sweet little sparrow Parvin had once awakened in his heart. He could see that he was beginning to float away into the heaven of happiness that Parvin had once opened up for him.

Day Six

Suranjan picked up the morning paper along with his tea. He was in high spirits today. He had had a sound sleep the night before. After casting a cursory glance over the paper, he called Maya.

"What has happened to you? Why are you so glum all the time?"

"Nothing's the matter with me. You are the one who has been behaving strangely. You haven't sat beside Baba even once."

"I don't like seeing a man, quite hale and hearty till the other day, now lying immobile on the bed. What I dislike all the more is your whimpering cries all the time by his bedside. Why, by the way, did Ma return the money I gave her? Does she have plenty of it?"

"Ma has sold her ornaments."

"She has done the right thing. I don't like the ornaments at all."

"You are saying this now. But you did present a pearl-studded ring to Parvin Apa."

"Then I was quite young, the world looked colorful, I lacked maturity. That's why I gave it."

"Well, have you matured now?" Maya asked with a smile.

Suranjan saw a flicker of a smile on Maya's face after a long time. In his bid to keep her cheerful, he drew her attention to the front page news and said, "Do you see? Peace processions have appeared on Dhaka streets. We, irrespective of our class, community and religion, are and will be in Bangladesh. All-party peace processions are boldly declaring: resist communalism. They are giving calls to thwart the disruptionists and looters. Violence in India is on the wane. The acquisition of the mosque land by the Uttar Pradesh government in that country has been ruled illegal by the High Court. Narasimha Rao has stated it is not the central government but the BJP-run Uttar Pradesh government which is responsible for the demolition of the Babri mosque. The army continues to be deployed in West Bengal, Gujarat and Maharashtra. The leftists have virtually declared a crusade against the fundamentalists. A rally is being held today at the *Paltan Maidan* by the Communist party of Bangladesh. The Awami League has asked for the formation of peace brigades for preserving communal harmony. The city's coordination committee has demanded the arrest of Nizami Kader mullahs for instigating riots. The Committee for the Extermination of Killers and Informers is also holding a rally today. All-party peace processions will march in the Tongi area. The slogan of the cultural front is: Bangladesh will surely put an end to communal forces. Fifteen prominent citizens have said in a statement that the task of maintaining communal harmony should be shared by all. Colonel Akbar has demanded the banning of fascist organizations like Jamat. A combined council for the preservation of communal amity has been formed in Barisal. The Dhaka University Teachers Association has said that the sanctity of the month observing victory after the country's liberation will be destroyed in the event of communal outrage. Twenty-eight people have been arrested on charges of temple destruction at Dhamrai. Jyoti Basu, West Bengal's chief minister, has regretted that India has lost face before the world."

"You read only the heartening news," said Maya, sitting crosslegged on the bed. She pulled the paper from Suranjan and said, "What about the rest of the news? Ten thousand families homeless at Bhola. Seven hundred houses burned in Chittagong. The temple at Kishoreganj ransacked. Section 144 at Pirozepur. Seven hundred houses at Meersarai of Seetakunda set on fire."

"I don't want to hear bad news today. I'm in a jovial mood."

"Why, has your heart cheered up at the news of Parvin Apa's decision to divorce her husband? She came yesterday. She is beaten up by her husband every night."

"Why now? Didn't she find the expected boundless peace by marrying a Muslim? No, dear, not because of Parvin. Now my mind has found its berth somewhere else. Not a Muslim girl this time. No pleas to convert in a tear-choked voice."

Maya laughed aloud. It had been a long time since she laughed.

Suranjan suddenly turned grave and asked, "How is Baba's condition now? Won't he recover quickly?"

"He's much better now. His speech has become much clearer. With my support, he can go to the toilet now, and can also eat soft food. Oh, yes, listen, Belal Bhai came last evening to look for you. He advised you not to venture out of the house, which he thought would be risky."

"Oh."

Suranjan sprang up. Maya asked, "What's the matter? Looks like you're going out."

"Am I the sort of a chap to sit idly at home?"

"You don't know how worried Ma is when you go out. Dada, please don't go. I also feel so scared."

"The money will have to be returned to Pulak. Do you have some money? After all, you're an earning girl. Why don't you give me something from your fund for my cigarettes?"

"No, I won't give you anything to buy cigarettes. I don't want you to die so soon."

Maya raised her voice in protest, yet she finally came out with a hundred-taka note. In her childhood, schoolmates used to pester her with cries of "Hindu, Hindu Tulshi leaf, Hindus only eat beef." Coming back home a snivelling wretch, Maya had asked Suranjan, "Am I supposed to be a Hindu? Now tell me, Dada, am I really a Hindu?"

"Yes," Suranjan had affirmed.

"Then I won't be a Hindu. If I'm one, they harass me constantly."

After listening to her complaint, Sudhamay had said, "Who says you are a Hindu? You are a human being. There's nothing on earth which is greater than that."

Suranjan from his heart felt his reverence for Sudhamay. He had never seen a greater idealist, a greater personality with such a rational, intelligent and conscientious approach. To him Sudhamay was the epitome of godliness. How many persons with his broadness of mind and tolerance could be found in this world?

In 1964, Sudhamay coined the slogan: East Pakistan, put down your foot to resist. The riots of that time were stopped in their track. Sheikh Mujibur himself intervened to stop the violence. The Ayub Khan government took the initiative in fomenting the riots in its bid to turn the tide of the movement against it. The government brought criminal cases against student and political leaders. Sudhamay was the accused in a case. He didn't like to muse on the past. Still, memories loomed before him with all their starkness. What had he gained by devoting himself to the country's cause? The country had been slipping into the hands of the fundamentalists since 1975. The people were listless still, even after realizing everything. Was the present generation so unaware? The blood that had been spilled on the streets to demand Bengali as the state language, the blood of the mass uprisings of 1969, the blood of three million people in the liberation war of 1971—wasn't the same blood flowing in their veins now? Where was that heat of excitement that had hurled Sudhamay into the movements of those days? Where were those spirited youths? Why were they so cold? Was fundamentalism striking its roots in the secular country of Bangladesh? Weren't they aware of the approach of unimaginably hard times? Sudhamay sought to muster all his strength to get up from bed. But he couldn't. His face turned dark in anguish and unexpressed wrath.

"The Enemy Property Act" of the Ayub Khan regime

was reintroduced under a new name by the Law Minister of the Awami League, which he rechristened as the Acquired Properties Act. The properties left by the Hindus who had left the country were called enemy properties. Were Sudhamay's maternal and paternal uncles enemies of the country? They had huge mansions in Dhaka and properties in Sonargaon, Narasingdi, Kishoregunj, Faridpur and so on. Those houses had now been converted into colleges, veterinary hospitals, family planning offices, income tax offices, registration offices, and the like. When he was a boy, Sudhamay used to come to the house of his Uncle Anil. At that huge estate on Ramkrishna Road, ten horses were kept. His uncle would let him ride them. Sudhamay now lived in a dark, damp house at Tikatuli while the government had taken possession of that enormous house of his uncle. Had the renamed law, that is, the Acquired Property Act, been designed to favor the closest living heirs, the distress of those who had chosen to stay would have been alleviated. Sudhamay had suggested this change in the legislation to many political bigwigs. But no one had paid any heed to him. He felt weary in his present immobile, inactive state. He found no reason to go on living. He could see that his death wouldn't be of concern to anyone. Rather, Kiranmayee would be relieved of keeping a virtual vigil through the night and nursing him.

During the 1965 Indo-Pakistan War, the Enemy Property Act was enforced because of the communal malice of the colonial Pakistani ruling clique. Sudhamay was indeed surprised when the same legislation was allowed to remain effective through trickery even after Bangladesh's independence. Was it not a matter of shame for a free country, for the Bengali people? This act deprived about twenty

171

million people of their fundamental human, democratic and civil rights in a single stroke. Through this legislation, which contravened all the principles of equal rights, social and political, these twenty million people were being irrevocably evicted from their hearths and homes, to their supreme misfortune. Hence, the Hindus could hardly be blamed for their feeling of insecurity. This was followed by the planting of the seeds of communal discord. The constitution of Bangladesh, despite assurances of equal security and rights for all citizens, was being distorted by this act, which showed extreme disrespect for national independence and sovereignty by violating the basic tenets of the administrative structure.

It was rather paradoxical that the constitution of the People's Republic of Bangladesh stated in its following clauses and subclauses:

26. (1). The laws contrary to the rules and regulations laid down in this part should be treated as null and void as this becomes effective.

26. (2). The state will not frame any legislation which violates any principle mentioned in this part and any such act, if passed earlier, shall be treated as null and void depending upon the extent of its contravention.

27. All the citizens will be equally treated in the eyes of the law and entitled to seek legal protection.

28. (1). The state will show no discrimination to any citizen on the grounds of religion, community, caste, sex or place of birth.

31. It shall be an inalienable right of every citizen to seek legal protection as well as treatment according to the provisions of law. Even the persons living in Bangladesh temporarily will not be deprived of this right. Without the

sanction of the law, no measure can be taken against any person that can lead to the loss of his or her life, freedom, physical existence, reputation or property.

Clause 112 clearly stated: "All authorities, executive and judicial, in the Republic shall act in aid of the Supreme Court."

The sections of the Defense of Pakistan Act, 1965, read thus:

a. any state, or sovereign of a state at war with or engaged in military operation against Pakistan, or

b. any individual resident in enemy territory, or

c. any body of persons constituted or incorporated in enemy territory, or in or under the laws of a state at war with, or engaged in military operation against, Pakistan, or

d. any other person or body of persons declared by the central government to be an enemy, or

e. any body of persons (whether incorporated or not) carrying on business in any place, if and so long as the body is controlled by a person who under this rule is an enemy, or

f. in respect of any business carried on in enemy territory and individual or a body of persons (whether incorporated or not) carrying on that business.

Clause 169. 1. stated: enemy subject means:

a. any individual who possesses the nationality of a state at war with, or engaged in military operation against, Pakistan, or having possessed such nationality at any time has lost . . . without acquiring another nationality, or

b. any body of persons constituted or incorporated in or under the laws of such state.

169. 4. Enemy property means: any property for the time being belonging to or held or managed on behalf of

SHAME

an enemy as defined in Rule 161, an enemy subject or an enemy firm, but does not include the property which is evacuee property under the Pakistan (administration of evacuee property) Act, 1957 (xii of 1957).

Moreover, it was stated:

> Where an individual enemy subject dies in Pakistan, any property, which, individually before his death belonged to or was held by him, or was managed on his behalf, may notwithstanding his death continue to be regarded as enemy property for the purpose of Rule 182.

The communal riots in the partition year of 1947 made millions in East Bengal flee to India. The then Pakistan government enforced East Bengal Evacuees (Administration of Property) Act VIII of 1949, the East Bengal Evacuees (Restoration of Possession) Act XXIII of 1951, East Bengal Evacuees (Administration of Immovable Property) Act XXIV of 1951.

The East Bengal Evacuees (Administration of Immovable Property) Act XXIV of 1951 stated:

> The evacuee committees constituted under this Act shall not take charge of any evacuee property.
>
> 1. if the sole owner or all the co-sharer owners of the property object to the management of such property by the committee on the grounds that he or they has or have made other arrangements for the management and utilization of the property and if the committee is satisfied that the arrangement so made [is] proper and adequate, or
>
> 2. if an objection is filed and allowed under this section.

This act further stated:

the property shall be vested on the application of the evacuees and it shall be vested with the right to dispose of property as he likes.

In 1957, the Pakistan government, after amending this act further, enforced Pakistan (Administration of Evacuee Property) Act XII of 1957. This act stated:

properties of any person who is resident in any place in the territories now comprising India or in any area occupied by India and is unable to occupy, supervise or manage in person his property in Pakistan or is being occupied, supervised or managed by a person.

Even this act hadn't caused that much inconvenience to the Hindus as did the subsequent East Pakistan Disturbed Persons and Rehabilitation Ordinance, 1964.

The Pakistan government declared an emergency because of the Indo-Pak war of 1965. It enforced on September 6, 1965, Defense of Pakistan Rules, 1965, in accordance with Defense of Pakistan Ordinance No. XXIII.

In Section 182 of Defense of Pakistan Rules, 1965, it was stated:

with a view to preventing the payment of money to an enemy firm, and to provide for the administration and disposal by way of transfer or otherwise of enemy property and matters connected therewith or incidental thereto, the Central Government may appoint a custodian of enemy property in Pakistan and one or more Deputy Custodians or Assistant Custodians of enemy

175

property for such local areas as may be prescribed and may, by order, vest or provide for and regulate the vesting in the prescribed custodian such enemy properties as may be prescribed.

On the basis of this draconian section all such properties covered by the Pakistan Defense Act and Rules were vested with the government.

Instead of a promise to give full guarantee to enemy property owners' rights and interests in the event of their being imprisoned or the imposition of restrictions on their movements during the wartime situation and difficulties in supervising or managing these properties, the Pakistan central government, as a temporary measure, imposed Enemy Property (Custody and Registration) Order, 1965, and later, Enemy Property (Land and Building) Administration and Disposal Order, 1966, to bring under their purview the vesting of the power to realize money and compensation for these properties and keeping their separate accounts along with the charge of their supervision and management with an official.

Even after the end of the Indo-Pak War, the government, in its bid to keep the earlier act operational, imposed Enemy Property (Continuance of Emergency Provision) Ordinance No. 1 of 1969. Although India was a friendly power in the country's liberation war and no warlike conditions existed between the two countries, the Presidential Order No. 29/1972, which renamed the earlier act as Bangladesh Vesting of Property and Assets Order, vested all the enemy properties said to be of a permanent nature, hitherto lying in charge of the custodian of the Pakistan government, with the Bangladesh government. In reality, the Enemy Property (Continuance of Emergency Provision) Ordinance was kept in force in blatant violation of the assurance to maintain the people's human dignity, social rights and uniform status for all. Just as in the Pakistani regime, the power of supervision and management of enemy properties were left with the government even after the emergence of a free Bangladesh in a grossly unfair manner. Ignoring popular demand for the restoration of lawful rights, the Enemy Property (Continuance of Emergency Provision) Repeal Act XLV of 1974 was imposed. It was indeed a new subterfuge in the name of cancellation of earlier legislation to retain all the powers vested with the Pakistani government over the properties of those who were not permanent residents of Bangladesh or whoever "has ceased to be a permanent resident," so that the supervision and management of such properties could be done through a government-appointed committee of administrators. This committee took charge of all such properties in the context of either its own initiative or the request of a nonresident or a government directive. This new legislation indeed expanded the scope of its Pakistani predecessor by including even those properties not previously brought under the official jurisdiction in the pre-independence era. But even before this act could become effective, Ordinance No. XCIII was promulgated in 1976. This order said:

> Those properties which were vested under the Act shall be administered, controlled, managed and disposed of by transfer or otherwise by the government on such officer or authority as Government may direct.

Hardly had a year had passed when a circular was issued on May 23, 1976, which said:

> ten *kathas* of vacant nonagricultural land shall be given long-term lease to a person deserving to get it, realizing full market value as premium and proper rent, that nonagricultural lands situated in business centers shall be settled in open auction with the highest bidder.

In other words, fifteen to twenty million people in Bangladesh who owned nonagricultural land would have their land auctioned off, and the government, for its part, would enjoy the benefits of long-term taxes from it. Section 37 of this circular empowered the local petty revenue officers to track down all such landed properties and reward the people who could supply information about their location. Section 38 further gave entitlement of such rewards to different officials engaged in this work like Additional District Magistrate (Revenue), all Subdivisional Officers, Circle Officers (Revenue) and all the personnel of the Land and Land Revenue Department. Lured by this reward, these people, in the name of tracing the vested properties, had evicted the Hindus from their homesteads or portions of properties held by them.

After 1966, the East Pakistan government conducted a land survey. This showed that many people had left the country after the partition of 1947 and the riots of 1950 and 1954, leaving the responsibility of maintaining their properties to other members of their households. Ponds, gardens, family cremation grounds, religious centers and temples as well as both agricultural and nonagricultural lands had been listed as enemy property. Even properties of the

Hindus who hadn't left the country were brought under the purview of this order. However, the properties of the Muslims who had left likewise for other countries were spared. No survey was conducted to locate their properties. According to law, the property of the absentee member of a Hindu joint family went to the possession of the eldest surviving members of the family. Yet, even such properties were taken over by the government.

Sudhamay thought about Niaz Hussain, Fajlul Alam, Anwar Ahmed and others like them he had seen depart for London or the United States. Their distant relatives were living in their village homes. Some of them had left their houses in the charge of caretakers, some had let them out and were collecting rents from other people without any hindrance. It was rather strange that their properties were never treated as enemy properties. Sudhamay wanted to get up. He was perspiring. He found no one in his room, neither Maya nor Kiranmayee. Where had they gone, he wondered.

Suranjan, walking down a road in the old part of Dhaka, found that even after moving around this city many times over, he couldn't erase the memory of Mymensingh. He was born in that town where, although it was much smaller, he had spent his childhood and youth. As he dipped his feet in Dhaka's Buriganga river, his mind traveled back to the Brahmaputra river. Only a man determined to deny his birth could become oblivious of the soil where he was born and the river that flowed alongside it. Gautam, along with his family, was leaving the country forever. They did not consider themselves safe and secure in this country. Suranjan's maternal uncle came from Calcutta about five years ago. Visiting Brahmanbaria, which had been his land, he wept like a child. Kiranmayee had asked him, "Would you like to go to Calcutta with your uncle?" Suranjan spurned the proposal.

A party assignment took him to Mymensingh about four or six years ago. Seeing the flitting images of lush green paddy fields, trees on the skyline, huts, haystacks, children merrily floundering in the marshy tracts or catching fish with the help of handspun towels, the simple, wonder-struck faces of peasants looking at the speeding train, Suranjan, seated on the windowside in the train compartment, could see the visage of his own country on this canvas of impressions. The poet Jibanananda Das, after being charmed with this image of his country, never wanted to see any other scene in the world. Suranjan was jolted out of his reverie, finding the station Ramlakshmanpur renamed as Ahmed Bari. He also saw to his amazement the continuation of that renaming spree: Kalir bazar had turned into Fatima bazar, and Krishna Nagar had become Aulia Nagar. The process of Islamization now going on all over the country had not spared the small stations in his Mymensingh district. To blot out the Hindu identity from the names of places and institutions, where Muslim names couldn't be immediately found, abbreviation was resorted to. Thus Brahman Baria became B. Baria, the famous Braja Mohan College of Barisal turned into B.M. College and Murari Chand College of Sylhet reduced to M.C. College. What Suranjan feared was that these educational institutions, too, would soon be called Mohammad Ali College or Serajuddaula College. Twenty-one years after the renaming of Jinnah Hall of Dhaka University after the great revolutionary Surya Sen in the post-in-

180

dependence period, those who were opposed to the country's freedom were now describing that martyr as a dacoit and questioning the rationality of associating the name of a dacoit with the university. This obviously implied the veiled demand of restoring the old name. One was not too sure about the possibility of the government's bending to the demand.

The ruling Bangladesh nationalist party had come to power aided by the fundamentalists. That was why its leaders, too, were looking after the interests of their allies.

Walking in the old Dhaka areas, Suranjan found all the Hindu shops closed. On what assurance would their owners raise their shutters? Still, they opened the shops after the riots of 1990, and perhaps they would this time also. The skin of a Hindu was perhaps as thick as that of a rhinoceros. Otherwise, how could they possibly rebuild their broken homes? How could they reconstruct a plundered shop? Even if it was conceded that shattered houses and shops could be repaired with the help of building materials, how could broken minds be mended?

In the riot of 1990, Brahma Samaj at Patuatuli, the Shridhar temple of Shankhari Bazar and the Snake temple of Kayet tuli were sacked and then set on fire. The famous homeopathic medicine shop of M. Bhattacharyya at Patuatuli, the Hotel Raj, Dhakeshwari Jewelers, Kashmiri Briryani House, Rupashree Jewelers, Fergreen Jewelers, Alpana Jewelers, New Ghosh Jewelers, Manashi Jewelers, Mitali Jewelers, some stores of Shankhari Bazar, Anannya Laundry, Krishna Hair Dresser, Tire Tube Repairing, Saha Conteen, the floating hotel at Sadar Ghat called Ujala, Pathanibas, all these were looted and burned down. The same thing happened to the municipal sweepers colony at

Naya Bazar, and the slums of sweepers near Dhaka district court, Chunkutia Purbapara Harisabha temple of Keranigunj, the Kali temple, the temple of Meer Bag, Gosham Bazar akhra, the Durga temple of Shubhadya, Gosain's Bagh temple of Chandranikara, the Kali temple of Paschim Para, the cremation ground, the Ramkani temple of Tegharia Pubanadi, the Durga temple at the market of Kalindi Barishu, Kali temple, the temple of the snake goddess Manasa—all had been subjected to looting and image smashing. Fifty rented houses at Shubhadya Khejurbag, including the residence of Rabi Mishra, son of Pyari Mohan Mishra, were burned down. The same fate befell the houses of Bhabatosh Ghosh and Paritosh Ghosh, of Tegharia, the Hindu areas at Mandail of Kalindi, and three hundred houses of Rishipara in Bangaon. Suranjan had witnessed much of this carnage, and he had heard about some from others.

Suranjan had been walking around aimlessly for some time now, but he did not really know where to go. Who was close to him in this city of Dhaka? With whom could he sit and talk for a while? Today Maya had given him one hundred takas after overcoming her initial hesitation. He was reluctant to spend the money in his front pocket. He thought of buying a packet of Bangla Fives. But that would only start the process of spending and use up the money in no time. He never cared about money. What he received from Sudhamay to pay the tailor's bill had been spent on his friends. If one of them wanted to run away and get married, it was Suranjan who would provide the finances. Once he had given money to a boy named Rahmat. The poor chap's mother was in the hospital and he didn't have money to buy medicines for her. Suranjan unhesitatingly gave him the money he had been keeping to pay his examination fees. Could he now possibly go to Ratna's place? Ratna Mitra? Could not Ratna, even after marriage, stick to her maiden name? What prompted girls to change their surnames after marriage? Must they always tie themselves to the shirt tails of their fathers before marriage and to the husband's afterward? All nonsense. Suranjan wanted to drop his surname Dutta. The caste and religious differences were indeed bringing doom to man. The Bengalis, irrespective of being Hindu or Muslim, should maintain their Bengali identity in their names. Many times he had thought of renaming his sister "Neelanjana Maya." What then could his own name have been? "Nibir Suranjan"? "Suranjan Sudha"? "Nikhil Suranjan"?* If he pursued this way, he wouldn't have to be smeared with the color of religion. He had noticed a propensity among the Bengali Muslims to go in for Arabic names. Even the most progressive-minded among them, who would ceaselessly proclaim Bengali culture, would invariably call his own child outlandish names like Faisal Rahman, Toudihul Islam or Abu Bakar. Why should it be so? Why should a Bengali have an Arabic name? Suranjan would not name his daughter Srotashwini Bhalobasa (River of Love) or Athai Neelima (Boundless Azure). The second name came closer to Maya's other name, Neelanjana. This name could be kept exclusively for Maya's daughter.

Suranjan went on walking. Aimless ambling, yet when he stepped out of his house he thought of doing a great deal. But once out he could think of no destination. As if

---

*Meaning, respectively, Suranjan the intimate, Suranjan the nectar and Suranjan the universal.

everyone were busy, running frantically on his own errand. Only he had nothing to do. He didn't have anything to occupy him. He wanted to talk to someone in this city of terror. Could he go to Dulal's place at Bangsal? Or to the house of Mahadebda at Azimpur? He could drop in at Kajal Debnath's house in Ispahani Colony. Why was he remembering the names of Hindus today in search of places to go? Belal came to his house yesterday, so he could pay a return visit to him. Hyder also paid him a visit, so his house could also be visited. But if he went to their houses, the topic of the Babri mosque would invariably touch off sparks. The same cycle of what was happening in India, how many died there, what was the latest about the BJP leaders, in which places the army had been called out, who were arrested, which party was banned, what would happen in the future. He no longer cared to hear all this. The Jamat of this country hardly differed from the BJP there. Both had an identical objective: to put fundamentalism on a solid foundation. If only religion-based politics could be banned from both countries! Religion weighed so heavily on the Third World countries, like a massive stone, that their starving, timid, persecuted people perhaps stood no chance of liberation. He cherished a saying of Karl Marx which he muttered as he walked through the crowd. Religious hardship is the other face of real hardship and is also a protest against the real hardship. Religion is the sigh of persecuted beings, the heart of a heartless world, just as it is the soul of a soulless society. Religion is the opium of the people.

Aimlessly wandering through Wari, Nababpur, Nayabazar, the Court area, Rajani Basak Lane, Begumbazar, Suranjan finally went to Kajal's house. As it happened in the case of almost all the Hindus, Kajal was at home. There were only two alternatives for them: either to hide themselves somewhere outside their houses or to stay put at home, making as little sound as possible. Suranjan, craving talk as he was, felt happy to find Kajal at home. Some others were there in Kajal's room: Subhash Sinha, Tapas Pal, Dilip Dey, Nirmal Chatterjee, Anjan Majumdar, Jatin Chakravarty, Zai-ur-Rahman, and Kabir Chowdhury.

"What's the matter? I find quite an assembly of Hindus."

No one but Suranjan laughed at his utterance. "What's the news, why are you in such low spirits, just because of the killing of Hindus?" Suranjan asked.

"Is there any reason to be happy?" Subhash said.

Kajal Debnath was actively involved with the Hindu, Buddhist, and Christian Unity Council. Suranjan had considered this outfit also as a communal party. Any support for this organization simply removed the foundation from the demand to ban all religion-based political parties. Kajal, however, maintained that after being disillusioned in the wake of a forty-year wait, he had been forced to join this organization just for self-defense.

"Has Khaleda even once admitted the continuation of communal riots in the country? Never once has she cared to visit the devastated areas," one member of the gathering said. Kajal immediately intervened, saying, "What has the Awami League done beyond issuing some statements? Such statements have been made by a rabidly communal set-up like Jamat-i-Islami. In the last election, a propaganda program was launched to misdirect the people into thinking that if the Awami League was voted back into power, the religious expression "Bismillah" would be dropped from the constitution. Now unable to capture power, the Awami Leaguers were thinking that their stance against the eighth amendment of the constitution would erode their popularity. It was difficult to say if the Awami League was only targeting votes or was keen on sticking firmly to its ideology. If their choice was the latter, why aren't they now speaking out against the coming bill?"

"They were perhaps thinking of getting power first. Then changes, if necessary, can be brought about," Zai-ur-Rahman said, trying to defend the Awami League.

"No one can be trusted. All the parties, once they are seated in the saddle of power, will sing in praise of Islam and adopt an anti-India stance. These are the issues that sway public opinion easily in this country," Kajal said, nodding his head.

Suddenly Suranjan, sidetracking the course of discussion, swung back to his old query. "But Kajalda, don't you think it would be better to form a noncommunal group rather than this communal association? And why is Zai-ur-Rahman not a member of your council, may I ask?"

Jatin Chakravarty intervened in a grave voice: "It's not our inability that kept Zai-ur-Rahman out. It's the failure of those people who have planted a state religion. We didn't have to set up such a council for so long. So what is compelling us to go in for such a move? Bangladesh hasn't come into being simply on its own. All the people, irrespective of being Hindu, Buddhist, Christian or Muslim made their contribution to its creation. But to declare state patronage for a particular religion is to invite a feeling of separatism in the minds of people believing in other religions. No one loves his country any less than the others. But seeing their own religion being relegated to second- or third-class status just because of their being non-Muslims is quite a deadly blow to their egos. Can they be blamed for their preference for communalism over nationalism?"

Since the reply was meant for Suranjan, he said in a low voice, "But what is the point in maintaining such a communal outfit in a modern state?"

Jatin Chakravarty immediately added without waiting for a pause: "But who has forced the religious minorities to form this sort of community-based organization? Aren't the promoters of the state religion responsible for it? The state loses its national identity the moment the religion of a particular community is declared the state religion. And any state with a state religion can be proclaimed a theocratic state any time. This state is turning into a communal state so rapidly, it will be ridiculous to talk of national integration at this juncture. The minorities, because of their suffering, are realizing that they are being duped by the eighth amendment."

"Do you think that the Muslims are going to gain from Islam's being declared as the state religion? Or from the state being branded theocratic? I certainly don't think so."

"That's true. If not today, some day the Muslims, too, will come to realize it."

"The Awami League, however, could play a commendable role at this time," Anjan commented.

Suranjan said, "True, but the bill mooted by the Awami League doesn't have any provision for scrapping the eighth amendment. The most indisputable condition for democracy is secularism and any modern man having faith in a democratic system realizes it. What's the point of declaring Islam as the state religion in a country that already has an 86 percent Muslim population? I don't understand. The Muslims in Bangladesh are quite religious-minded. They hardly need a state religion for themselves."

Jatinbabu made a slight movement in his cramped position and said, "There can't be any compromise on the question of principle. The Awami League, to defend itself against adverse propaganda, is going for a sort of compromise."

Subhash, who had so long been listening to the different angles, said, "In fact, instead of taking the Jamat and BNP to task for all these misdeeds, we've been training our guns on the Awami League." Interrupting him, Kajal said, "We know them as proven enemies. Hence they are not worth any discussion. We indeed get hurt when we notice deviation on the part of those in whom we put our faith."

Kabir Chowdhury suddenly cut in, saying, "So far you are speaking on secularism, which, you must know, means viewing all religions equally. There's no question of discrimination on this score. And in plain and simple language secularism means materialism, that is, a total detachment of the state from religion."

Kajal Debnath said rather agitatedly, "It was the triumph of Muslim fundamentalism during the partition that led to the creation of Pakistan. Hindu fundamentalism was defeated in India. Its defeat has made India a modern, democratic and secular state. For the security of the Indian Muslims, the Hindus in this country were given the despicable name of *jimmis*; the real motive behind such a declaration was to take possession of the Hindu properties by hook or crook. It's nothing surprising if the Hindus get scared when fresh Islamic clamors are made in the style of the Pakistani regime. The Hindus won't be able to survive in this country unless the state is declared secular. So we further demand the scrapping of the Enemy Property Act. There's hardly a Hindu in the administration. They have never been given secretary-level posts since the Pakistani days. There's only a handful of Hindus in the army, and they hardly ever get promoted. I don't think there's a single Hindu in the navy or air force."

Nirmal said, "Kajalda, no Hindu till this day has reached the rank of brigadier or major general in the army. There is one among seventy colonels, eight among four hundred fifty lieutenant colonels, forty among one thousand majors, eight among one thousand three hundred captains, three among nine hundred second lieutenants, and five hundred among eighty thousand soldiers. Of the forty thousand in the BDR, only three hundred are Hindus. For the secretary's post there have been no Buddhists or Christians—why mention the absence of Hindus only? None among the additional secretaries, either. Only one among one hundred thirty-four joint secretaries."

Kajal resumed, "Is there a single Hindu in the Foreign Service? I don't think so."

Subhash was seated on a wicker stool. He stood up to say, "No, Kajalda, there's none."

The floor was carpeted. Sitting on the carpet, Suranjan leaned against a cushion. He was enjoying the trend of discussion.

Kabir Chowdhury said, "From the Pakistani days till now, during the Awami League regime in Bangladesh, only Manoranjan Dhar was sent as Bangladeshi ambassador to Japan for a short while."

"Hindus are scrupulously avoided in the selection of candidates for higher studies or for training in foreign countries. No Hindu is in possession of a good profit-making business concern at present. Even licenses for starting a business are rarely given to a Hindu unless he has a Muslim partner. Besides, no loans are approved for financial organizations to a Hindu intending to start an industry," Kajal said.

"Quite so," Anjan added. "I have worn out the soles of my shoes in a bid to get loans for my garment business. Yet I didn't get any help from the banks. Then I had to rope in Afsar and that worked."

Subhash piped up, "Have you noticed one thing? The TV and radio broadcasts begin with quotations from the Koran, which is mentioned as a holy book. When similarly excerpts from the Gita or Tripitak are read out, these books are never described in such a way."

Suranjan said, "In fact, no religious scriptures can be called holy. All of them are full of shit. All this can easily be left out. Rather, a demand for ending all religious preachings on radio or TV should be made."

A silence descended on the debate's participants. Suranjan felt like having a cup of tea, but possibly there were no such arrangements in this household. He could stretch himself out on the carpet. He would like to enjoy this outpouring of pains suffered by all the others.

Kajal Debnath, after a break, resumed: "In all official functions, at every meeting, the program begins with *suras* from the Koran. But the Gita is strictly avoided. The Hindus in government service have only two holidays of their own. They can't even take leave if they want to. Each organization makes proclamations about mosque construction. But there's never any reference to temple construction. Every year, hundreds of millions of takas are being spent for either construction of new mosques or repair of the old ones. But has there ever been any allocation for the maintenance of temples, churches or pagodas?"

Suranjan raised his head and said, "Do you feel happy only with the broadcast of religious scriptures like the Gita? Will you feel great if temple construction is permitted? The twenty-first century is knocking at our door and we are still inviting religion to guide our society and state. Better say, all basic principles of the state, society and education should be free from religious interference. Secularism of the constitution does not mean that from now on the Gita, like the Koran, should also be compulsorily read. In schools, colleges and universities all religious functions, prayers, the teaching of religious texts and the glorification of the lives of religious persons should be banned. Also banned should be political leaders' aid to religious activities. Any political leader participating in a religious function and patronizing it should be expelled from his party. Religious propaganda must be discontinued in the government media. No one should be asked to state his religion in his application form for a job."

Kajal Debnath laughed at Suranjan's outpourings. He said, "Your imagination is running wild. Your suggestions are practicable in secular states but not in this country."

Subhash was fidgeting to join the discussion. Finding a gap, he slipped in, "Today we held a meeting outside the Press Club on behalf of the Bangladesh Student-Youth Unity Council. We submitted a memorandum to the Home Minister demanding reconstruction of damaged temples, relief and rehabilitation for the helpless displaced people, punishment for the guilty and the banning of communal politics."

Suranjan lifted his head from the cushion and said, "Not a single demand of yours will be conceded to by the government."

Kabir Chowdhury said, "How can you expect him to

accept your demands? The Home Minister himself was a *Rajakar* at one time. The story goes that he used to mount guard over a Pakistani camp at his sentry post on the Kachpur bridge."

Saidur Rahaman said, "Those *Rajakars* have now come to power. Sheikh Mujibur pardoned them. Zia-ur-Rahman invited them to share power. Ershad has made them all the more powerful. And Khaleda Zia Begum is now at the helm of the country with their direct support."

"I heard that Sebakhola temple at Cox Bazar has been torn down. There was a memorial temple at a cremation place and that, too, has gone the same way. The Central Kali temple in Idgaon Bazar of Jalalabad, the community Durga Puja temple of Hindupara, the the Hali temple, the club room of Macchuapara have been completely burned down. The community Durga Puja temple of Hindupara at Islamabad, the Durga temple, Adwaita Chintahari monastery, the house of the monastery head, and five other family temples have been totally gutted. The Hari temple at Boalkhali has been looted. Also destroyed are eight temples, six houses, and two shops of Choufaldandi. In all, one hundred sixty-nine families from the Hindu locality were robbed of all their possessions. Five more shops in the market area have been looted; Hindus are being assaulted everywhere. The paddy storage silos of all Hindu households have been set on fire by sprinkling kerosene on them. The temple of Sarbang, too, has been smashed and later set afire. The Bhairabbari of Ukhia has been totally destroyed. The Kalibari of Teknaj and the house of its priest have been set on fire. Three temples and eleven houses at Maheshkhali were also set ablaze. Four religious Gita schools, too, have been set on fire. The same goes for the Kali and Hari temples of Kalarmar Bazar. Six temples, including the Kali temple and Nat Mandir of Baraghop market at Katubdia have been set on fire. Four smithies in the market have also been plundered. All the household articles of fifty-one fishermen's families at Ali Akbar Dail have been completely burned down. Three children have been roasted alive at Kutubdia as a result of indiscriminate arson. The community Kali temple at Idgarh of Ramu and Hari temple of Jele Para have been pulled down and then set on fire. Many houses at Fateh Kharkul have been destroyed by fire . . ."

Stopping this long narration by Tapas Pal, Suranjan said, "To hell with those tales of looting and arson. Better sing a song."

"A song!" Everyone was surprised. Could anyone sing at a time like this? Was this day like any other? All over the country Hindu houses, temples and shops were being looted and set on fire. How could Suranjan have such a fancy for songs?

Suranjan, however, setting aside the bewildering topic of singing, said all of a sudden, "I'm feeling very hungry. Kajalda, could you possibly offer me a meal of rice?"

"Rice at such an odd hour?" Some members of the assembly expressed surprise.

Suranjan was feeling like gobbling rice to his heart's content. He was overcome by a desire to have a plateful of dried fish. Flies would be droning around. He would drive them away with his left hand, while with the right he would be gulping down rice. Once he had seen Ramratia, sweeper of Rajbari School, sitting in the courtyard of their Brahma Palli house gorging down rice. She had brought Maya back home from school. Suffering from a severe stomach upset, Maya couldn't make it to the school toilet. She fouled herself in the school ground and was crying. The headmistress sent her back home escorted by Ramratia. Kiranmayee offered a meal of rice to Ramratia. That someone could eat rice with such a deep sense of satisfaction, Suranjan wouldn't have believed had he not been witness to the scene. Now he was insisting on having rice before a roomful of men. Was he going off his rocker? Perhaps not. Otherwise he wouldn't have had to let out all the cries of agony that had gathered in his heart. Wouldn't it strike a note of violent discord if he broke out into a cry in the midst of all these serious discussions? He had been roaming around in the sun. He was supposed to call on Pulak to return the money he had borrowed from him the other day. He hadn't yet spent the hundred takas given him by Maya. He would have to go to Pulak's place even at night. At the same time he was feeling hungry and sleepy.

Through his slumber, Suranjan heard someone continuing that dreary narrative of the holocaust: Basana Rani Chowdhury of Loharkanda village in Narasingdi had been driven out of her home. Her son was forced to sign a blank stamped paper at the point of a dagger. They left with the warning that if anyone got to know about this deal, they would kill Basana Rani and her two sons. Did Basana look like Kiranmayee? Was she as soft, innocent and harmless as Kiranmayee? As gentle and peace-loving? The henchmen of Yunus Sardar of Ramjanpur in Madarihat raped two girls, Sabita Rani and Pushpa Rani. At Dumuria in Khulna, two sisters, Archana Rani Biswas and Bhagabati Biswas, were dragged down from the van in which they were returning from market only to be raped at the house of Wajed Ali. Who were these men? What were their names? Something like Madhi, Shaokat, Aminur. At Patia in Chittagong, Uttam Das, son of Parimal Das, was killed by Badsha Mian, Nur Islam and Nur Hussain as they forced their way into the victim's room at about three in the morning. For filing a case against the assailants, Uttam's family was now facing the threat of eviction from their home. Sabita Rani, a student at Baralekha school in Sylhet, was kidnapped by one Nijamuddin and the members of his gang while she was studying at night in her room. She was never heard of again. Shephali Rani, daughter of Nripendra Chandra Datta of Bagura, was forcibly taken away and subsequently converted to Islam. The administration was of no help. Surrounding Shuro and Bagdanga villages in Jessore on all sides, armed mobs looted the Hindu houses, beat up the people severely and gang-raped eleven women the whole night. Then what? Still someone was curious to know. Were the eyes of the one who wanted to know dilating in fear or hatred, or was he feeling a strange sensation?

Suranjan's eyes were closed. He was feeling sleepy. He didn't have that much patience left to find out who was bursting with curiosity to hear about the fate of a wandering family of three Hindus of the Ghoshbag area of Noakhali, Sabitribala Ray, her husband, Mohanbanshi Ray, and their young daughter, Abdul Halim. Nanu, Abdur Rab, Bacchu Mian and their associates of Alipur raided Sabitribala's house and snatched at dagger point eighteen thousand takas that she had collected by selling her cultivable land to defray the marriage expenses of her daughter. They threatened to kill her if she refused to write a deed in their favor and leave the country for India. They also took all the cows belonging to the family before their departure. What would happen if Sabitri and her family members didn't go to India? What else could happen? They would just be killed. Three hundred sixty milkmen's families of Sapmari village at Sherpur had been forced to leave the country following persecution by fundamentalists. At Katiadi in Kishoreganj, some Muslim informers had forcibly acquired through forged deeds the landed properties of Charu Chandra De Sarkar, Sumanta Mohan De Sarkar, Jatindra Mohan De Sarkar and Dinesh Chandra De Sarkar. A move was afoot to acquire the lands of Ranjan Rajbhar of Dapunia in Mymensingh district and evict him eventually through identical methods. Ranjan's two sisters were forcibly converted, married to Muslims and then driven off after a few days. The Muslim sharecroppers had forcibly grabbed seven acres of paddy land belonging to Narayan Chandra Kundu, a resident of Balighata village at Jaipur. They had also constructed their own houses on that land.

Suranjan wanted to fall asleep, but he couldn't. He didn't want to listen to these harrowing tales, yet the voice of someone came floating in: Armed with guns, Ali Master, Abul Basher, Shaheed Morol and others plundered in commando style the houses of six Hindu families of Chargotkul in Narayanganj. They robbed Subhash Mandal, Santosh, Netai and Khetra Mohan of all their belongings and then evicted them from their home.

Someone called Suranjan, "Get up, Suranjan. Get up, eat now, the rice is ready."

The caller seemed to be Kajal. Maya called him in this manner with a pleading voice: Dada, food has been served, please come to the table. He would buy some sleeping tablets with the money received from Maya. It seemed he hadn't slept for quite some days. He was eaten by bedbugs at night. He remembered Kiranmayee crushing the bedbugs with the hand fan in his childhood. He would ask Maya to finish off all the bedbugs in his bed tonight. They seemed to nibble even within his head. Suranjan felt his head was swimming. He was overcome by nausea.

In the midst of all this, a voice droned on: "His home is at Rajbari." It was perhaps Tapas's voice. "In our place, thirty temples and their adjoining houses have been consigned to the flames." Another voice chimed in, keeping pace with the oncoming evening: "Listen to what has happened in Noakhali. Seven houses and the Adharchand hermitage in Sundalpur village have been looted and burned down. After looting three houses in Jagadananda village, the raiders set fire to them. Ghoshgram, Maijdi and Sonapur have lost their temples. Added to this list are Akhanda hermitage of Durgapur village, Qutubpur, Gopalpur and Sundarpur besides several temples of Chhay Ani Bazar. Ten temples and eighteen houses have been set on fire at Babupur, Tetuia, Mahidpur, Rajganj Bazar, Tengir per, Kajir Hat, Rasulpur, Jamidar Haat, Choumohani, Porabari and Bhadabhadri villages. The same has happened to nineteen houses in Rajpur village at Companigunj besides molestation of women. In Ramdi village a man called Biplab Bhowmick was hacked to death with long choppers."

Suranjan only wished he could seal his ears with cotton balls. The talk was centering on the single topic of the Babri mosque demolition along with the rampage and arson all around. Oh, if only he could find a deserted island! Better, if he could go to Mymensingh. This sort of destruction or burning of houses figured somewhat less in that region. He could have cooled the burning sensation all over his body if only he had had a daylong bath in the river Brahmaputra.

Suranjan got up with a jerk. Many of the people assembled in the room had already left. He also made a move to go. Kajal said, "Rice is there on the table. Just eat it up. You dozed off at this odd hour of the day. Are you feeling sick?"

Suranjan turned and twisted to limber himself up and said, "No, Kajalda, I won't eat. Don't feel like eating. Not feeling well."

"Does that make any sense?"

"Perhaps it doesn't. But what can I do? I feel hungry at one moment, next moment the pinch disappears. Belches are bringing a sour taste to my mouth, my chest is burning with acidity. I often feel sleepy, but when I try to fall asleep, it just eludes me."

Touching his shoulder, Jatin Chakravarty said, "You seem to have broken down, Suranjan. But can we afford to be so dejected at this hour? Be firm. Somehow or other we'll have to survive."

Suranjan stood bowing his head. Jatinda's words to some extent echoed Sudhamay's. For a long time, he hadn't sat at his father's bedside. He wouldn't stay out for long today. Kajal's place was the meeting spot for various people. Fervent discussion would linger in endless circles. Serious talk on politics and culture would go on till late at night. Suranjan would pay heed to them sometimes; sometimes he would not.

He left, leaving the meal untouched on the table. He hadn't taken a meal at home for quite some time, but today

198

he would. He would sit at the dining table together with Maya, Kiranmayee and Sudhamay. A great distance had separated him from them, although he was to be blamed for this. No more would he allow this barrier between himself and the others in the house. Light-hearted as he was in the morning, he would talk with them in the same high spirits and laugh merrily, conjuring up his boyhood days when he would eat homemade cakes with the sun on his back. They would all become his close friends, not in the usual way of family relationships like father-son or brother-sister. Today he wouldn't call on anyone else. Neither Pulak nor Ratna. He would go straightaway to Tikatuli and take whatever meager food was offered to him; he would go on talking with his family till late at night and then fall into a sound sleep.

Kajal walked him to the front gate. He said with great warmth and concern, "You are not doing the right thing by staying out of your house in this manner. We move around within a very limited area, never venturing out of it. Those who came to this house today—all of them are from nearby areas. I wonder how you can move about freely all over the city alone. Anything may happen at any time."

Without talking further, Suranjan started walking at a brisk pace. He had money with him, so he could hire a rickshaw easily. But he was hesitant to spend the money loaned to him by Maya. He hadn't smoked for the whole day. He now felt a craving for a smoke despite his hesitation about using Maya's money. He felt quite royal as he bought a packet of Bangla Fives at a shop. Walking up to the Kakrail crossing he hired a rickshaw. The city turned somnolent rather early these days, like a sick man who retired to bed at an early hour. But what was the sickness the city had been suffering from? He remembered a friend

199

who had a big painful boil on his buttock. He would scream in pain throughout the day, but would be scared at the sight of medicines or an injection syringe. Could it be that the city, too, now had a boil on its buttock? So it seemed to Suranjan.

"Maya, can you tell what has happened to Suranjan? Where is he moving about at this hour, can you guess?" asked Sudhamay.

"He told me he would be going to Pulakda's place. Must have become engrossed in talk there."

"But does that mean he won't return home before evening?"

"Who knows? At least, I don't understand. Should have returned by this time."

"Can't he even once think about how we at home worry so about him? Doesn't it occur to him now is the time to come back home?"

Maya intervened to stop Sudhamay from talking. "Please don't talk so much. You feel difficulty in speaking and you shouldn't exert yourself either. Just keep quiet on the bed. It's time for you to eat and, after that, if you want me to read to you, I'll be happy to do so. You must go to sleep at ten after you've taken your sleeping pill. By then Dada will surely be back, so don't worry."

"With your nursing, I'm coming around quite fast. Otherwise, I would have been lying on the bed for a few more days. But recovery has its risks as well."

"What sort of risks?" asked Maya, crushing the boiled rice to make it softer.

Sudhamay, beaming with a smile, said, "You're feeding me, Kiranmayee is massaging my arms and feet, pressing

200

my forehead! Shall I get this much love and care when I am
fully cured? Then I'll have to face the drudgery of attending to my patients, do the daily shopping at the
market and even quarrel with you." Sudhamay laughed
aloud. Maya gazed at Sudhamay's joyous face with un-
blinking eyes. For the first time since his illness, Sudhamay
was smiling today.

He had earlier told Kiranmayee, "Open all the windows today. I don't like this darkness in the room. Let the
air move freely. I haven't felt the nip of winter till now.
Does a feeling of freshness go well only with the spring-
time? In my younger days, I would paste posters on the
wall, braving the chilly wind in winter. I'd then have just a
thin cotton shirt on. I had moved to the hilly areas of
Sushong Durgapur with the communist leader, Mani
Singh. Do you know anything about the Tonk movement
or rebellion by Hajong tribesmen of those days?"

Kiranmayee, too, was in a good mood. She said, "I
heard lots of these stories from you after our marriage.
Didn't you spend a night with Mani Singh in an unknown
house at Netrakona?"

"Kiran, did Suranjan put on woolens when he went out?"
Sudhamay asked. Pursing her lips, Maya said: "Not at all,
just like your younger days, merely a thin cotton shirt. He is
a modern-day revolutionary. Natural wind hardly bothers
him. He is more busy coping with the winds of time."

Kiranmayee's voice also showed streaks of anger:
"Where does he go, what does he eat, or does he eat at all?
No one knows. He is becoming more and more wild as the
days go by."

Just then, there was a mild knock on the door. Was that
Suranjan? Kiranmayee left Sudhamay's bedside for the

door. Suranjan knocked on the front door in this manner. Of course, if he was too late at night he entered his room straightaway from outside. Most of the time the door that led directly to his room was locked from the outside, which facilitated his entry, but he also knew how to open the door if it had been locked from within. Since it wasn't too late, it must be Suranjan. Maya was mixing boiled pulse with the softly cooked rice for Sudhamay. She would see to it that the food was quite soft lest Sudhamay have difficulty in swallowing it. He had been on a liquid diet for quite a long time. The doctor had now advised partially solid food. *Shing* fish in light gravy had been cooked for him. Maya was about to take a little gravy with rice when that light knock could be heard. Kiranmayee, standing at the door, was asking who it was. Did she train her ears to listen to the reply from the other side? But hardly had Kiranmayee opened the door, when seven or eight youths burst into the room. Some four of them were carrying thick sticks. Before she could see any others, they just swarmed past Kiran-mayee to get inside. They were in their early twenties. Two of them were dressed in skullcaps, *pyjamas*, and *punjabis*, three others were in shirts and trousers. After storming in, they started smashing up and hurling whatever they could lay their hands on: tables, chairs, cupboard, television, radio, utensils, glasses, books, dressing table, pedestal fan, just like a demented pack of animals and absolutely tight-lipped. Sudhamay tried to raise himself, but failed. Touching the door, Kiranmayee stood petrified. What a grisly scene! One of them took out a long chopper and shouted, "You bastards, you have demolished the Babri mosque. Do you think we will let you go in one piece?"

Not a single article in the room was left unbroken.

Everything came crashing down. The whole room was ransacked before anyone could realize what was happening. Maya, too, was still, silent. She screamed as one of the raiders pulled her, grabbing her hand. Kiranmayee's patience, too, snapped. She also shrieked. Sudhamay only groaned. He was incapable of articulating anything. He saw before his own eyes that Maya was being dragged out. She was trying to free herself by catching the railing of his cot. Kiranmayee came running and tried to protect Maya with both her arms. Ignoring her bid to stand her ground while screaming all the time, the intruders pulled Maya away. Kiranmayee ran after the abductors with frantic pleas: "My sons, please let her go. Please leave my daughter."

Two autorickshaws were waiting outside on the road. Maya's palm was still sticky with the rice she was kneading for Sudhamay. Her clothes were in disarray as she screamed, wild-eyed, "Ma! O, Ma!" And she was looking at Kiranmayee with piteously distressed eyes. Applying all of her fragile strength, Kiranmayee couldn't hold her back. Brushing aside the menacing long chopper, Kiranmayee grappled single-handedly with two of the kidnappers in her desperate bid to save Maya. But she failed against their brute strength. She started running after the two speeding autorickshaws, trying to draw the attention of pedestrians with pitiful shouts of, "They are taking away my daughter! Dada, please save her!" At the corner of the street, exhausted and at the end of her strength, she stopped. Her loosened hair streaming down, barefooted, Kiranmayee pleaded with shopkeeper Mati Mian, "Please try to help me, Dada. Some people forcibly snatched away Maya, my daughter." All her pleadings were ignored with cold, detached stares, as if she were a demented woman of the street, babbling nonsense. Kiranmayee ran into the night, in a vain and ineffectual pursuit of her vanished daughter.

Suranjan was surprised to find the door of the house wide open. Everything bore the signs of plunder. The table was upside down, littered with books, the beds were without mattresses and sheets. The clothes rack was broken with clothes strewn all over the room. He felt suffocated. He entered another room. The floor was full of shards of broken glasses, overturned chairs without handrests, torn books, broken medicine bottles. Sudhamay lay face down on the ground and was groaning. Maya and Kiranmayee couldn't be seen anywhere. Suranjan was scared to ask what had happened. Why was Sudhamay lying on the floor? And where were the others? Suranjan could notice that his voice was trembling as he eventually forced the questions out.

Slowly, through the mist of agony, Sudhamay said, "They have taken away Maya."

Suranjan was violently shaken right to his depths. Gasping out the words, he asked, "Taken away? Who has done it? When?"

Sudhamay lay still. He had lost all his power of movement as well as his ability to call anyone. Suranjan, with great care, picked him up and put him back on the bed. He was breathing stertorously and perspiring.

"Where is Ma?" Suranjan asked feebly.

Sudhamay's face had turned blue in dismay and frustration. His whole body was shaking violently. Something disastrous might happen if his blood pressure took a big jump. What would Suranjan do now—look after Sudhamay or search for Maya? He couldn't decide anything. He was also trembling all over. He heard angry swirls of water within his head. At its center was the fascinating face of Maya, soft like a helpless kitten hemmed in by a pack of ferocious dogs. Suranjan swept out of the room. Before he left, he just touched Sudhamay's inert arm, saying, "I'll bring back Maya at any cost, Baba."

He knocked sharply on Hyder's door. He banged the door so loudly that Hyder himself came rushing to open it.

He was startled to see the look of Suranjan. He asked anxiously, "What's the matter, Suranjan? What has happened to you?"

Suranjan couldn't utter anything at first. Clotted agony choked his voice.

"Maya has been abducted," he said, his voice trailing off to a whisper. He did not have to explain who had taken Maya.

"When did it happen?"

Suranjan said nothing in reply. Why was it important to know when Maya had been abducted? Wasn't it news enough to know that they had taken her? Hyder's forehead showed creases of worry. He had just returned home after attending a party meeting. In fact, he had been about to change into his night clothes when Suranjan had arrived. Suranjan kept on staring at Hyder dumbly. He was looking like someone all of whose belongings had been swept away in a flash flood. The hand that he rested on the door was trembling. He clasped his arm to stop its tremor.

Touching his shoulder, Hyder said, "Please calm down and let me see what can be done."

As Hyder's hand brushed his shoulder, Suranjan burst into tears with a piercing cry. Gripping Hyder with both his arms, he said, "Please bring back Maya, Hyder. Please bring her back."

Suranjan started bowing down as he wept, dropping at Hyder's feet. Hyder was staggered. He had never seen his tough, hard friend weeping so unabashedly. He brought him to his feet. Hyder was yet to have his dinner and he was hungry, too. Still, saying, "Let's go out and see," he went out, taking Suranjan on the pillion of his Honda motorcycle, and set out for the maze of lanes in the Tikatuli area. He entered houses totally unfamiliar to Suranjan. He talked in whispers with some owners of dimly lit betel leaf and cigarette shops. After Tikatuli, Hyder's Honda went speeding around English Road, Nababpur, Lakshmibazar, Lalmohan Saha Street, Bakshi Bazar, Abhay Das Lane, Narinda Alu Bazar, Thatari Bazar, Parry Das Road, Urdu Road, Chak Bazar. Suranjan had no clue whom Hyder was looking for. They made forays into some filthy lanes full of knee-deep, murky water and knocked at some dark, obscure houses. He tried to think, whenever Hyder got down, that he would perhaps chance upon Maya at this place. Maya must have been trussed up and beaten, perhaps at this place, or something worse might have happened to her. Suranjan trained his ears to listen for the sound of Maya's wails.

Hearing such a shriek near Lakshmibazar, Suranjan asked Hyder to stop his two-wheeler. He said, "Just listen. Doesn't that sound like Maya crying?"

They chased the sound. They were disappointed to find a child was crying in a two-storeyed mud house. Hyder went on combing areas. The night advanced inexorably. Suranjan didn't stop. Groups of angry-eyed youths in different lanes made Suranjan think perhaps it was one of these bands that was keeping his innocent, soft-faced sister confined.

206

"Hyder, why can't you trace her as yet? Why?"

"I'm trying my best."

"She must be found by tonight at any cost."

"I'm trying to locate each and every rowdy that I know. I've looked in every place possible. What can I do if I still don't find her?"

Suranjan went on chain-smoking cigarettes bought with the money given by Maya.

"Let's have something to eat at Superstar. I'm hungry."

Hyder ordered two plates of butter-fried handmade flat loaf and mutton curry. Suranjan was not averse to eating. Yet, the piece of loaf remained stuck in his hand, he couldn't reach it into his mouth. As the time passed, a feeling of emptiness spread within him. Hyder was gobbling food rapidly. He lit a cigarette. Suranjan urged him to hurry up. "Let's get up, she hasn't been traced as yet."

"Where else can I try? I've left no place unsearched. You saw it yourself."

"Dhaka is a small city. How can you say that it's not possible to find Maya here. Let's go to the police station."

When informed, the police, showing a wooden face, just wrote down the name and address of the missing person in their report. And that was that. Coming out of the police station, Suranjan said, "I don't think they are going to take any action."

"May do something."

"Let's go to the Wari side. Do you know anyone in that area?"

"I've engaged my party boys in the search operation. They will also look for her. Please don't be worried."

Hyder had tried his best. Yet Suranjan felt like he was

being bitten by the wasps of anxiety. Hyder's Honda went round old areas in the city throughout the night. The drinking and gambling dens of hoodlums and hooligans, the smugglers' hideouts. All the places were peeped into. The time rolled on to the first morning call for prayer from the mosques. Suranjan previously liked the tune of the *ajan*, set in raag Bhairab. Today it sounded discordant to him. The *ajan* indicated the end of the night, and Maya had still not been found! Hyder shut off the engine of his Honda at Tikatuli. He tried to console him, "Don't lose heart, Suranjan. We'll have another go today. Let's see what can be done."

In the midst of the wreckage Kiranmayee sat with her eyes showing distressed eagerness fixed on the door. Sudhamay, despite his immobility, remained awake with the hope that Suranjan would return with Maya. They saw their son returning alone. Maya wasn't there. Both of them were struck dumb as the weary, unsuccessful Suranjan staggered in with his head down. Then would Maya never be found? They cringed in fear as the grim possibility loomed large in their minds. All the doors and windows were tightly shut, leaving no scope for ventilation. The air was trapped inside the room. A dank smell was everywhere. They were seated with their hands, arms and feet all curled up. They were mute, anguished and terrified. They looked like spooks. Suranjan didn't feel like talking to them. All the questions were concentrated in their eyes. But the reply was one and invariable: Maya couldn't be found.

Spreading his feet, Suranjan slumped on the floor. He felt nausea. Maya must have been gang-raped by this time. Well, couldn't it be that Maya, as had been the case when she was a six-year-old child, would stage a comeback?

Suranjan had kept the door open hoping for her return, to let her come back in an unconcerned manner, as she did in her childhood. Let her come back to this small, devastated, totally ruined household. Hyder had given him word that he would continue the search for her. When such an assurance had been given, could Suranjan nurse a dream about her return? Why did they take Maya away? Just because she was a Hindu? And how great a price would the Hindus have to pay in bloodletting, the rape of their women, the robbing of their properties, for their bare survival in this country? Would they, like tortoises, have to draw their heads in to survive in this country? For how many days? Suranjan sought a reply for himself. But he failed to get it.

Kiranmayee sat in a corner of the room leaning against the wall. She muttered, not for anyone in particular, but perhaps to herself, "They said: 'We have come to see if you are well. We are local boys. Please open the door.' How old will they be, barely twenty or twenty-one. Can I be equal in strength to them? I frantically wailed from door to door in this locality begging for help. All of them silently listened or made a show of sympathy. But no one lifted a finger. One of the raiders was called Rafique by a boy with a skullcap on his head. . . . She had hidden herself for some days at Parul's place. She would have survived had she stayed there till now. Won't Maya come back? Leaving her, they could have burned down this house. Or didn't they do it because the landlord is a Muslim? Still, it would have been better if they had killed me instead. If only they could spare the innocent girl. My life has nearly come to an end and hers has just begun."

Suranjan all of a sudden felt violently dizzy. Rushing to the toilet, he threw up in a spasm of retches.

Day Seven

The verandah was awash with sunrays. The black-and-white cat was walking about on its own. Was it looking for fish bones, or was it searching for Maya? Maya would carry it in her arms. It would snuggle under her quilt to sleep. Did it know that Maya wasn't here?

Maya must have been crying a lot, calling frantically, "Dada, dada," to take her out of this hellhole. Had they tied her up with ropes around her hands and feet, and stuffed a cloth in her mouth as a gag to smother her screams? The first time she had been forcibly abducted, she was only six. She was now twenty-one. The two ages were not the same. The purpose of taking away girls of two different ages was not the same either. Suranjan could guess what seven people could do to a twenty-one-year-old girl. His entire body shuddered in helpless frustration, in sheer agony. He felt he had become as stiff as a corpse. Was he still alive? Surely, but Maya was certainly gone. Yet her absence couldn't deter her relatives from living. No one could share his life with others. There was hardly a more selfish being than man.

True, Hyder was searching for Maya. Still, Suranjan gained the impression he had not been that serious. Suranjan had used a Muslim to track down the offenders, who were also Muslims. Just like applying a thorn to pick out another thorn embedded in the flesh. As he was watching the cat lying in the sun, Suranjan was suddenly overcome with a suspicion that Hyder perhaps knew about Maya's abductors. When he was taking food with great zest on that night of the search at Superstar restaurant, his face showed no sign of anxiety. After his meal, he belched following the satisfying dinner, then puffed out plenty of cigarette smoke with the satisfaction of a contented man, showing hardly a sign of concern for searching anyone out with any sense of urgency. He liked roaming around the city all through the night like a nocturnal animal. Was he then pandering to this fascination of his? Didn't he have the least intention of getting Maya back? Whatever urge he might have shown was in fact the mere motion of perfunctorily repaying the debt of friendship. He hadn't shown any real insistence at the police station. He had exhorted his party comrades to go in on the search, but after talking party matters with them as if the party matters demanded greater precedence and the care for Maya was of secondary importance. Was it because the Hindus were treated as second-class citizens in this country?

Suranjan couldn't believe that Maya was not in the next room. As if he could see her exercising Sudhamay's inert right arm just looking in that direction. He believed that stepping into the room, he would hear that sweet brown girl saying, "Dada, please do something" in a sort of frantic pleading. He hadn't been able to do anything for the girl. All girls were usually importunate with their elder brothers with their plea, "Dada, buy this or that, take me out. . . ." Maya had indeed made such pleas, only Suranjan had failed to fulfill them. He had been busy with himself all the time. He had been exclusively occupied with his friends, politics, party meetings. Near and dear ones like Maya and Kiranmayee had not mattered to him at all. Had his ideal of turning each and every person in the country into a conscientious being succeeded?

At the stroke of nine in the morning, Suranjan rushed out to Hyder's residence. The house was quite close by. Hyder was still asleep, and Suranjan had to wait for some time in the living room. One of the seven abductors was called Rafique. Hyder perhaps knew the boy. It might even be that Hyder was related to Rafique. Suranjan shuddered at the thought. Two hours later, Hyder woke up. Finding Suranjan waiting for him, he asked, "Has she returned?"

"Would I come to you had she come back?"

"Oh," Hyder's voice sounded utterly detached. He was wearing a *lungi* with his upper body bare. He scratched himself for some time and then said in a placid, unconcerned voice, "It's not so cold this winter, is it? There's also a meeting today at the home of the party chairperson. Possibly a move will be made to arrange a procession. When the demand to arrest Pakistani agent Galam Azain had reached its crescendo, just at that point this bloody riot spoiled everything. In fact, these are the BNP's stratagems to divert the real issue into a different direction."

"Well, Hyder," Suranjan said, coming to the point, "do you know any boy called Rafique?"

212

"Where from?"

"Can't say. He's about twenty-one or twenty-two. He may even be of this locality."

"I just don't know anyone like that. Still, I am engaging my men to track him down."

"Come, let's go out again. It's not right to delay. I can't look my parents in the face. Baba has already had a stroke. A greater disaster may strike him because of this present misfortune."

"It won't be proper for you to accompany me at this time."

"But why?"

"Why don't you understand? At least try to guess."

Why shouldn't Suranjan understand? He understood quite well the reason for Hyder's urging him to stay behind. It wouldn't be proper to keep his company because Suranjan was a Hindu and it would appear to be improper for a Hindu to abuse a Muslim, even if that Muslim were a thief or a hooligan or a murderer. It was perhaps indicative of further insolence to rescue a Hindu girl from the clutches of Muslims.

Suranjan left. Where would he go? Home? He didn't feel like going back to the utter desolation of that bleak place. Just like the mythical swallow with the eternal thirst, his parents were hoping for his return with Maya. He did not intend to return home without her. Hyder said he had engaged his men to trace Maya. A belief that some day his men would escort Maya back to her home felt pleasant. Suspicion again crept into his mind about those people's sincerity. Why should they feel concerned for Maya? They were hardly bothered over Maya's prolonged absence. Why should the Muslims nurse any tender feelings for the

Hindus? No Muslim house had ever been attacked or looted. The targets of such marauding forays were only Suranjan's house or Gopal Halder's or Kajalendu Dey's. Suranjan didn't go back to his home. He roamed aimlessly along the streets, moved around the entire city in the quest for Maya. What had Maya done to deserve this fate? Was it such a crime to be a Hindu? Could it go to such an extent that his house would be pulled down? Could he be assaulted whenever it pleased the raiders? Could his wife and daughter be raped with impunity? Suranjan walked, and sometimes ran, without any particular sense of direction. He suspected any boy in his early twenties, thinking him to be the abductor of Maya. This feeling nagged at him.

He bought a packet of *muri* from a grocer's shop at Islampur. The shopkeeper cast a sidelong glance at him. Suranjan got the impression that this man, too, was aware of Maya's abduction. He just walked on blindly without any destination in his mind. He took a seat on the rubble of the devastated monastery at Nayabazar. He couldn't find ease. The topic of the Babri mosque would invariably be brought up anywhere he went. The other day, Selim blurted out, "If you could destroy the Babri mosque, then what's wrong with our smashing up temples?" Selim had been joking when he said this. But many serious thoughts are expressed through casual jokes.

If Maya came back home, of course, it might be like that. Let her at least come back, even if she had been raped. This led him to believe that Maya had returned. Suranjan trudged back home only to find two persons with their senses alert, sitting stone still, hoping for Maya to come back.

What could be more cruel and ruthless than the revelation about Maya's still not being found? Sinking his face in the pillow of his bed, Suranjan lay supine. The sound of Sudhamay's groaning reached him, piercing the night's stillness. Kiranmayee's feeble weeping, like the drone of crickets, also could be heard. All this kept Suranjan awake the whole night. If only he could lay his hand on a vial of poison, then all three of them would end their miserable existence by taking it. The agony of being torn in bits and pieces could be put to an end forever. What did they gain by staying alive? There was no point in remaining alive in Bangladesh as a Hindu.

Sudhamay guessed that something like cerebral thrombosis had struck him. He would have certainly been dead if the attack had accompanied by a hemorrhage. What was the harm if he were dead? Sudhamay was frantically wishing for a hemorrhage. He was half-dead; if only he could save Maya in exchange for his own life. She had a deep craving for life. She went to Parul's house all alone just to stay alive. It was only his sickness that had brought her back, only to be carried off by those cruel monsters. His sense of guilt, just like woodmites, caused a persistent pain in him. His vision became blurred repeatedly. He held out his hand to Kiranmayee. But no one was there. Suranjan wasn't near him, and Maya had just vanished. He felt thirsty—his tongue and throat had become parched with thirst.

He had caused Kiranmayee lots of suffering. She had been used to worshiping the household deity every day. After their marriage, she was told to give up that practice. At one time, Kiranmayee sang quite well. But the people around would call her a shameless woman for singing in public, pointing at her as an illustration of the immodesty of Hindu girls. So offended was Kiranmayee by these accusations that she had given up singing completely. When she finally stopped singing, how much support did she receive from Sudhamay? Perhaps he, too, was swayed by the thought that when people called it bad, there was no point in pursuing it. For twenty-one years, he had slept by Kiranmayee's side, but only to protect her chastity. What was the reason for his keeping guard over his wife's chastity? Wasn't this a sort of perversion? She never coveted expensive saris or ornaments. She had never insisted on having a particular sari or a pair of earrings of her own choice. Sudhamay would often ask, "Kiranmayee, are you keeping some sorrow from me?"

Kiranmayee would say, "No, not at all. All my pleasures and dreams are linked with this family. I don't crave any special pleasure for myself."

Sudhamay wanted to have a girl. Before the birth of Suranjan, he would place the stethoscope on the bulge of her abdomen and say, "I can hear the heartbeat of my daughter. Would you like to hear it?"

Sudhamay would say, "Daughters invariably look after the parents in their old age. Sons go about their own way after marriage. On the contrary, daughters often neglect their own husband and family to nurse their parents. This has been my experience in the hospital. It is the daughters whom I find nursing their ailing parents. Sons visit them like guests, no more."

Placing the earpieces of the stethoscope in Kiranmayee's ears, he would make her listen to the drumming of the fetus's heartbeat. While parents all over the world craved sons, Sudhamay alone wanted a daughter. Sudhamay even went to the extent of dressing baby Suranjan in a frock on outings. His long-cherished dream, however, came true following the birth of Maya. Sudhamay himself named his daughter Maya after his own mother. He would say, "One mother is gone, another has come in her place."

It was Maya who would administer medicines to Sudhamay during the nights. Now the time for his taking medicine had long passed. He called to his cherished daughter, "Maya, Maya. . . ." The neighbors were asleep and his anguished wail was heard only by Kiranmayee and Suranjan, who were both awake. It was also heard by the black-and-white cat.

Day Eight

The bloody riots that had broken out over India in the wake of the demolition of the Babri mosque at Ayodhya in Uttar Pradesh was grinding to a halt. The number of dead had already exceeded 1,800. Occasional clashes still caused tension at Kanpur and Bhopal. The army had been called out in states like Gujarat, Karnatak, Kerala, Andhra Pradesh, Assam and West Bengal. The offices of the banned parties had been locked up.

In Dhaka, all the parties were spontaneously staging processions for peace and communal harmony. So what? On the other hand, thirty girls on Shambhu-Golakpur had been raped, girls like Chanchala, Sandhya, and Mani. Nikunja Datta was killed. An old woman, Bhagabati died of heart failure in sheer panic. Girls had been raped at Golakpur in broad daylight. Even the girls sheltered in the Muslim houses were not spared. The betel nut storehouse of Nantu Halder with a stock of nearly one and a half

218

tonnes at Daser Haat market had been burned to ashes. The police, magistrates and the district magistrate were mute spectators when the temples in Bhola town were caught in the demolition spree. Jewelry shops had been looted while people looked on. A Hindu washerman's colony was burned to ashes. In Manikganj town, Lakshmi Mandap, Community Shib Bari, Dashora, Kalikhola, the area of goldsmiths, the beverage and cigarette stock center of Gadadhar Pal had been smashed up. There truckloads of rowdies launched attacks on Twara, Pukuria, Uthli, Mahadebpur, Joka and Shivalaya police station areas. In Betila village, about three kilometers from town, Hindu houses were looted. A similar attack was made on a hundred-year-old Nat Mandir at Betila. The fire which was set to Jiban Saha's house at Garpara also consumed his three cowsheds, as well as several hundred kilograms of paddy. All the Hindu shops in Terashree Bazar under Gheor police station, all the Hindu houses at Gangdubi, Baniajuri and Senpara were set on fire. A Hindu housewife at Senpara had also been raped. In Phirozepur, the Kali temple, the Sheetala temple, the Shiva temple, the Narayan temple, the temple of Madanmohan image, Akhrabari, the temple of Rayer Kathi Kalibari, Krishnanagar Rairasaraj Sevashram, the hermitage and temple of Dumurtala Sirguru Sangha, the Kali temple of Suresh Saha at South Dumurtala, Naren Saha's Manasa temple in the same place, the Manasa temple of Ramesh Shah and his residence, the Dumurtala community Kali temple, the household temples of Sucharan Mandal, Gauranga Halder, Narendranath Saha, the Kali temple beside Dumurtala High School, the temple of Panchadevi, the community Durga temple of Hularhat and firewood shop of Kartik Das, the Sanatan Ashram Kali temple at Kalakhali, Jujkhola Gourgovinda Sevashram, the Sanatan Dharma temple of Harisabha, the household temple of Ranajit Seal, Jujkhola community puja pandal, the community Durga temple beside Gabtala School, Bipin Halder's household temple at Kirshna Nagar, the community Kali temple at Namajpur, the temple and monastery of the Biswas household at Kalikathi, the Kali temple at Lairi, the community temple at Inder Haat under Swarupkathi police station, the Durga temple of the Kanai Biswas household at Inder Haat, the cinema hall owned by Nakul Saha, the Durga temple of Amal Guha's household, the household temple of Hemanta Seal, the Kali temple of Jadab Das under Mathabaria police station, all these were burned down. The Shiva temple at Mistiripara in Syedpur was also pulled down. The community temple at Ratandanga village under Narail district, the community temple at Ghona, the community cremation ground at Kurulia, the household temple of Nikhil Chandra Dey, the household temple of Kalipada Hajra, the household temple of Shibu Prasad Pal, the household temple of Dulal Chandra Chakravarty at Badan village, the household temple of Krishna Chandra Laskar, the community temple in Taltala village, the family temples of Baidyanath Saha, Sukumar Biswas and Pagla Biswas in Pankabilla village, the community temple in the same village and the Narayan Jiu temple of Daulatpur Purbapara under Lohagara police station were ransacked and destroyed. Ten temples in Khulna faced identical fates. Four or five temples in Rauli, Sobnadas and Baka village in Paikpara were ransacked and several houses looted. Two temples in the Talimpur area under Rupsa police station were demolished and the adjoining Hindu houses were looted. Three temples in Dighalia and

Senhati were sacked and set on fire on the night of December 8. Some processionists raided thirteen houses in Sahadebpur village in Feni. Led by one Moazzem Hussain, some two hundred people from Langalboa attacked the residence of Gobinda Prasad Ray. A man called Kamal Biswas, who had been seriously injured in the attack, was in his death throes.

Birupaksha, Nayan and Debabrata continued to spew these revolting tales of devastation. Suranjan lay on his back with his eyes closed. He didn't utter a single word after hearing all these narratives of destruction. None of them was aware that not only the houses in Bhola, Chittagong, Pirozepur, Sylhet and Comilla had been looted, but from this house at Tikatuli, a nice girl called Maya had also been snatched away. Women were somewhat akin to property. That was why, just like gold and other valuables, Maya had been whisked away by them.

"What's the matter, Suranjan, you are so silent, what has happened to you?" Debabrata asked.

"I want to drink. Isn't it possible to drink to my heart's content today?"

"Do you want to drink?"

"Yes, I will."

"I've money with me. Let someone go and get a bottle of whiskey."

"Do you mean to say you'll sit at home and drink? What about your parents?"

"Let 'em go to hell. I want to drink and I will. Biru, please go. You'll find it at either Sakura or Piyasi."

"But Suranjan."

"Don't hesitate so much, go now."

221

The sound of Kiranmayee's wailing from the other room reached them.

"Who's crying? Auntie?" Birupaksha asked.

"Once you are branded as a Hindu, can you escape tears?"

The three youths were dumfounded. They, too, were Hindus. But why should aunt alone cry, they wondered. A muffled cry also rose from their chest. Birupaksha rushed out of the room carrying the money. As if going away would spare him all his agony. Just like Suranjan, who was seeking escape through drink.

As soon as Birupaksha left, Suranjan said, "Well, Debabrata, can a mosque be set on fire?

"A mosque, you said? Are you crazy?"

"Come, let's burn down the 'Tara mosque' tonight."

"Debabrata cast puzzled glances in turn at Suranjan and Nayan.

"There are twenty million of us Hindus in the country. If we want, we can target the Baitul Mokarrumit mosque as well."

"You never identified yourself as a Hindu. Why are you doing so today?"

"I used to describe myself as a human being, a humanist. The Muslims did not allow me to remain a human being. It was they who made me a Hindu."

"You are changing very fast, Suranjan."

"That's not my fault."

"What do we gain by destroying a mosque? Will we get back our demolished temples?" Rubbing his nails on the broken handle of the chair, Debabrata said: "Perhaps not. But we can show we are capable of destruction. Mustn't we show at least for once that we, too, have the right to express

222

our anger? If the Babri mosque was a four-hundred-fifty-year-old structure, the home of Chaitanyadev, too, dated back five hundred years. Aren't the four- or five-hundred-year-old traditions being crushed in this country? I feel like razing the Sobhanbag mosque as well. Gulshan mosque was built with the help of the money supplied by Saudi Arabia. Come, let's occupy it for its conversion into a temple."

"What are you saying, Suranjan? You've really gone crazy. Didn't you previously think of digging lakes in place of temples and mosques and then releasing beautiful ducks on their water?"

"Did I say only that? I used to say: 'Let the pavilions of religion be ground to bits. Let the bricks of temples, mosques, *gurudawaras*, churches be burned in blind fire, and upon those heaps of destruction let lovely flower gardens grow, spreading their fragrance. Let children's schools and study halls grow. For the welfare of humanity, let prayer halls now be turned into hospitals, orphanages, schools, universities. Let prayer halls now become academies of art, fine arts centers, scientific research institutes. Let prayer halls now be turned into golden rice fields in radiant dawn, open fields, rivers, restless seas. From now on let religion's other name be humanity.' "

"Just the other day I read an article by Debesh Roy," said Debabrata. "He has written about the great maestro Bade Golam Ali singing playing that small harp-like swaramandal, singing *Hari Om Tatsat, Hari Om Tatsat*. Bade Golam sang that *bhajan* till his end. But those who escaped after stealthily installing the Ramlala image after demolishing the Babri mosque, those Hindus were incapable of hearing this devotional song. This song is not meant for Advani, or Ashoke Singhal, nor for Rashtriya Swamgsevak

Sangh or Bajrang Dal, those outfits of Hindu fanatics. Bade Golam Ali was a Muslim. Yet this devotional song *Hari Om Tatsat* remains beyond the hearing of those Muslims who believe that the only way to redress the demolition of the Babri mosque is to destroy temples."

"So you mean to say the smashing of a mosque is no real retaliation against the destruction of temples or mandirs? You are echoing my father's ideology. I hate him. I hate that old haggard."

Suranjan had been lying down. He now sprang up in excitement and stood erect.

"Calm down, Suranjan, calm down. What you are suggesting is not really a solution."

"No? Well, for your information, this is the only solution that I am looking for. I, too, want choppers, daggers and pistols in my hands. I want thick rods. Didn't they go and piss on the ruins of a mandir in old Dhaka? I also want to piss on their mosques!"

Debabrata whispered, "Suranjan, you are becoming communal."

"Yes, I am becoming communal. I am becoming communal . . . communal."

Debabrata and Suranjan had worked together in the same political party, but Debabrata could no longer recognize his old colleague. He was shocked beyond measure by Suranjan's behavior—he wanted to get drunk, he declared himself to be communal and he even abused his own father. Debabrata was horrified.

Riots can't be equated with floods in which rescue from their marooned state and later some relief supply can tide people over the crisis for the time being. Riots can't be

224

equated with fire either. Fire can be extinguished by throwing water on it. But during riots people keep the sense of humanity in suspension. The poison accumulated in the human mind finds a release through riots. Riots are not natural phenomena or disasters. Riots reflect the perversity of human nature. Sudhamay sighed as he mused over this concluding portion of his thought. Kiranmayee, after a long break, swung back to her god for whom she placed her head against the wall in the corner. Somewhere he had found a picture of Lord Krishna and his consort Radha, and she touched the picture with her forehead. Shedding his tears in silence, Sudhamay, his body immobile, wondered if either Radha or Krishna had enough strength to bring Maya back. They were nothing but pictures of mythical characters. Just a figment! How could they rescue Maya from the harsh, rigid, merciless clutches of the fundamentalists? He was not getting security in this country although he was its citizen, and as a citizen he had taken part in the movement for the recognition of Bengali as a state language, fought in the war to liberate it from the domination of Pakistanis. And from nowhere this mythical couple of Radha and Krishna would emerge to ensure security for them! These blind devotees had no other serious work to do. This irrational faith had made them oblivious of the realities reflected in the forcible occupation of his house by neighbors known to him since his birth, his countrymen living next door abducting his daughter. Yet you expect the naughty cottage cheese pilferer Krishna of the mythical tale to free you from your distress. And he would be assisted in his task by his mythical consort, Radha, who was Ayn Ghosh's wife. If you are to be rescued from your misery, the task can be undertaken only by those people

225

who fought for the country's liberation, waging the war as a single nation in a united front.

Sudhamay, in a tired, pathetic voice, called his wife, "Kiran, Kiran."

Kiranmayee went to him, moving mechanically like a robot. He asked, "Didn't Suranjan go out to find out Maya today?"

"I don't know."

"I heard Hyder had engaged men to trace her. Did he come?"

"No."

"Does it mean Maya can't be found?"

"I don't know."

"Would you please sit by my side for a while?"

Kiranmayee dropped to the bedside like an inanimate object. She just remained immobile. She neither reached her hand out for his inert limbs nor looked at her sick husband. The sound of clamorous shouts came from the other room. Sudhamay asked, "Why is Suranjan raising his voice so much? Didn't he go out to look up Hyder? Had I been fit as before I could have gone. If I had my former strength, nobody would have been able to touch Maya. I would have beat them to jelly. If only I were fit, I would have gone myself to bring Maya back home." Sudhamay made a frantic bid to raise himself, but slumped back on the bed. Kiranmayee made no move to help him get up. She kept her gaze fixed on the closed door, in anticipation of hearing the sound of a familiar knock heralding Maya's return.

"Just call your dear son for once. An unadulterated scoundrel! His sister is missing. And he is indulging in a drinking bout in the house with his friends, raising a big fracas. What a shame."

Kiranmayee neither went to call Suranjan nor asked Sudhamay to be calm. She just kept staring at the door. She had installed the picture of Radha-Krishna in the corner of the room. Now she was not going to abide by the dictates of her son or husband to stick to their atheist attitude. At this moment, no one but God alone could help her out.

Sudhamay made another move to raise himself. He wished to say, like Jonathan Swift: "We have so many religions that teach us to hate each other. But there are not enough religions that preach love. Human history has been sullied again and again by religious frictions, battles and calls for holy wars."

Sudhamay used to raise the slogan, "Hindus and Muslims are brothers" during the pre-partition riots of 1946. Such slogans still had to be raised even now. Why did such slogans have to be shouted for such a long time? For how many centuries would these slogans remain relevant to this subcontinent? If people didn't feel any inner urge to be noncommunal, no amount of slogan-shouting would be able to eradicate the germ of communalism.

Suranjan had come back from Hyder's house without finding him. Hyder was not at home; he had gone to Bhola to make an on-the-spot study of the distress of Hindus there. After his return, he must be oozing "ohs" and "ahs" of commiseration. People would applaud in appreciation. They would say: The Awami League workers are very sympathetic, very noncommunal, so in the next election Hindu votes should be cast for that party. He has no sympathy for Maya next door. He has gone to a distant place to express his sympathies to others like Maya!

Removing the seal from the bottle, he poured some

liquid freely down his throat. Others were not as keen as he was. Still, for the sake of keeping his company, they sipped their drink after diluting it with water. Suranjan's empty stomach churned with the liquor he was drinking.

"I used to love going for walks in the evening. Maya wanted to go with me. One of these days I must take her to Salbon bihar."

"From January 2, the Ulama Mashaekh will be going on a long march," said Birupaksha.

"What long march?"

"They are going to walk all the way to India for the reconstruction of the Babri mosque."

"Will they take Hindus in their long march? If they do so, I'll certainly be a volunteer. Will any one of you care to go?" Suranjan asked.

All of them remained silent and looked in one another's faces. Dababrata said with a hint of rebuke in his voice, "Why do you keep harping on Hindus and Muslims so much? You seem to have been inebriated with an overdose of Hinduism."

"Well, Debu, if the boys are not circumcised, they can be identified as Hindus. But how can the girls be spotted? Take Maya, for instance, if she is released on the road. Assume, for argument's sake, her hands and feet are tied up and her mouth taped. How can they know she is a Hindu? She will appear just like any Muslim girl with her nose, eyes, and mouth, feet and head all covered up."

Without replying to Suranjan's drunken query, Debabrata said, "At the time of Zia-ur-Rahman, a long march was undertaken on the issue of water from Farakka Barrage to the border. During Khaleda Zia Begum's regime, the year 1993 will commence with a long march with strong communal overtones demanding reconstruction of the Babri mosque. As the motivating factor behind the first march was not more water from Farakka, the proposed Babri mosque long march is also not aimed at the mosque's reconstruction. In fact, the Babri mosque issue is being harped on so much in order to convert the politics into a powerhouse of communalism and divert the people's attention from the mounting agitation against the Pakistani collaborator Gokam Azam. Also noticeable at this time is the 'airtight' silence of the government. Despite the waves of violence everywhere, the government has been parroting the theme of undisturbed communal harmony in the country."

Pulak entered the room at this juncture. He asked, "What's the matter, why you are keeping the door wide open?"

"The door is open. I have been drinking wine. I have been shouting. What's there to fear? If I die, I die. But why is it that you have come out of your house?"

"The situation is better now. So I ventured to come out."

"You villagers sit in your houses, closing the door, if the situation turns violent again. That's right, isn't it?" said Suranjan with loud laughter.

Pulak was shocked to see Suranjan drinking. He had cautiously come on a scooter, trying to attract as little attention as possible. He couldn't imagine the scene of a politically conscious youth like Suranjan drinking, doing nothing more than getting drunk at home! He couldn't believe his eyes. What had gone wrong? Why had his friend changed so dramatically?

Sipping his drink, Suranjan said, "Golam Azam and

Golam Azam. What's that to me? What do I gain if he is punished? I don't feel the least enthused to take part in a movement against him. The very name makes me sick. I feel like puking. The Pakistanis killed my two paternal uncles and three maternal uncles during the liberation war. I don't know why they allowed my father to stay alive. Possibly to enjoy the fun of freedom. Isn't he enjoying it now? Isn't Doctor Sudhamay Dutta now basking in the sunshine of freedom along with his wife, son and daughter?"

Suranjan was seated on the floor with his feet spread. Pulak was also sitting likewise. The room was dusty with broken chairs lying scattered, cigarette ashes thrown perfunctorily all over. The lone cupboard stood broken in a corner. Violent tempered as he was, Suranjan might have wrecked everything in his drunken state. The house was so quiet that possibly no one else was within.

Pulak said, "Ekram Hussain had been to Bhola. On his return, he said the police, administration and BNP people were describing the incidents there as a natural reaction to the Babri mosque demolition. It was nothing but the misdeeds of looters. In the Hindu eviction drive, village after village was burned to ashes. The air was filled with the smell of burning haystacks, granaries; nothing was spared. Everything was laid waste. All the households had been robbed of not only valuables and clothing, but also shoes, mattresses, quilts; even brooms were thrown in a big pile sprinkled with kerosene and set alight. Paddy fields and coconut groves were set on fire. The men had been forced to discard their *lungis*. They raped any girl they found, robbing her of her sari and ornaments. Many Hindus fled into the paddy fields. Nikunja Datta, a teacher at Shambhupur Khaser Haat School, was violently assaulted while he was hiding in a paddy field after they demanded his money. He would possibly succumb to his injuries. Slogans were raised at Bhola: "Hindus, if you want to live, leave Bangladesh for India." Hindus were being terrorized with threats like, "You will be cut to pieces to be given to the cows as fodder." Even relatively affluent Hindus faced an identical crisis. They, too, had nothing to call their own. Everything was burned. The loss of utensils forced them to drink water from makeshift cups made of coconut shell, or eat the meager food supplied by charity on banana leaves. Some were taking a single meal a day cooking wild roots and leaves. There were instances of daughters raped before their fathers, wives in the presence of husbands, brothers standing helpless witnesses to their sisters' supreme humiliation capped by the simultaneous ravishing of mother and daughters. Many Hindus were openly saying, "We would rather beg elsewhere. We won't stay here." Those who were coming to collect relief were saying, "We don't need it, please help us cross the border to leave for good." At the van of raiders at Shambhupur were M. A. Bashet and Siraj Patwari, who were now Jamat-turned-BNP activists. Not a single Hindu house in the Lord Hardinge area escaped arson. The house of Priyalal babu, a renowned freedom fighter, was not spared from destruction. In his village the men who conducted the attacks were Awami League leaders Abdul Kader, the chairman, and Belayet Hussain. All three power tillers for cultivation belonging to Babul Das were set on fire. When Ekram, who reported all this destruction, wanted to know what Babul's future plans were, he burst into tears, saying, "I shall leave as soon as I can."

Pulak would have perhaps continued with his narrative if he had not been rudely interrupted by Suranjan with the shout, "Shut up. Not a word more. If you utter one word more, I shall whip you."

Pulak was at first bewildered at Suranjan's violent outburst. He couldn't fathom Suranjan's strange behavior. Was it the spell of liquor? Might be. He smiled uneasily and looked at Debabrata.

For quite some time, they sat tongue-tied and silent. Suranjan alone remained busy emptying and replenishing his glass. He was not used to drinking. He was a casual drinker and that, too, in small quantities. But today he was willing to gulp down several bottles. The atmosphere in the room remained charged with a silent tension after Suranjan stopped Pulak with a violent reproof. In the midst of the prevailing stillness, everybody was stunned when Suranjan burst into tears. Resting his head on Pulak's shoulder, he went on crying loudly. Gradually he sank to the floor. In the dim light of the room, between the smell of drinks and the heart-rending cries of Suranjan, the stunned members in the room became stiff with apprehension. His shirt and trousers were unchanged. He hadn't had a bath or eaten any food. He rolled on the filthy floor in anguish and his dirty clothes became even more grimy. Finally he sobbed, "They abducted Maya last night."

"What did you say?" a startled Pulak said, turning toward Suranjan. Simultaneously Debabrata, Nayon, and Birupaksha turned toward Suranjan as well.

Suranjan's body was still heaving with spasms of weeping. The drink was left untouched. Some glasses overturned, spilling the liquid on the floor. Maya was not there—this was enough to reduce all other things to insignificance. No one could get his voice back. Suranjan's agony couldn't be mitigated with pat consolations given to a sick person like, "Don't think about it, everything will be all right." While the room was still sunk in silence, Belal entered. He took note of the prevailing atmosphere. Touching Suranjan, who was still on the floor, he asked, "I hear Maya has been taken away."

Suranjan didn't raise his head.

"Have you lodged a complaint with the police?"

Suranjan still kept his face pressed to the ground. Belal looked at the others, expecting a reply. They indicated by gesture that they, too, weren't aware of this.

"Have you made any inquiries as to who the offenders could have been?"

Suranjan still did not raise his head.

Belal sat on the bed and said, "What a bad time we're in. All the rogues and hoodlums have found an opportunity to do whatever they like. On the other hand, 'we' are being constantly killed and maimed in India."

"What do you mean by 'we'?"

"The Muslims, who are being merrily hacked by the BJP."

"Oh," came the monosyllabic exclamation.

"Listening to the news from the other side, the people here have lost their sanity. Whom should I blame? There 'we' are dying, and here 'you' are. What was the need for the demolition of such an old mosque? In the quest for the birthplace of Ram, a mythological, epic character, the Indians started digging up the mosque. Some day they'll claim their monkey god Hanuman was born at the site of Tajmahal. Then they will just destroy Tajmahal. And it is said that secularism is being practiced in India! Why are they now abducting Maya? The villains of the piece are, in fact, Advani and Joshi. I hear the situation at Metiaburuj in Calcutta is horrible."

Suranjan lay on the floor like an unclaimed body. Belal's sorrow became overshadowed by the wail of Kiranmayee and the groaning of Sudhamay from the next room.

"Maya will return certainly. After all, they can't devour a girl like Maya alive. Ask Auntie to be patient. And why are you wailing like a woman? Can you solve the problem by crying? And you, gentlemen, why are you sitting idle? You can find out where the girl has gone."

Birupaksha said, "We came to know of the incident just now. Is it possible to trace anyone who has been abducted? And where can we go in search of her?"

"Those chaps must be hooligans or heroine addicts, possibly of this very locality. They must have noticed her and, having gotten the opportunity, abducted her. Are normal people capable of doing such a heinous thing? The new generation has just gone to the dogs. The main reason is economic uncertainty, do you understand?"

Birupaksha lowered his head. None of them was acquainted with Belal. Belal was excited. He took out a packet of Benson and Hedges and a lighter. But the cigarette remained unlit in his hand. He said, "Is drinking any solution to the problem? You just say, can drinking solve anything? Has there been any massive outbreak of riots in this country? This is not a riot. It is the craving for tasting sweets that forces the boys to loot sweetmeat shops. In India, nearly six thousand riots have occurred. Thousands of Muslims have been killed. How many Hindus have died here? Truckloads of police have been posted in the Hindu areas."

No one said anything. Not even Suranjan. He didn't feel like talking. He felt very sleepy. Belal left his cigarette unlit. Saying he had business somewhere nearby, he left. One by one, the others, too, went out.

Day Nine

Gopal's house had been looted. The house was next to Suranjan's. A ten- or twelve-year-old girl, Gopal's younger sister, came to Suranjan's house. She looked at the wreckage. She paced the rooms silently. Lying on his bed, Suranjan observed the girl. Her eyes were terror-stricken even at this tender age. Standing at Suranjan's doorstep, the girl looked wide-eyed. Suranjan had lain on the floor through the night. The sun-bathed verandah told him the day had advanced well into the morning. He beckoned the girl to come near him and asked," What's your name?"

"Madol."

"Where do you study?"

"Shere-Bangla Girls' School."

The school was previously known as "Nari Shiksha Mandir." It was founded by the revolutionary leader Ms. Leela Nag. Was her name remembered anymore these days? When convention demanded that girls remain home-bound, she approached every house to encourage the girls to get enrolled in her school. It was by sheer dint of her individual labor that she built up this girls' school. That school was still there, which meant the same school building stood in the same place. But the name had been changed. Possibly there was a ban against uttering Leela Nag's name. Who knew if there was a similar unwritten restriction on the name "Nari Shiksha Mandir"? This was another way of distorting the names of educational institutions, as with abbreviations like B. M. College or M. C. College. The expanded names might vividly reveal Hinduism in the land of Muslims. A conspiracy was hatched in 1971 by the Pakistanis to Islamize two hundred forty street names in Dhaka. Lalmohan Poddar Land was called Abdul Karim Gaznavi Road, Shankhari Nagar Road became Gul Badan Street, Bakhtiar Khilji Road replaced Nabin Chand Goswamy Road, Kali Charan Saha Road was renamed as Gazi Salauddin Road, Rayer Bazar turned into Sultanganj, Shashi Bhushan Chatterji Lane became known as Syed Salim Street, Indira Road was made Anar Kali Road, and so on.

The girl asked, "Why are you sleeping on the floor?"

"I like the feel of the ground."

"I, too, like the touch of the ground. We had a courtyard in this house. Now we are moving to a new house where there is no courtyard. Hence, no touch of earth under the feet."

"Then you won't be able to play."

The girl sat near Suranjan's head, leaning against a leg of the cot. She seemed to like his company. She sighed frequently and said, "I feel very bad about leaving because of my attachment to the house! The word *maya*, "attachment," reminiscent of his sister, Maya's, name, opened a raw wound in Suranjan's heart. He asked the girl to come closer to him. As if the girl were a replica of Maya, who, in her childhood, would like talking with her Dada about her school, her sports. For a long time, he hadn't talked with Maya sitting by his side. As children, Suranjan and Maya would build earthen houses on the riverside in the afternoons. During the night the river would wash them away. One by one he remembered his days with little Maya, when their tongues would turn red after consuming colored sweets; when they would go to the tribal festival of Mahua Malua; when skipping out of the house, they would roam through the dense expanse of white *Kash* flowers on the riverside. . . . Suranjan reached his hand out to the girl. Her hands were as soft as Maya's. Whose hands were now holding Maya's? Must be some ruthless, cruel, rough hands. Was Maya trying to run away? She must be wanting to run, yet couldn't. He went on holding the hand of the girl named Madol. As if she were Maya. If he released her hand, somebody would take her away and tie her up firmly. Madol asked, "Why is your hand trembling so much?"

"Is it? I'm also feeling a deep attachment for you. You said you would be going away."

"But we're not going to India, we're going to Mirpur. Subal and his family are leaving for India."

"What were you doing when they entered your house?"

"I was on the verandah, crying. I was so scared! They've taken away our television, as well as the jewelry box from the cupboard. They have also taken away all the money that Baba had."

"Didn't they say anything to you?"

"Before leaving they gave me a couple of hard slaps on my cheek and said, 'Shut up and stop crying.' "

"Didn't they do anything else? Didn't they want to take you away?"

"No, they are perhaps beating up Mayadi severely, right? They've beaten up my Dada as well. Dada was asleep. They struck him on his head with a bamboo stick. He bled a lot."

Suranjan thought, had Maya been as young as Madol, she would have perhaps been spared. She would not have been dragged away in that manner. How many of them had raped Maya? Five, seven, or more? Was she bleeding much?

"Madol, would you like to take a walk with me?"

"Ma will be worried."

"We'll tell your ma before going."

Maya would often insist, "Dada, will you take me to Cox Bazar? Let us go to Madhupur forest. I would also like to visit the Sundarbans." Reading Jibananda Das's poem "Banalata Sen," she suggested a visit to Natore. Suranjan never attached any importance to Maya's importunities. He would say, "Get rid of those silly ideas. Better go to the slum areas at Tejgaon, see how the people are living there. It's much better to get an intimate view of human life than watching those inanimate trees and stones." Maya's enthusiasm would shrink from the cold waters sprinkled by Suranjan. Now Suranjan thought, What had he gained by watching and caring about human life? Had his dream for the well-being of the people been fulfilled? What had he achieved by thinking constantly of the movement of peasants and workers, the rise of the proletariat? In the end, socialism met with a disastrous end and Lenin's statue was hurled down with ropes. In the same way he had to accept the ignominy of defeat. A youth like him, who had always gone around singing in praise of humanity, had his house subjected to the most inhuman, barbaric attack.

Madol slowly made a move to leave. Her soft hand, like Maya's, slid away from his.

Hyder had not turned up today either. He must have gotten cold feet, although his excuse was that he did not want to get involved. He didn't want to get entangled in fresh trouble. Suranjan, too, realized the futility of searching for Maya. If Maya came back at all, she would do so as she had at the age of six. He felt emptiness enveloping him.

When Maya was at Parul's, the house appeared to be empty, but he did not have the feeling of such dire distress. He knew that Maya was safe and she would return. Now the house had the eerie stillness of the graveyard. As if someone had died. As Suranjan looked at the empty whisky bottle, overturned glasses near his feet, and scattered books, the tears that should have been in his eyes remained bottled up in his heart.

This time his Muslim friends like Kamal or Rabiul had not cared to inquire about his state. They were perhaps thinking, let everyone to whom it matters save his own skin. Belal, when he came the previous night, also echoed in the same vein: "Why did you smash our Babri mosque?" Suranjan mused, the Babri mosque was a structure located in India. Why should Belal feel any sense of belonging to it? And how could the Hindus like Suranjan be held responsible for its demolition? Suranjan, for that matter, had never been to India. Then how could he be involved in its destruction? Was Belal equating the Hindus in this country with their counterparts in India? Did they mean Suranjan was also a party to the destruction of the mosque by the Hindus in that country? Could Suranjan be placed on the same scale with the Hindu fundamentalists at Ayodhya? Was he not a citizen of this country as were Belal, Kamal and Hyder? Was he basically a Hindu alone? Did the onus of mosque demolition in India rest on Suranjan? Could country and nationality be deemed less important than religion? Well, that might be the line of thinking of uneducated, weak-minded persons who sought to survive on the plank of religion alone. But why should Belal figure among them? Belal was highly educated, a freedom fighter. Why should he get bogged down in the shit of religion? He found no answers to these questions. Kiranmayee had silently placed two bananas and some biscuits on the table. He felt like drinking the rest of the whisky bottle instead of touching those bananas and biscuits. He had been repeatedly visited by Maya while he lay in a drunken stupor last night. When he came to his senses, her face came in a flash again. If he closed his eyes the scene of her being torn apart by a pack of dogs loomed large.

Hyder didn't even care to inform him if Maya had been located or not. Suranjan had sought his help for his greater familiarity with the underworld. Otherwise, he could have plunged himself in the maze of alleys in search of her. Of course, the rapists didn't need the cover of alleys to pounce upon the Hindu girls anymore; they could easily go about their way openly. So was the looting perpetrated in the same unabashed way. One didn't require any particular protection to persecute the Hindus, because all such acts had the tacit support of the government. Sheikh Hasina said just the other day that communal harmony in the country would have to be maintained for the sake of protecting the lives and property of one hundred forty million Muslims in India. Why would Sheikh Hasina have to bother about the safety of the Muslims in India, first of all? Wasn't it imperative that communal amity be secured for defending the basic rights of the people in this country? Why should he have to show more compassion for the lives and property of the Indian Muslims than for those of the citizens of his own country? Was it to be concluded that the Awami League, too, was using the same spices of "anti-India stand" and "cause of Islam" with which a rabidly communal organization like Jamat-i-Islami was cooking for the consumption of the people? Was it then a stratagem to cover the communalists with an Islamic mask? Communal harmony should not be preserved in the interest of Indian Muslims; the most basic and fundamental reason behind the move should have been the preservation of the fundamental constitutional rights of Bangladesh's own citizens. The Hindus in this country, as free citizens, were equally entitled to enjoy the acknowledged right to practice their own religion and conviction and the protection of their life and property. The Hindus would live just like any other person not because of the kindness of any religion or political party, but because of the enshrining of their basic rights in the constitutional tenets. Why, then, should Suranjan have to seek shelter from Belal or Hyder and depend on their sympathy for his survival?

When the house of a student union leader, Kamal Bhowmik, at Mirsarai in Chittagong was set on fire, his aunt was burned alive. Three children were also roasted alive when the Hindu areas at Kutubdia were attacked by arsonists. In the same way ended the life of Surya Mohan of Nathpara in Satkania. When a resident of Mirsarai, Basudev, was asked about the identity of the attackers, he said, "Those who kill us during the night return to offer their sympathy during

242

the day, saying 'Our heart bleeds in agony for you.' " To the same question, Jatra Mohan Nag of Khajuria said, "Better shoot me to put an end to my suffering, that will be best." On the other hand, after six days of unrestrained communal violence, all the noncommunal political parties in Bangladesh, in conjunction with the national coordination committee and combined cultural alliance, had formed an all-party platform to preach communal harmony. The organization was set up only when the flames of the communal flare-up were dying down. Even this outfit, barring the holding of a rally and a peace procession, had failed to launch any concrete program. A demand would be made from a mass rally to impose a ban on the Jamat Shibir Freedom party. It was, however, not known what importance this demand would gain from the new communal harmony committee. Its leaders were totally silent about what their programs would be in the event this demand to ban Jamat was turned down by the government. Some of the committee members had suggested initiating criminal cases against the looters. But one of the victims, a devotee of the ravaged Shanir akhra, had made it clear that he was not in favor of suing the attackers whom he knew. This was because he believed that the opposition parties, which had failed to give them protection at the time of attack, couldn't be expected to give the required security after the filing of the case. Suranjan was sure that other victims of violence would react to the proposal in an identical manner. Hence, this call for starting cases against the offenders was nothing but a political gimmick.

The democratic forces had failed miserably to work out a speedy program to counter communal violence. Communal forces, on the other hand, were far better consolidated and they went ahead with their destructive program quite fast. The republican political parties, after forming the all-party harmony committee after dragging their feet for a week, had no reason to be complacent. Many members of the intelligentsia felt quite satisfied at the thought that there had been far fewer incidents of communal disturbances in Bangladesh than India. But Suranjan failed to understand why these people could not realize that the riots in Bangladesh were always one-sided. The Hindus here never launched retaliatory counterattacks like the Indian Muslims. That was why the attacks here never evoked counterstrikes. In all three countries in this subcontinent the ruling parties had joined hands with the fundamentalist-fascist axis powers to gain political mileage. Fundamentalists were gaining strength in the bargain as they were in India, Tajikistan, Afghanistan, Pakistan, Algeria, Egypt, Iran and Serbia. Their single aim was to strike at the root of the democratic forces. The German government had banned two fascist organizations for burning alive three Turkish women. In India, too, all the fundamentalist parties had been banned, although it was not certain how long this restriction would persist. They had been banned in Algeria also. Egypt's government had dealt firmly with them. A war was raging in Tajikistan between the communists and fundamentalists. But never once, even in an unguarded moment, had the Bangladesh government pondered the issue. It might have been possible elsewhere, but in this country religion-based politics would continue to rule the roost, or so thought Suranjan.

Thanks to the fanatically communal parties in India, the ruling BNP government had been able to divert the people's attention from the rising tide of the movement against Golam Azam and canalize it along communal channels. In this matter, the Jamat Sibir Freedom party and other communal parties helped the government with their activities. Jamat-i-Islami was now feeling very relieved to be able to deflect the people's attention from the movement demanding trial for the Pakistani collaborator Golam Azam. The combined cultural alliance-led procession had raised slogans like "Bangladesh will now resist the communal hoodlums." Oh, Bangladesh. Smoking a cigarette, Suranjan fumed, "You swine of a nation." He repeated this abusive epithet. He felt happy. He suddenly laughed out loud, although his own laughter sound fiendish to his ears.

Madol kept herself glued to Kiranmayee. She said, "Auntie, we are going away to Mirpur. There the ruffians won't be able to reach us."

"Why won't they?"

"Mirpur is far away."

Madol was under the impression that the hooligans were concentrated in Tikatuli alone; they didn't go to far-away places like Mirpur. Kiranmayee wondered whether those who looted the Hindu houses, or destroyed and burned them, or abducted girls like Maya could be called ruffians? Those ruffians were not supposed to discriminate between Hindus and Muslims; they would attack all the houses rather indiscriminately. The ruffians would feel insulted by being compared to those who looted or abducted for religious purposes.

Sudhamay was in bed. He couldn't do anything else but lie there. What was the use of staying alive in this immobile, disabled condition? Making hell out of Kiranmayee's life for nothing. She absorbed all sufferings silently, never showing any sign of fatigue. After shedding tears throughout the night, could she feel like lighting up the stove? Still, she had to do it. The starving stomach caused pains. Suranjan had virtually given up taking baths or meals. Kiranmayee, too, was going almost the same way. Sudhamay hardly felt any desire for eating. Maya still had not returned. Would she not come back again? If only he could bring back Maya, even at the cost of his life. What if he could proclaim while standing at an intersection: "I want Maya back, I have a right to demand her return."

The word "right" now seemed spooky to Sudhamay. In 1946, when Sudhamay was very young, after taking sweets at a shop, he asked for a glass of water. He said *paani*, which is a Muslim expression, and not *jal*, which the Hindus use. Some Muslims looked at him sharply. Was it fear that compelled him to say *paani* instead of *jal*? Possibly. Relations between the Hindus and Muslims were quite tense in the town at that time.

The British realized that unless they could disrupt Hindu-Muslim unity and friendly relations, they wouldn't be able to keep India under colonial rule and their exploitation. From their cunning was born the divide-and-rule policy. Sudhamay thought that it could be that just because 90 percent of Muslims were landless peasants while an equal percentage of Hindus were landowners, this craving for land possession bred the Hindu-Muslim clash as conflict over land had led to revolution in Russia and China. Under the patronage of the British, the Muslim League was born in Bengal in 1906 on the basis of communal principle. This party was responsible for poisoning the social and political life in India with the venom of communalism. Of course, the Congress party, too, could not be absolved from blame. After 1947, for twenty-four long years, the Pakistani rulers, acting as collaborators with imperialism, had usurped the democratic rights of the country's citizens by raising the bogeys of anti-India feeling, Islam, and communalism. Sudhamay heaved a sigh of relief after getting back those democratic rights in 1971. But he now felt suffocated every now and then.

After the liberation of Bangladesh, secularism was given the status of one of the four founding principles of the country's constitution. It was an invincible armor against the revival of communalism. But communalism staged a comeback after August 15, 1995. Other evil forces, like violence, fundamentalism, religious fanaticism and autocracy, became allied with communalism. To give communal thoughts a patina of acceptability, an ideological basis was needed. Before the emergence of Pakistan, this basis was called the theory of two nations. After 1975, it assumed the garb of Bangladeshi nationalism. The people, erasing their thousand-year-old tradition of being Bengalis, would have to identify themselves as Bangladeshi. Just like Bangladeshi cows, asses, paddy and jute, the people, too, now came to be known as Bangladeshi. In 1988, after the eighth amendment to the constitution of Bangladesh, it was written: "The state religion of the Republic is now Islam, but other religions may be practiced in peace and harmony in the Republic." Why this "may be" here? Why not "shall be"? Regarding fundamental rights, it was stated, of course, that "the state will show no discrimination to any citizen on the grounds of religion, community, caste, sex or place of birth." Although there was a guarantee against the practice of discrimination, discrimination was very much evident; otherwise, why was Maya allowed to be abducted? Why did they use abusive expressions like "son of a *malaun*"? Did only the *goondas* use this abusive language? No. Then all that had happened was not sheer rowdyism, it was something else. The situation was worsening every day with Islamic educational institutions like *madrasa* on the rise in place of the usual secular educational institutions, along with a spate in the number of mosques, Islamic religious rallies, and the blaring of the *ajan* over the loudspeakers. In a single locality, there was a mosque for every three houses along with its array of loudspeakers all around. The use of loudspeakers, however, was restricted during the Hindu puja festivals. But if these facilities were to be used, why should the Muslims be given the exclusive right to them? In section 28 of the United Nations' universal charter of human rights, it has been stated that every person has the right to express his thoughts, follow the dictates of conscience and practice religion freely. These rights entitle any person to change his religion or conviction and teach, preach, pray, and observe his or her own religion individually or collectively, in the open or secretly.

If that was true, then why should the Hindu temples be destroyed? Although Sudhamay personally didn't have any faith in the temples, he was still opposed to their exclusive and wanton demolition. Wasn't there any penal provision for punishing the people involved in these acts of sack and burning? The penal code had provisions of one, two or, at most, three years' imprisonment for these offenses.

The sickness around him overshadowed Sudhamay's personal illness. The country was gradually becoming sick. After many years' struggle the Bengalis were freed from the grasp of Pakistani rule. The free country had its own constitution that declared: "We, the people of Bangladesh, having proclaimed our independence on the 26th day of March 1971 and through a historic struggle for national liberation, established the independent, sovereign People's Republic of Bangladesh.

"Pledging that the high ideals of nationalism, socialism, democracy and secularism, which inspired our heroic people to dedicate themselves to, and our brave martyrs to sacrifice their lives in, the national liberation struggle, shall be the fundamental principles of the constitution."

"Struggle for national liberation" was changed in 1978 to "a historic war for national independence." Not only that, there were more changes: ". . . high ideals of absolute trust and faith in the Almighty Allah, nationalism, democracy, and socialism, meaning economic and social justice." Moreover, "liberation war" became "independence."

In a change from the constitution of 1972, at the beginning of the 1978 constitution *Bismillahir Rahamanir Rahim* (in the name of benevolent, great, merciful Allah) was inserted. Article 12 of the constitution was completely deleted. The article was entitled Secularism and Freedom of Religion:

> The principle of secularism shall be realized by the elimination of
>   a. communalism in all its forms
>   b. the granting by the State of political status in favor of any religion
>   c. the abuses of religion for political purposes
>   d. any discrimination against, or persecution of, persons practicing a particular religion.

After the total elimination of the article on secularism Article 25(2) added that the "State, on the basis of Islamic cohesion, will be active in consolidating, preserving, and strengthening the brotherhood among different Muslim countries."

Article 6 of the 1972 constitution said: "The citizenship of Bangladesh shall be determined by law; citizens of Bangladesh shall be known as Bengals."

Ziaur Rahaman made it, "The citizens of Bangladesh shall be known as Bangladeshis."

Darkness descended on Sudhamay's eyes. Why should the room seem so dark even before noon had advanced? Was it that his eyesight was failing? Or he hadn't changed his spectacles for quite a long time? Or was a cataract developing in his eyes or were tears welling up in his eyes to blur his vision?

Suranjan, too, was strangely changing. He never cared to sit even once by Sudhamay's bedside. Ever since Maya was hustled out, he had never bothered to step inside this room even unwittingly. From this room, Sudhamay could hear the noise of drinking bouts taking place in the other room. Was the boy getting spoiled? He had never seen Suranjan drinking at home. Perhaps he no longer cared for anyone. Had he then forgotten about Maya in just a few days? Sudhamay couldn't persuade himself to believe this. The sudden silence of his son heightened his anxiety. Was the boy going downhill?

Suranjan wouldn't go anywhere. He had realized the futility of searching for Maya. It was better to stay put at home. If he went out, he would have to hear comments like, "Those infidels, those sons of devils destroyed the Babri mosque. All of them should be severely thrashed to make them leave for India." Suranjan had become tired of hearing such abuse. He no longer believed in the statements of any Socialist party leader or any leftist leader. He had heard many a leftist calling him "a son of a *malaun*." Krishna Binode Roy was known to all as Kabir Bhai. Barin Datta had to change his name to Abus Salam. Which party could be trusted when even the eminent Communist party leaders didn't feel secure with their Hindu names? Or would he enroll himself as a member of the Jamat? Straightaway, he would approach its leader, Nizami, with a flourish of "Huzur Assalamu Alaikum." Next day bold newspaper headlines would scream out: A HINDU JOINS JAMAT-I-ISLAMI. It is said that Jamat-i-Islami was able to secure votes even in Jagannath Hall.* Of course, because of its tremendous financial resources, it got the votes. If anyone was assured of a monthly income of five thousand takas, who would then refuse to vote Jamat?

But Suranjan was keen on settling his score with the leftist parties, which, after raising his hopes, had eventually sunk him in the abysmal depth of frustration. In fact, these very party people had relinquished their memberships one by one and had joined the other parties. They changed their stand as well. Following the death of Comrade Farhad, all Muslim rituals were strictly observed at the office of the Communist party of Bangladesh with great fanfare. His funeral, too, was held with Islamic rituals. Why was it so? Why did communists finally have to take shelter under the Islamic flag? It must be to escape the embarrassment of being branded as atheists. But even so, could they save themselves? Even after such a show, could they earn the

*The Hindu student hostel of Dhaka University.

251

confidence of the people? Suranjan didn't blame the people; the real offenders, he felt, were the directionless so-called leftist leaders themselves.

The number of *madrasas* was on the rise. This system was indeed quite efficacious in crippling a country economically. It was Sheikh Mujibur himself who took the initiative in setting up *madrasas* in villages, who had ruined this country!

The nation, which had fought a liberation war in 1971 and launched the language movement, was now in a disastrous condition of unbelievable magnitude. Where was that awareness of Bengali nationalism? Where was that consciousness that proclaimed that the Hindus, Muslims and Buddhists of Bengal belonged to the nation of Bengalis? Suranjan felt very lonely. As if he were not a Bengali, not even a human being. He was just a Hindu, a two-legged animal which had become a foreigner in his own land.

In the country's administrative structure, there was a separate ministry called the religious affairs ministry. The allocation under this head last year was quite generous. Suranjan would certainly call it so. Under the nondevelopment head was this grant for the promotion of religion. The Islamic Foundation, Dhaka, got 1,500,000 takas; the Waqaf (religious properties) administration got 800,000 takas; sanctions for other religious matters, 26,000,000 takas; the Jakat (charity) administration fund, 2,200,000 takas. The Islamic mission institution received 220,000 takas, the minorities 250,000 takas. The free supply of power to the mosques, 12,000,000 takas. The free supply of water to the mosques, 5,000,000 takas. The Tara mosque of Dacce got 300,000 takas. The total allocations came to 84,570,000 takas. The maintenance of the Baitul Mokarram mosque cost 1,500,000 takas. Total nondevelopmental allocations, including those for teaching and consolidation of development-based programs and its expansion, amounted to 109,338,000 takas. The minorities in the country numbered 250 million. To sanction a mere 250,000 takas for their religion was quite funny indeed!

Religion figured even in developmental expenditures: for the religion ministry: 2,000,000 takas. The compilation and publication of an Islamic encyclopedia: 2,000,000 takas. The project for the Islamic cultural center of the Islamic Foundation: 19,000,000 takas. The publication research and translation program of the Islamic Foundation: 16,875,000 takas. Plan for teaching Imams (religious heads), the library development program of the Islamic Foundation: 1,500,000 takas. Mosque library scheme: 2,500,000 takas. The expansion of Islamic cultural centers in new districts, Imam training centers and training academies: 15,000,000 takas. A grand total on development of 56,895,000 takas. There were subdivisions within the allocation of 260,000 takas for other religious purposes. For Islamic religious occasions and festivals: 500,000 takas. For program-based grants for different Islamic religious organizations: 2,860,000 takas. For the repair and maintenance of different mosques in the country under the supervision of honorable members of Parliament: 20,000,000 takas. The allocation for religious representatives coming from or going abroad amounted to 1,000,000 takas. Subscriptions or donations to international religious institutions came to 640,000 takas. The rehabilitation of neo-Muslims and distressed persons came to 1,000,000 takas. The total allocation for religious purposes under development and nondevelopment headings amounted to 166,213,000 takas.

The allocation for the rehabilitation of neo-Muslims was quite amusing. One million takas had been earmarked for this account. But no allotment had been made for the minorities under the heading of development. It was indeed reprehensible to allot such huge amounts to lure others into converting to a particular religion in a multi-religion, multi-caste poor country. The economic backbone of the country was shattered. Had anyone cared to know what was the load of foreign debt for each person? How rational was the allocation of such an enormous amount for Islamic affairs in a crippled economy of this sort? The lopsided allocation in this budget was also disrupting the national integrity of the country. Did anyone care to consider these factors at all?

As Suranjan was musing over these matters, Kajal Debnath opened the door and entered.

"What's the matter? You are still lying in bed at this hour? Has Maya come back?"

"No." Suranjan said, emitting a deep sigh.

"Tell me if I can do anything. We must do something."

"What can you do?"

Kajal Debnath had salt-and-pepper hair and was over forty. He was dressed in a loose shirt, with wrinkles of anxiety furrowing his forehead. He took out a packet of cigarettes and offered one to Suranjan.

Suranjan accepted. He hadn't bought cigarettes for quite some time. Whom could he ask for money? Certainly not Kiranmayee. He had stopped visiting the other room simply out of shame. As if he alone suffered the ignominy of losing Maya! He felt shame all the more because he alone bothered about the country too much, he alone was keen to prove the largely noncommunal attitude of the people of this nation.

He was too embarrassed to present himself before an idealist, honest and upright person like Sudhamay.

Suranjan went on smoking on an empty stomach. If Maya were there, she would have objected with the warning: "Dada, you are smoking on an empty stomach only to invite cancer that will kill you."

It wouldn't have been bad if he had cancer. He would have waited for death just lying down. He wouldn't have to live for the fulfillment of any expectation.

Kajal Debnath was at a loss over what to do now. He said, "Today they took away your sister, tomorrow it will be my daughter's turn. And this sort of thing will surely happen. Today they hit Gautam on his head. Just wait, it may be you or I tomorrow."

Suranjan said, "Could you tell me what we are basically, human beings or Hindus?"

Kajal looked around the room and said, "They came to this room as well, didn't they?"

"Yes."

"What was Maya doing at the time?"

"Heard she was preparing food for Baba."

"Couldn't she hit them back?"

"How could she? They were armed with thick clubs, iron rods. And what power does a Hindu have to touch a Muslim? In India, the minority Muslims venture counterstrikes. When two sides fight it out, it can be called a riot, which, in fact, was occurring in that country. And the people describe the incidents in this country as riots. What is happening here is nothing but communal terrorism. It can be termed persecution or torture. One side is thoroughly beating up or killing the other."

"Do you think Maya will come back some day?"

"Don't know." Suranjan invariably felt a choking sensation at the mention of Maya's name. An emptiness prevailed in his heart.

"Kajalda, what else happened in the country?"

Kajal Debnath blew a ring of smoke toward the ceiling of the room. He then began his dreadful litany: Twenty-eight thousand seven hundred commercial establishments, three thousand six hundred temples were totally or partially devastated. Twelve people were killed. The total damage was more than 20 million takas. Village after village had been laid waste. Forty-three districts had been caught in this orgy of violence. Two thousand six hundred women had been raped and molested. The most severely damaged temples were the five-hundred-year-old temple of the great saint Gauranga Mahaprabhu, which was located in Sylhet; the several-hundred-year-old Kali temple at Baniachang; Kaibalyadham at Chittagong; Tulshidham; Madanmohan Akhra at Bhola; and Ramkrishna Mission outposts at Sunamgunj and Faridpur.

Suranjan asked, "Didn't the government offer any aid?"

"No. Not only was the government not forthcoming, it didn't allow any other social service organizations to offer relief. Of course, some nongovernment organizations come forward on their own initiative. Thousands of people are still spending their days and nights under the canopy of the open sky. These displaced people have no clothes to put on, no food, no home. Some of the raped women have become dumb with shock, they can't talk. The businessmen, having lost everything, are sitting idle. Still, they are being robbed of what scanty possessions they could salvage, and forced to give up their lands to the grabbers.

256

The damage caused to the properties amounts to 750 million takas in Barishal Division, 200 million takas in Chittagong and 100 million takas in Dhaka Division, with Khulna and Rajsahi following with 10 million takas each. That makes a grand total of 1,070,000,000 takas. Added to this are the losses sustained by the commercial establishments amounting to 220 million takas and the damaged and devastated temples at another 570 million takas."

"I can't take it anymore, Kajalda, I just can't."

"Do you know what's the worst aspect of this? A mass exodus. There is no way to stop a massive migration of people this time. The official circles, of course, maintain that there is no migration of Hindus. Didn't the noted Calcutta magazine *Desh* write once that every year, about one hundred fifty thousand Bangladeshis are infiltrating into India and the bulk of them are not going back? During the last two decades, more than half a million minorities have been forced to leave this country. Just look at the census report that says that in 1941 the Muslims constituted 70.3 percent of the East Bengal population as against 28.3 percent Hindus. In 1951, the Muslims rose to 76.5 and Hindus dropped to 22.0. This 'Muslims up' and 'Hindus down' trend continued, showing the former at 80.4 and the latter at 18.5 in 1961. In 1974 it was 85.4 and 13.5; in 1981 the figures were 86.7 and 12.1, and in 1991 the Muslims swelled to 87.4 percent and Hindus shrank to 12.6. What does all this mean? In each census the number of Muslims was going up and the Hindu population was continuously shrinking. If their number dwindles, where are they going? The official version of 'no Hindu migration' is then being contradicted by the census figures. Why this discrepancy? Now they have decided to tinker with the census report? There won't be any separate counting of Hindus and Muslims any more."

"Why?"

"Because otherwise the uncomfortable fact of the continuous drop in the number of Hindus will be known to people."

"Then this government can be said to be quite crafty, isn't that so, Kajalda?" said Suranjan, stretching his arms.

Kajal Debnath lit another cigarette without adding anything to his narrative. Then he asked, "Is there an ashtray?"

"Why not treat the entire room as a giant ashtray?"

"I would like to meet your parents, but I really have no words of consolation for them." Kajal Debnath hung his head in shame. He felt so dispirited, as if it were his own brother who had kidnapped Maya.

Maya again. Suranjan's chest felt like exploding in a volcanic eruption. He quickly changed the topic: "Well, Kajalda, Jinnah said that from now on we all would be Pakistanis; there wouldn't be any Hindu-Muslim divide. Has there, after his ensuring utterance, been any decrease in the migration of Hindus to India?"

"Jinnah was an Ismailia Khoja community member. Although Muslims, the members of this community follow the Hindu inheritance laws. His real surname was Khojani. His name was Jhinabhai Khojani. He retained just the Jhina part of the name and dropped the rest. Despite Jinnah's assurance, Hindus became victims of discrimination. Otherwise, why should more than a million Hindus leave East Pakistan even before June 1948? They became known as refugees in India."

"Many Muslims also came here following riots in West Bengal."

"Yes, but most of those Muslims who came from Assam and West Bengal also went back to their places of origin following the signing of the Nehru-Liaquat Ali Pact between the Indian and Pakistani governments, which stipulated that the minorities of both countries would enjoy equal rights irrespective of their religions. The pact assured them of their rights to life, property and culture along with the ensuring of freedom of speech and of religion. Those people who came here returned to India on the basis of the conditions of this pact. But those who had left here never came back. Despite their remaining on the other side, the exodus of minorities for India was stopped for the time being. But it started again following the passing of two laws in the Pakistani legislature in 1951, the East Bengal Evacuee Property Act and the East Bengal Evacuees Act, which acted as fresh stimulants to the minorities to leave the country. Eventually the number of such people soon swelled to three and a half million. Your father must know all this."

"Baba never speaks to me about these things. He would just blow up if the question of leaving the country was broached. He can't tolerate this."

"We don't entertain the idea of quitting the country. But those who are going away for good are doing so secretly. So how can you prevent it? Some sort of assurance must be given to them. After all, no one leaves his own land willingly. Isn't there a saying in the scriptures that he is happiest who doesn't live outside his land? The Muslims are rather a wandering people. There is historical evidence of their moving from one country to another. But a Hindu holds his land close to his heart."

While talking, Kajal Debnath walked to the verandah, possibly to smother his own emotion.

Coming back, he said, "My soul is screaming for a cup of tea. Come, let's go out to a tea shop."

Suranjan didn't change his dress. He hadn't bathed and had been virtually without food for quite some time. Still, he hoisted himself out of bed and said, "Let's go, then. By staying in bed continuously, all my body joints seem to have become rusty."

Suranjan went out, leaving the door open. After all, what was the point in closing it? After that fateful night, there was hardly anything in the house worth taking. Walking with him, Kajal Debnath asked, "Are you eating at home regularly?"

"Ma leaves food in my room; sometimes I eat, sometimes I don't. Nor do I feel like eating. I just don't like to." Suranjan ran his fingers through is hair, not to arrange it, but to get over the agony within him.

Suranjan picked up the broken thread of their conversation: "Kajalda, perhaps the rate of Hindu migration dropped somewhat during 1969–70."

"The six-point movement was launched in 1966. The mass uprising was in 1969, the general elections in 1970, and then there was the liberation war of 1971. During this period the rate of Hindu migration had indeed gone down. A large number of Hindus left the country between 1955 and 1960. But the exodus went into full swing between 1960 and 1965. During this period about one million Hindus left the country. The beginning of the liberation war saw the massive exodus of one hundred million who took shelter in India. Returning home at the end of the war, many Hindus that saw their houses and other properties had been illegally occupied. Some then trekked back to India, some stayed behind in the faint hope of recovering what they had lost. They hoped for safety from the newly independent country. Then you must have noticed that even in 1974, the Mujibur government did nothing but change the name of the Enemy Property Act, retaining all its draconian contents. Zia-ur-Rahman restored the anti-freedom communal forces to power and deleted the secularism part from the constitution. Then Ershad started the Islamic revivalism movement. Ershad announced on December 22, 1982, that from now on the principles of the Koran and Islam would be the foundation of the new constitution. Who could have thought that even after being exploited in the name of religion for twenty-four long years, religion would bounce back into politics with such a flourish?"

They stopped outside a tea stall. Kajal Debnath, gazing hard at Suranjan, said, "You appear to be quite inattentive. You are asking questions which you should know the answers to. Why? Seems you have been suffering from a tremendous restlessness. Calm down, Suranjan. Why should a talented boy like you suffer from frustration?"

They sat at a table facing each other. Kajal Debnath asked Suranjan, "Will you eat anything with your tea?"

Suranjan nodded his head. Yes, he would like to eat something. He ate two *singaras*. Kajal Debnath also ate a *singara*. After eating he said to the boy in the shop, "Can we have some *paani*?"

Suranjan heard the word *paani*.

At home, Kajal Debnath would say *jal* to mean water. But here he used the word used by the Muslims, *paani*. Was it just the outcome of practicing to say so outside? Or was it out of fear? Although keen on knowing from Kajal, he couldn't ask. He felt they were being watched by many pairs of eyes. He sipped his tea quite fast. Was it out of fear? Why was he getting so frightened? His tongue was scalded, for the tea was very hot. The youth watching him intently from the next table had a goatee on his chin and wore a knitted cap on his head. He could be in his early twenties. Suranjan had an impression that this boy must have been among Maya's kidnappers; otherwise why should he be listening so attentively to their conversation? Suranjan also noticed a smirk on his face. Was he taunting him to remind him what a nice game they had had with his sister?

Suranjan couldn't finish his tea. He said, "Let's go, Kajalda. I don't like it any more."

"What's the big hurry?"

"I'm not feeling well."

Day Ten

In 1954 the National Assembly totaled 309 members, seventy-two of whom belonged to minorities. In 1970, the number took a downward plunge to eleven out of 300; in 1973, twelve out of 315; in 1979, just eight out of 330; and in 1986, seven out of 330. The number further declined to four in 1988 and rose slightly to become twelve out of 330 in 1991. In the Bangladesh army, there was not a single brigadier or major general from the minorities. Just one colonel out of seventy; only forty majors out of 1,000; eight captains out of 1,300; three second lieutenants out of 900; and, of infantrymen, barely 500 out of a total of 80,000. Out of the same number of policemen, only 2,000 belonged to religious minorities. Out of 60,000 in BDR only 300 were Hindus. No additional Inspector General of Police let alone Inspector General. Out of a total of 870 police officers, minorities accounted for only fifty-three.

There was no minority community member of high

rank in the Home, External Affairs and Defense ministries. The situation in the secretariat was worse. There was no secretary or additional secretary from the minorities. Of 134 joint secretaries, there were only three and just twenty-five deputy secretaries from a contingent of 463. Of 46,894 first-class officers of the self-governing organizations, minorities numbered 350. Among government, semi-government, or local self-governing institutions' first- and second-class officers the minorities figured less than 5 percent of the total number. Among 152 Customs and Excise senior officials, there was a lone minority member. The percentage was just 1 in the case of state sector industrial units, 3 to 4 percent among the employees and less than 1 percent among workers. There was not a single Hindu in the rank of chairman or managing director or branch manager in the entire banking industry, including the country's state bank. Industrial licenses were hard to come by for the Hindus unless they had Muslim partners. Besides no state-controlled bank, particularly industrial finance organizations, ever sanctioned any loan to a Hindu entrepreneur.

Suranjan hadn't had a wink of sleep the previous night. He had come under the spell of intense dislike for everything. Kiranmayee came once into his room in the morning. Perhaps she wanted to ask if Maya had been traced at all, or would she have to drag herself through another day without her daughter? Kiranmayee, too, had become quite listless these days. She had deep dark circles under her eyes, and her grim face was devoid of any smile or words. Suranjan lay sprawled on the bed as if he were asleep. He didn't make Kiranmayee guess the pain gnawing at him from within. She would silently place the dishes with his meals twice every day. Suranjan occasionally felt angry. Was she made of stone? Her husband was crippled, her daughter missing, her son there only nominally. Still why didn't she have any complaint against anyone? Kiranmayee led a strange life, like a zombie, without any complaint or feeling—a strange, still life!

He decided he would sleep the day out. He needed sleep. He hadn't slept for a long time. If he closed his eyes he could visualize the inexorable approach of a sharp claw toward him. He felt suffocated. But those hands kept on coming at him, one following the other, to throttle him. He couldn't relax, peace eluded him.

Nanigopal had come from Manikganj with his family, consisting of his wife, son, and daughter. He was distantly related to Sudhamay. The signs of plunder in the room failed to surprise him. He simply asked, "Your house, too, was not spared?"

Lalita, Nanigopal's wife, had kept the part in her hair, although she had erased the vermilion mark of a married Hindu woman and covered her head with the loose end of her sari. Taking Kirnamayee's hands in her own, she shrieked, "Oh, Boudi!" Her daughter stood petrified. Sudhamay couldn't remember her name. She would be about Maya's age or perhaps a little younger. Sudhamay kept on staring at the girl. His eyes again became hazy. Maya wasn't there. He couldn't bring himself to believe that Maya wasn't there in the house. He felt she was there. Maybe she was next door or out tutoring, and would be back in the afternoon. Everybody in the house secretly entertained the conviction that, though raped and tortured, with wounds all over her body, Maya would come back some day.

"Dada, we'll no longer stay in this country. I've a grown daughter now. I feel so scared. No one knows what's going to happen or when."

Looking away from the girl, Sudhamay said, "Don't mention anything about going away to me. I heard the family of Gautam in the next house is leaving. What do you think you are doing? You speak of quitting every now and then. Aren't there any rowdies in your promised land? Is that country totally free from terror? Girls are at risk in every country. Isn't there a couplet that says, 'Sighs on this bank of the river, all the happiness nestles on the other side'? That's what you're thinking."

Nanigopal was dressed in *pyjamas* and *punjabi*, usually used by Muslims. He had a stubble of beard on his face. Pressing his forehead with his palms he sat silently. Lalita suddenly began to cry once more. Kiranmayee made no move to comfort her or to talk to her. She could not even bring herself to say that Maya had been abducted. Nanigopal was bothered not so much about his wife as about his daughter. Who could say when the kidnappers would be coming for his daughter, Anjali. He said, "Dada, Lalita had a relative at Chandpur in Feni. He was hustled away by the property-grabbers, then they killed him. Don't you know that at Pingail in Jaidebpur, the fourteen-year-old daughter of Ashwini Kumar Ray was forcibly taken away and then raped? The girl died later. Similarly, the daughter of Harendranath Hira of Bedgram in Gopalgunj, Nandita Rani Hira, was kidnapped. At Banccharampur, Khitish chandra Debnath's daughter Karunabala met with the same fate at the hands of the Muslims. Added to this list are: Tandra Rani, daughter of Shobha Rani of Kalinath Bazar in Bhola; Sudhir Chandra Das's daughter Mukti

266

Rani at Adalatpara in Tangail, who was abducted by a businessman named Abdul Kayum; the daughter of Purna Chandra Burman at Bhaluka and Jayanti Rani; the daughter of Inkari Saha at Taragunj in Rangpur district. Haven't you heard all this?"

"When did all this happen?" Sudhamay asked in a tired voice. Nanigopal said, "In 1989."

"And you have kept in your memory such old incidents?"

"Can all these be forgotten?"

"Why don't you know the cases of the Muslim girls like Pari Banu, Andwara, Manowara, Sufia, Sultana? They, too, were kidnapped, raped and tortured."

Nanigopal reverted to his earlier posture of pressing his forehead. He said, "I heard about your illness. It's the worries about our own survival that deterred us from coming to see you. I thought just before our departure, I'd see you. Tonight we are leaving for the border station of Benapol. I couldn't sell off my property. I've asked a cousin of Lalita to try it out."

Sudhamay came to realize that he couldn't make Nanigopal change his mind. He just couldn't find a reason for leaving the country in this manner. If the number of Hindus opting to stay further dropped, the persecution of those remaining would mount all the more. Who would then be the gainers—those who were leaving or others who would be staying back? Sudhamay concluded that no one would gain, everyone would be losers. It would be a loss for the poor, a loss for all the members of the minority communities. Sudhamay had a craving to know how many Hindu deaths in this country would be enough to pay for the sins of Indian Hindu fundamentalists in the

SHAME

past, present and future. If he knew, he could at least increase the requisite number of deaths by committing suicide. He would insist that others take a similar course if
that could bring any sense of security to the surviving
Hindus.

Shafique Ahmed's wife came to their house in the afternoon. Her name was Aleya Begum. She used to drop in
quite frequently in the past. But these days, she had
stopped her visits. Similarly, Hyder's parents had also
stayed away from this house. Sudhamay could understand
Kiranmayee's loneliness. Seeing Aleya Begum, Kiranmayee was a bit surprised. Nobody was expected nowa-
days to visit this house which had the look of a deserted
dwelling. Seeing the smiling face of Aleya Begum, her dazzling sari and ornaments, Sudhamay wondered if Kiranmayee was feeling downcast. Perhaps he had treated Kiranmayee wrongly all along. He had forced a girl from an
educated and affluent family into his straightened, cheer-
less household and thereafter denied her basic physical
yearnings for twenty-one long years. Sudhamay had always placed his own interest about everything; otherwise
he should have asked her to marry again. Had he made
this request, would she have gone away? Did she secretly
nurture a dream of an equally resplendent life like Aleya
Begum's? She was human, after all. She could have gone
away had she liked. Fearing this possibility, Sudhamay
had stayed close to Kiranmayee as much as possible, re-
fraining from inviting his friends to his home. Now lying
on his sick bed, Sudhamay blamed himself for preferring
to forsake his friends even at the cost of becoming lonely
lest Kiranmayee feel any attraction for any of the callers to

268

the house. This selfishness gave his love for Kiranmayee a fierce intensity to keep her permanently attached to him. At least he wanted it to happen like that. But could love meet all one's needs? After such a long time, Sudhamay now felt that love alone couldn't fill the vacuum left in a life that required other things as well.

Aleya Begum saw the wreckage in the house, Sudhamay's immobilized condition, and heard the incident of Maya's kidnapping with appropriate punctuations of sympathetic "ahs" and "uhs." At one time she said, "Well, Boudi, don't you have any relatives in India?"

"Yes, all my relatives are there."

"Then why are you left here?"

"This is our country, that's why."

Aleya Begum was surprised at Kiranmayee's reply. Perhaps because she realized for the first time that this country belonged to Kiranmayee also. Aleya Begum was perhaps wondering if Kiranmayee could be equally emphatic as she in claiming this country to be hers. Sudhamay understood at that moment that Kiranmayee and Aleya could not be regarded in the same light. A fine line of distinction was somehow emerging.

Day Eleven

Today was Victory Day. The country became independent on this day. The word "independence" stung Suranjan like the bite of a poisonous insect. The day was being observed all over the country. Parades were being staged. An air of merriment was everywhere. Only Suranjan did not partake in this festivity. In past years on this day, Suranjan would go out early in the morning, take part in different functions, and sing rousing songs riding on a truck. Now he thought how he had wasted his time in these meaningless exercises. What sort of freedom had he gained? How had he benefited from the independence of Bangladesh? "Victory to Bangla. Victory of Bangla"; "The sun has arisen on the eastern horizon"; "Blood red, blood red"; "The golden Bangla of Rabindranath and Bangladesh of Nazrul, the beautiful Bangla of Jibanananda Das has no end to its loveliness"; "Those who brought about freedom in exchange for a seaful of blood, we'll never forget them";

270

"We fight to save a flower, we fight for a smiling face"—all these songs that he had sung earlier came back, sending waves reverberating through his heart. Only he couldn't respond. He didn't want to hear these songs. He deliberately trampled all the flowers of pleasant memories in his heart.

His daylong stay in bed gave birth to a wish. He nurtured this secret wish and kept it alive so that it could grow up, sending out its branches. He made it stronger and in his mind reared this wish plant up to the flowering stage, even smelling its fragrance. After nursing the wish throughout the day, he went out of the house at around eight in the evening. He hired a rickshaw, giving the driver the freedom to go wherever he liked. The rickshaw, after going around Topkhana, Vijaynagar, Kakrail and Magbazar, brought him to Ramna. Suranjan watched the nighttime illumination. Did these well-lighted streets know he was a Hindu boy? Had they known, the asphalt underneath would have split open. Unless this wish were fulfilled today, the fire that was burning in every cell of his body would never be put out. He wouldn't be able to wrest himself free from this suffocating life unless he carried out his wish. What he would do wouldn't solve any problem; still, it would give him some respite, reduce a bit of his pain.

Suranjan asked the rickshaw puller to stop outside the Bar Council. He lit a cigarette. Suranjan had virtually given up the hope of getting back Maya. He would inform his parents not to nourish their hope of having her back. Let them seek consolation in the presumption that Maya had died in a street accident. Suranjan could no longer bear the lonely, helpless condition of a man like Sudhamay, who, till the other day, had been quite active. He now groaned throughout the day, suffering the pain of not having Maya back in his arms. Maya must have been treated the way carrion is, torn apart by vultures. They must be feasting on her. Were they enjoying her flesh just as cannibals did? These thoughts stirred up a terrible pain within Suranjan. It was as though he himself were being devoured by a pack of seven hyenas.

The cigarette was still unfinished in his hand when a girl sauntered up to Suranjan. Her face looked unusually bright under the glow of neon lights. She must have put on lots of makeup. She was around twenty.

Throwing the cigarette away, Suranjan beckoned to the girl. The girl stood by the cab swinging her body provocatively and smiling.

Suranjan asked her name.

"Pinky," the girl said, giggling.

"Tell me your full name."

"Shamima Begum."

"Your father's name?"

"Abdul Jalil."

"Your home?"

"Rangpur."

"What did you say your name was?"

"Shamima."

The girl was somewhat surprised at the number of questions. No one did that. What sort of customer was he, she wondered. Suranjan looked sharply at Shamima. Was she lying? Perhaps not.

"Okay, get into the rickshaw."

The girl did as she was told. Suranjan directed the rickshaw puller to go toward Tikatuli. He didn't talk with Shamima any more during the rest of the journey. Nor did he cast a glance at her. He remained unmoved by her constant chatter, nestling close to him, suddenly breaking into a line or two of song, laughing and leaning on him. He smoked thoughtfully. The rickshaw puller, too, appeared to be in a jovial mood. He drove his vehicle in a zigzag. He sang an occasional refrain from Hindi film songs. The city was dressed up in red and blue illumination. Suranjan was going ahead with his plan in a cool, calculated manner and he was cold sober.

He had locked his room from the outside so that he could silently slip into the room without calling anyone to the front door. Entering the room, Shamima said, "What about my fee? Nothing has been fixed."

Suranjan cut her short, saying, "Shut up, not a word more."

The room wore the same disheveled look. The bedsheet was hanging out. No sound came from the other room. Perhaps they had fallen asleep. Straining his ears, Suranjan could hear Sudhamay groaning. Did he realize that his beloved son had picked up a girl from the street and brought her in? He for his part did not view Shamima as a common tart. She was a Muslim girl to him. He would just rape Shamima, nothing but rape. He made the room dark. He tore away her clothes, making her lie on the floor. He dug his nails into the girl's abdomen and sank his teeth into her breast. Suranjan could understand he was not making love to the girl but was wantonly pulling her hair, biting her cheek, throat and breasts, and scratching deep marks on her stomach, buttocks and thighs. She was a common streetwalker used to rough treatment from her customers. But she occasionally cried out in pain. Her cries gave Suranjan a strange pleasure. He crushed the girl with a grim determination to cause all the more pain to her and rape her. The girl, despite the pain, was amazed. She, too, had never had such a violent customer, who was virtually ripping her apart. Like a doe trying to escape from the clutches of a tiger, the girl collected her clothes to rush for the door.

Suranjan was now quite gentle. He was feeling relieved of the weight he had been carrying. He had been able to fulfill the wish that had been haunting him throughout the day. He would feel overjoyed if he could now kick the girl out of the house. His chest started heaving again. Would he now aim a solid kick at this Muslim girl? The girl stood still. She didn't know whether she could leave now or would have to stay the whole night. Since she had been forbidden to talk, she couldn't say anything out of fright.

Where was Maya now? Did they tie her up in a closed room and rape her, all seven of them? Maya must have suffered like hell. Did she shout for help? When Maya was in her teens, once, while having a nightmare, she screamed, "Dada, Dada!" Suranjan, rushing to her, found her trembling all over even in the midst of sleep. He had asked, "What is it, Maya, why are you trembling?" Her tremors didn't stop even after waking up. She was still deeply engrossed in her dream story, which she narrated: "You and I had gone to a very beautiful village. We were walking through lush green paddy fields, talking between ourselves. One or two other people were also walking with us talking in bits. Suddenly I found the paddy fields had disappeared. I was standing in a desolate place alone and you were no longer with me. Rather, I saw some men were rushing to catch hold of me. I was then running in fright, looking up for you." Poor Maya! Again his breathing became deeper. He seemed to hear Maya crying quite loudly.

But nobody could hear her shrieks. Her cries could reach no one. She was crying, perhaps in a closed room surrounded by a pack of wild animals. Where could Maya possibly be now? It was a small place, yet he didn't know if his dear sister was in a garbage bin or brothel or floating on the water of the river Buriganga. Where was Maya? He wanted to drive away this girl standing near him by taking her by the nape of her neck.

The girl was scared at the wildness of Suranjan. She dressed rapidly and said, "Now pay me off."

"Take care, get lost now." Suranjan jumped up in anger. Opening the door, Shamima took one step out and looked pathetic, with blood oozing from the bite marks on her cheek. "Please give me at least ten takas," she pleaded.

Anger was rising in Suranjan in leaps and bounds. But he softened looking at the helpless, sad eyes of the girl. A poor girl, who earned by offering herself to others. The worthless social system, instead of using her labor or other qualities, was pushing her further down into the gutter. She would certainly buy some rice to smother her hunger with her meager earnings. Who knew how many times she went without eating? Suranjan took out ten takas from his trousers pocket and gave them to Shamima. he asked, "You are a Muslim, right?"

"Yes."

"You are prone to changing your names. Have you done anything like that?"

"No."

"Okay, now go."

Shamima went away. Suranjan felt quite relieved. He would not nurse any sadness today. Today was Victory Day. All were in a festive mood, bursting crackers in remembrance of the day twenty-one years ago. Shamima came to Suranjan's room on this day. Bravo, freedom, bravo. Suranjan wanted to snap his fingers loudly or he would break into a popular inspiring song: "My world begins and ends with Bangladesh, my life and death is Bangladesh."

It was remiss on his part not to have told his name to Shamima. He should have said that his name was Suranjan Dutta. Then she would have realized that the man who had made her bloody by scratching and biting her was a Hindu. The Hindus, too, were capable of rape; they, too, were equipped with nails for scratching and teeth for biting. Shamima was merely a harmless, innocent girl, but still she was a Muslim. Even if he could deliver a mild slap to a Muslim, he would derive great pleasure from that.

His night was spent in tremendous restlessness, almost without any sensibility. He spent the night alone, in eerie silence, in the midst of a feeling of utter insecurity, beneath the wings of dark terror. He couldn't sleep. he wanted to take his own small revenge, but could not. Suranjan, to his utter amazement, found that throughout the night he was feeling pity for the poor girl Shamima. No jealousy, no anger. If he were devoid of these feelings, then how could he call this revenge? Then it was sort of a defeat for him. Was Suranjan defeated? Then he must have been. He couldn't deceive Shamima. She had already been a victim of deceit. To her rape and normal intercourse were hardly different. Suranjan was curled on his bed in shame and agony. Though it was quite late at night, sleep continued to elude him. Was he then getting spoiled? The incident of the Babri mosque had spoiled him. He could clearly realize that the rot had begun in his heart. Why was he suffering so much for the girl whom he had ravished by scratching and biting her? If only he could wipe the blood from her cheek with his own handkerchief before she left! Would he be able to meet the girl again? If he could by waiting for her at the crossing of the Bar Council, he would certainly ask for her pardon. He was feeling hot even on this winter night. He threw off the quilt. The bedsheet, too, lay in a crumpled bundle near his feet. On the dirty mattress, Suranjan lay like a dog with his knees touching his forehead.

In the morning, feeling no enthusiasm to get up, he stayed in bed suppressing the tremendous urge to urinate. Kiranmayee brought his tea. But he didn't feel like tasting it. He felt nauseated. He wanted to have a hot shower. But where would he find hot water? They had a pond in their Brahma Palli house. The water was extremely cold during the winter. Still, he couldn't have dreamed of having a bath without swimming in the pond. Today he wanted to swim again, but where could he find a pond? And where was that deep water? He didn't want to wash in the bathroom with a measured amount of water. Why should every aspect of life have to be measured?

Day Twelve

Suranjan left his bed at ten in the morning. He was brushing his teeth standing on the verandah. He could hear Khadem Ali's son Asraf telling Kiranmayee, "Auntie, Putu saw a girl like Maya floating in the canal under the iron bridge at Gendaria yesterday evening."

Suranjan's hand holding the toothbrush became stiff and rigid like stone. He had the feeling of an electric current passing through his entire body. No sound of crying came from within.

The house was totally still. The slightest sound, it seemed, would bring back heavy echoes from all parts of it. It was as if no one but he had been living in this house during the last thousand years. Standing on the verandah, Suranjan recalled the gaiety of yesterday's Victory Day celebrations; the city had not fully arisen from slumber as yet. He stood there, toothbrush in hand. Hyder was walking down the road. Seeing Suranjan, he stopped as a show of courtesy. He slowly came up to Suranjan and asked, "How are you?"

"Quite well," Suranjan said with a smile.

Invariably the question of Maya would have arisen, but Hyder refrained from asking. He silently stood leaning against the railing. He said, "Yesterday the men of the fundamentalist Jamat Shibir smashed the memorial plaque of the mass grave at the Rajshahi University."

Spitting out a glob of toothpaste from his mouth, Suranjan asked, "What do you mean by mass grave?"

"You don't know what mass grave means!" Hyder exclaimed, staring at Suranjan in surprise.

Shaking his head, Suranjan pleaded his ignorance.

Hyder's face darkened in insult. He failed to understand how Suranjan, being a leader of the liberation war consciousness-awakening center, could say so. The Shibir followers had demolished the memorial plaque of the mass war grave, so let them. They had arms with them. They were putting them to use. Who would resist them? Gradually they would demolish "invincible Bangla," the sculpture dedicated to the memory of the Liberation War, and would destroy the "Bravo Bangladesh" statue of a freedom fighter at Jaidevpur. Who could resist this? There would be just occasional protest meetings or processions. Slogans like "Stop the politics of Jamat Shibir Youth Command" would be raised by some progressive political parties. That much! What would happen then? Suranjan answered without speaking: "Trash."

After standing for some time with his head bowed, Hyder said, "You might have heard Parvin is here now. She is divorced." Suranjan listened silently, making no comment. Parvin's divorce failed to evoke any reaction. Instead, he felt she had been rightly served. She preferred a Muslim to a Hindu. How did she feel now? Suranjan had already raped Parvin in his mind. In the morning, at this present stage of brushing his teeth halfway through, the feeling of rape lost much of its poignancy. Still a bit of the taste of the mental rape remained in his mind.

After some time Hyder said, "I'm going." Suranjan didn't object.

Sudhamay had reached the point where he could sit up unaided. Leaning against the pillows, he sought out sounds in this silent house. Sudhamay thought that of all the members of this family, Maya had the greatest urge to remain alive. Had he not become ill, Maya wouldn't have to come from Parul's house to meet this catastrophe. Someone said her body was found under a bridge. But who would go to identify the body? Sudhamay knew no one would go, for everyone believed that Maya would come back some day. If the body was really identified as Maya's, then the hope of her return today, tomorrow, in a month or two, or even years later, would evaporate. There are some hopes, right or wrong, that help people survive in this world. After a long while he called Suranjan and asked him to sit by his side. In a broken voice he said, "I feel so ashamed to live with doors and windows closed."

"You feel ashamed? I feel angry."

"I feel also quite worried about you!" Sudhamay wanted to keep his left hand on his son's back.

"Why?"

"You return home so late. Haripada came yesterday. He told me how bad the situation was at Bhola. Thousands of people were spending their days under the sky, they were totally shelterless. The women were being raped."

"What's new about that?"

"Certainly something new. Had anything like this ever happened before? That's why I feel so concerned about you."

"Are you concerned only about me? Why aren't you scared about yourself and Ma? You're Hindus as well."

"What can they do to us?"

"They could chop off your heads and hurl them in the Buriganga river. You are yet to understand the people of this country. They'll have Hindus for their breakfast. They won't discriminate between the young and the old."

Folds of irritation appeared on Sudhamay's forehead. He said, "Do you not belong to this country?"

"No, I can no longer think of myself as someone of his land although I am trying to. But the task appears impossible. When others like Kajalda spoke about the discrimination between Muslims and Hindus, I felt bad. I used to say there was lots to do in this country besides keeping count of what was happening to the Hindus and how many of them were dying. My contention was that there was no point in wasting time over these things. But slowly I've realized that he was right. And I, too, am changing. But this shouldn't have happened to me, Baba." Suranjan's voice became choked.

Sudhamay kept his hand on his son's back. He said, "The people are coming forward. Lots is being written in newspapers. The voice of protest has been raised. The writers and intellectuals are writing every day."

"All these activities will lead to nothing," Suranjan said in an angry voice.

"One group of people has come out with long choppers and axes. Nothing can be done to resist them by raising slogans, protesting with bare arms and shouts. Long chopper should be met with long chopper. It was sheer foolishness to fight bare-handed against armed people."

"Should we then give up our ideals?"

"What ideals? All bogus."

Sudhamay's hair had turned grayer during the last few days. His cheeks now looked hollow. He had virtually shrunk to half his former self. Still, his mind was unwavering. He said, "The people are still protesting against injustice and wrong. In how many countries is even this much possible? This right to protest."

Suranjan didn't reply. He presumed that the country's name would soon be changed from "People's Republic of Bangladesh" to "Islamic Republic of Bangladesh." The country would be ruled by the Islamic laws. The women would disappear behind the black veil that covers them head to foot. The number of people with caps, beards and *punjabis* would increase on the roads. The schools, colleges, universities would be eliminated. Mosques and *madrasas* would increase rapidly. Then all Hindus would be killed. The very thought sent shudders through Suranjan. Just like a trapped frog inside a well, he had to stay put at home most of the time. The sight or sound of movement outside or slogans of protest or revenge forced them to bolt their doors from inside instead of rushing out and joining in. Such ventures were far more fraught with risk for them. The Muslims could unhesitatingly raise slogans for the realization of their demands, but the Hindus couldn't. A Hindu couldn't raise his voice in protest against the injustice against his community members as forcefully as a Muslim could do on behalf of the Hindus. His voice would be choked, all the more so in the fear that this boldness might lead to the slitting of his throat during the night. Ahmed Sharif was allowed to remain alive even after being declared a *murtadd,* but if Sudhamay uttered unpalatable words, he would be silently killed. A vociferously protesting Hindu wouldn't be tolerated by a militant Muslim, not even by a progressive Muslim. Suranjan felt like laughing out loud at the thought of progressive people defining themselves as Hindus or Muslims. Actually, nobody with any religious identity could be progressive! Suranjan would have previously considered himself a modern, progressive man. Now he was beginning to feel like a Hindu. Was he becoming rotten? Perhaps so. In a broken voice Sudhamay asked Suranjan to come closer to him and then asked, "Won't it be possible to find Maya?"

"Don't know."

"Kiran hasn't been able to sleep for even a single night ever since. She also thinks about you. If anything happens to you ..."

"If I'm destined to die, then let me die. So many people are dying every day."

"Now I can sit on my own. With Kiran's support, I can now go to the toilet. But I won't be able to attend to my patients unless fully recovered. We have yet to pay two months' rent. If you do something, a job perhaps ..."

"I would never serve under anyone."

"The family actually. . . . We no longer have that landed property. We've had a taste of life that comes from paddy from the granary, fish from the pond, and milk from our cows. You have not seen anything like that. I have even sold all the land that we had in the village. Had I not, I could have erected a thatched hut there to spend the remaining years of my life."

Suranjan burst out in a rebuking voice, "Why are you talking like a fool? Would you have survived in the village? There the armed men of the village chief would have beaten you up to snatch everything from you."

"Why do you disbelieve each and everyone? Isn't there a good soul anywhere in the country?"

"No, there is none."

"You are being needlessly pessimistic."

"Not for nothing."

"What about your friends? You studied communism for such a long time, participated in so many movements. The people with whom you moved and worked, are they not worth any trust?"

"No, all of them are communal-minded."

"I think you, too, are becoming communal."

"Yes, quite so. This country is turning me into a communal-minded being. It's not my fault."

"This country has made you communal?" Sudhamay exclaimed disbelievingly.

"Yes, this very country."

Suranjan laid emphasis on the word "country." Sudhamay maintained silence. The floor was still littered with pieces of broken glass. They might have pierce their feet. If not their feet, they had certainly pierced their hearts.

Suranjan stayed in bed throughout the day. He felt not at all inclined to go anywhere. Would he go to the iron bridge once, to see the floating, decomposed, disfigured body of Maya? No, he wouldn't go anywhere today.

Later that afternoon, Suranjan paced the cemented courtyard. At one time he hurled down all the books in his room into the courtyard. Kiranmayee thought that he was spreading the books in the sun, perhaps the ones infested with insects: *Das Kapital,* works of Lenin, works of Marx and Engels, Morgan, Gorky, Dostoevsky, Tolstoy, Jean Paul Sartre, Pavlov, Rabindranath, Manik Bandopadhyay, Nehru, Azad; brick-sized books on sociology, economics, politics and history. He started tearing their pages; he made a huge heap of them in the courtyard, lit a match, and set fire to the whole pile.

The flames treated the torn pages in the way a Muslim fanatic is expected to treat a Hindu. Smoke enveloped the entire courtyard. Smelling something burning, Kiranmayee came rushing out. Suranjan laughingly said, "Do you want to warm yourself? Then you are welcome."

Kiranmayee asked wearily, "Have you gone mad?"

"You're right, Ma. For a long time I have been quite a normal being. Now I am going off my rocker. Only the hopping mad can enjoy the bliss of peace."

Standing near the door, Kiranmayee watched Suranjan's book-burning spree. She had no thought of putting out the flames by bringing bucketsful of water from the tap. Dark smoke shrouded Suranjan. It seemed to Kiranmayee that Suranjan, in the name of burning books, was, in fact, setting fire to himself.

Sudhamay thought that this lively boy of sharp intellect, who, he believed, would suck out poison from others' minds, was now himself relishing a drink of venom. The poison was turning him blue. His lying in bed silently, shouting at his friends, bringing a whore into his room at night, abusing the Muslims, book burning—all these were signs of his unexpressed and accumulated grievances. He nurtured a strong resentment against his family, society, the state, everything. And he burned himself in the resultant fire of an inferiority complex.

Suranjan was quite delighted at the sight of the fire. The Hindu houses had gone up in flames in this manner all over the country. Such blazing flames! Were only the houses and temples burned, not the minds of the people? He wouldn't follow the ideals of Sudhamay any longer. Sudhamay was a believer in a leftist ideology in which he had also reared Suranjan. Now he didn't believe in any of that. Many leftists had also branded him as a *malaun*. He had been hearing the word *malaun* since his boyhood. Whenever there was an argument with his schoolmates, after some time they would call him "son of *malaun*." Tears welled up in his burning eyes. He failed to understand the source of these tears. Was it due to any pain or the smoke emanating from the burned ideals? Suranjan was much more at ease with himself when everything was burned. Lying down on his bed, whenever he had caught a glimpse of these books, the principles enunciated in them had constantly chewed him up. He no longer cared for their principles. If only he could plant a royal kick on the backsides of these convictions! Why should he be a receptacle of these useless conceptions? All the more so when people took the cup of knowledge to their lips without caring to take it to their heart? Why should he alone take all this to heart?

The fire ritual over, Suranjan wanted to enjoy a long sleep. But sleep eluded him. The image of Ratna flashed through his mind. He hadn't seen her for a long time. How was she doing? He could read the message of her deep, dark eyes. She needn't say anything more. She must be thinking, one day Suranjan would knock on her door, would spend the whole night talking with her over umpteen cups of tea. Suranjan thought of going to her house tonight. He would say, "Do you think that only I should come to see you? Mustn't one feel the need to reciprocate?"

Suranjan was convinced that Ratna would come to his place on a melancholy evening. She would say, "Everything appeared to be so empty, Suranjan." Suranjan had not enjoyed any pleasure for a pretty long time. Parvin would embrace him, saying, "You are mine and mine alone. I'll kiss you at least one hundred times." They would detach themselves at Kiranmayee's sudden intrusion. Marrying a Muslim wouldn't have stirred up any problem. That was why she had sought it. Ratna didn't suffer from any problem of caste or creed. He would surrender his burned-out life to her. When Suranjan was musing on all this, he decided to go to Ratna's place, cleansing his mind of all the dirt and putting on a clean shirt. At that moment someone knocked at the door. Opening the door he found Ratna. She looked quite decked out with a dazzling sari, her wrists showing glitters of tinkling bangles. Suranjan was overwhelmed by her sweet, enrapturing smile. "Please come in," Suranjan said; but while speaking this welcome, he noticed a handsome young man behind her. But where was he going to offer a seat to Ratna? The entire room was in a mess. Still with the customary "Please be seated," he pointed to a broken chair. Ratna said smilingly, "Guess whom I've brought with me?"

Suranjan had not met Ratna's brother and wondered whether the young man was he. Suranjan didn't allow much time for Suranjan to think. Reflecting the tinkle of her bangles in her voice, she said, "This is Humayun, my husband."

In a moment a tremendous whirlwind swept over his mind, uprooting the last tree which he had marked to be his final shelter. After wasting the greater part of his life in a squandering spree, he had dreamed of settling down with Ratna to start a happy family. But to his shock, Ratna, in her quest for surviving in a terror-stricken country, had chosen a Muslim husband. Suranjan's face darkened in anger and humiliation. He would now have to welcome Ratna and her possibly affluent husband in his disheveled, poor room, exchange niceties over cups of tea, and engage in the farce of polite pleasantries with the ritualistic "Please do come again" after shaking hands with him. No, Suranjan wouldn't do anything like that. He was in no mood for such courtesies. He stunned the two guests in his room by suddenly blurting out, "I'm going out on urgent business, I don't have any time to spare for you." They felt so insulted that they stormed out with only a brief "Sorry." Suranjan closed the door with a bang and stood leaning against it. He stayed in that position for a long time. He came back to his senses when Kiranmayee, entering the room, said, "Have you returned the money that you took out as a loan?" The word "loan" pierced his heart. He looked in the face of Kiranmayee, but did not say anything.

Suranjan felt suffocated. The room appeared to be a cast iron box he was unable to open. He loitered on the verandah for some time. Yet he could not escape the overwhelming grief which engulfed him like a torrential rain. Kiranmayee silently placed a cup of tea on the table. Suranjan looked at it but did not reach out his hand to take it. He lay down for a while, but got up again. Should he go once and for all to the iron bridge? The thought sent tremors through his chest. It seemed that he would find his own decomposed body floating in the murky drain below

288

the bridge. The house was quiet as a still pool of water. Its three inmates moved about in silence like marine insects sliding on water. No one could hear the patter of the other's footsteps.

This ghostly silence was suddenly broken by Kiranmayee. She, without any apparent reason, burst into piercing cries. With the penetrating sharpness of her wails, Sudhamay hoisted himself into a sitting position, Suranjan came rushing out. He found Kiranmayee crying her heart out, leaning her head against the wall. This was not a cry that could be stopped with consoling words. It was the bursting dam of tears which had accumulated in her heart over a long time. Nothing could stop this spillover. Sudhamay had his chin on his chest, keeping still. The loud lamentations erupting from Kiranmayee's wails pierced his heart. There was no end to it. No one asked the reason for such an eruption of sorrow. There was no need. Both Sudhamay and Suranjan knew why.

Suranjan was standing at the door. He entered noiselessly to keep from interrupting Kiranmayee's cries. All his dreams were now in shambles, all the structures built with his mind were broken to pieces and burned and reduced to ashes. As Kiranmayee had shattered the long unbroken silence of this house, so did Suranjan suddenly scream "*Baba.*"

Sudhamay looked at him startled. Suranjan grasped his hands and said fervently, "Baba, I thought it over last night. I know you won't accept it. Still I'm insisting, please keep my word. Please do it. Let's go away from here."

Sudhamay asked, "Where?"

"To India."

"India!" Sudhamay shuddered in such a manner as if he had heard a strange, hitherto unknown word which was something obscene, forbidden. Its articulation was a criminal act to him.

Slowly Kiranmayee's cries came to a grinding halt. She groaned and groaned till she slumped to the floor.

Sudhamay's forehead showed crinkles of extreme annoyance. He said furiously, "Is India your father's or grandfather's home? Who of your distant forefathers or any other relatives were born there? You want to run away from your own homeland. . . . Doesn't it make you feel ashamed?"

"What are we going to do with this country? What does it have to offer to you? To me? To Maya? What has prompted my mother to cry? Why do you groan all night? Why can't I sleep?"

"Riots occur in every country. Is India free from this? Aren't the people dying there? Do you keep any track of deaths there?"

"Riots were not that bad. But, Baba, here no riots break out. Muslims are just killing the Hindus in an absolutely one-sided manner."

"You are thinking of yourself as a Hindu," said Sudhamay, making an effort to raise himself from the bed in excitement. But Suranjan restrained him with both his arms. He said, "However much we proclaim ourselves as atheists or humanists, still the stigma of being a Hindu will stick to us. They'll call us *malauns*. The more I love this country, the more it'll move away from me. The more we love the people of this land, the more quickly we'll be ostracized. They can't be trusted, Baba. You have treated so many Muslim families without charging them any fees. But how many beneficiaries of your generosity have stood by us in these dark days? All of us would have gone the

290

way that led to Maya's body floating under the bridge. Baba, let's go away from here." Suranjan leaned on Sudhamay as he appealed with great emotion.

"Will that restore Maya?"

"Maya will never return, Baba, she'll never come back," Suranjan said through a spasm of agony.

Sudhamay slumped on the bed. His body lay sprawled, absolutely slackened. He mumbled, "If Maya couldn't be saved, then who else's do we need to save?"

"Our own. Should we stay here to grieve over what we've lost? And that, too, in midst of dangerous insecurity! Better let's go away."

"What shall I do there?"

"Something will turn up. Besides, what are we doing here? Are we quite well here, living with great joy?"

"The rootless life . . ."

"What are you going to do with the roots, Baba? If the roots really meant something, why then are we under the compulsion to keep our doors and windows closed? You'll have to live the life of a frog entrapped permanently in a well. They have become quite used to raiding our houses and slitting our throats any time they like. I feel ashamed to live this life of a holed-up rat. I am gripped by anger, but I can't do anything. Can I give vent to my feelings by setting a couple of their houses on fire? Shall we go on watching ourselves being humiliated and rendered powerless? Do we have the right to talk back or strike beat a Muslim who slaps me for nothing? So, come, let's go away."

"Now the situation is cooling down. Why are you worrying so much. Life doesn't run on emotions alone."

"Who says the situation is cooling down? That's all on the surface. Ferocity burns unabated just underneath. They are laying traps for us, showing all their fierce claws and fangs. Why did you have to throw away your *dhoti* to put on *pyjamas*? Why don't you have the freedom to dress as you choose? Come, let's go away."

Sudhamay gritted his teeth in anger. He said, "No, I won't go. Go away if you like."

"Then you won't go?"

"No," Sudhamay said, looking away in disgust and revulsion.

"Again I'm telling you, Baba, let's go away," Suranjan said, placing his hand on his father's shoulder. His voice showed signs of his agony, silent tears.

Sudhamay said with his earlier resoluteness, "No." This emphatic "no" landed on Suranjan's back like an iron rod.

Suranjan accepted his failure. He knew he wouldn't succeed in convincing his father. A man of rigid character like Sudhamay would prefer to stick to his place despite all the disgraces heaped upon him. He would go falling face down on the ground.

Kiranmayee was not crying any more. She was bending toward a picture of Radha-Krishna. Earlier Suranjan had seen an idol of the elephant god, Ganesh. Possibly that had been smashed by the Muslim raiders. Perhaps she kept this picture concealed somewhere. Now she was praying, almost prostrate, to Lord Krishna, asking for security, freedom from anxiety, surety and an untroubled life.

Upstream in the river of frustration Suranjan found himself to be the lone swimmer. The night wore on. He felt absolutely alone. There was no one to stand by his side. He felt like an alien in his own country. He, with all his rationality, intelligence, and conscience started shrinking within. His rational, broad, liberal mind in this country of strikes, curfews and unmitigated terror became hedged in on all sides. He couldn't find unpolluted air to breathe in his room with its closed door and windows. As if everyone were waiting with bated breath for a violent death. It was not Maya now, but the blind sense of self-preservation that became uppermost in everybody's mind. They were becoming increasingly isolated. None of their Muslim friends or neighbors who cared to look them up could give them any assurance of the safety of their lives such as the Muslims enjoyed. They couldn't assure the members of this family: Don't feel hesitant, don't cringe in fear. You may walk freely without any feeling of terror, work without any hindrance, laugh openly, go to sleep without any worry.

Day Thirteen

Suranjan fell asleep in the early hours of the morning. He had a strange dream. He was walking all alone by a riverside. Suddenly a huge wave sucked him into the depths; he was drowning, despite his frenetic urge to live, he was caught up in the suction of the eddy with no one offering a helping hand to pull him out of this distressing situation. He started sweating, and went down and down in the swirling unknown water. Suddenly he was startled. His face paled in fear. The whirlpool was sucking him down to an abysmal depth; he was shouting for help, reaching out his hand to cling to a straw for survival in the midst of the dream. Just then he found a hand that would rescue him, clasping which he would regain his strength, the strong hand of Sudhamay.

Resting on Kiranmayee, Sudhamay had walked to him. Slowly he was regaining his lost power. He was seated near Suranjan's head. His eyes flickered like the light of distant stars.

"Baba?"

A mute question throbbed in Suranjan's heart. It was early morning. Through a chink in the closed windows, light was filtering in. Sudhamay said, "Come, let's go away."

Suranjan was staggered. He asked, "Where will we go, Baba?"

Sudhamay said, "India."

Sudhamay felt ashamed, his voice shook; but still for the first time in his life he had talked about leaving the land. The mountain that he had built up within him was crumbling day by day.

Glossary

ajan—call to prayer for the faithful Muslim, performed five times a day (Arabic)

akhra—place where people gather to sing devotional songs and dance

apa—a polite way of addressing an older sister or woman (Muslim)

ashram—Hindu monastery where monks reside, organize charitable activities, and house travelers

Awami League—political party of Bangladesh, the leading party during the war of liberation in 1971

Ayodhya—a place in Uttar Pradesh, India, where the Babri mosque was situated

baba—father (Hindu)

Bajrang Dal—group in the Hindu fundamentalist movement

BDR—Bangladesh Rifles, infantry unit that controls border security

Bengali—an Indo-European language derived from Sanskrit, spoken by approximately 120 million people in Bangladesh and 70 million in India. The people who belong to the Bengali language and culture.

bhai—brother, a way of addressing other men

bigha—square measure, approximately 1,340 square meters

biharis—Muslims from the Indian state of Bihar. They migrated in 1947 to what was then East Pakistan. During the war of 1971 they supported the Pakistan army.

bismillah—"In the name of God" (Arabic)

BJP (Bharatlya Janata party)—Hindu ultranational fundamentalist party

BNP (Bangladesh National party)—formed by Zia-ur Rahman during his military regime

boudi—sister-in-law, older brother's wife. Also used when addressing older persons or a friend's wife (Hindu)

CPB—Communist party of Bangladesh

dada or da—polite way of addressing an older brother or man

dal—lentil soup

dhoti—long piece of cloth, usually white, draped around the waist, worn by Hindu men.

didi or di—polite way of addressing an older sister or woman

Durga—Hindu goddess

Eid—Muslim religious occasion (Arabic)

Ershad, H. M.—Lt. General, president of Bangladesh, 1983–1990

Farakka—a dam in the Ganga river of India. The river Ganga flows to the Padina river of Bangladesh. The people of Bangladesh want to break the dam because they need water. This is a big political issue in Bangladesh.

gosol—bath, as Bengali Muslims call it

Gita, Bhagavad Gita—religious book of the Hindus

goonda—hooligan

haj—the Muslim pilgrimage to Mecca (Arabic)

Hajong rebellion—land labor against the landlord in the late 1940s

Harnad Nath—Muslim religious song

Hanuman—the Hindu monkey god who helps the god Rama in the Sanskrit epic *Ramayana*

jal—water as Bengali Hindus call it

Jamat-i-Islami—fundamentalist Muslim party

Jinnah, Muhammad Ali—the founder and first president of Pakistan. Leader of the Muslim League in undivided British India.

Kali—Hindu goddess

kantha—hand-stitched light quilt

kar sevak—voluntary religious worker (Hindu)

katha—square measure, approximately 67 sq. meters

Khaleda Zia Begum—the present prime minister of Bangladesh, chairperson of the BNP

pyjamas—long and loose trousers, usually worn by Muslims.

lungi—piece of cloth draped around the waist, worn by Bengalis (mostly Muslims)

madrasa—Muslim religious school

malaun—something refused from heaven. This word is used to insult Hindus (Arabic)

mandir—Hindu temple

maulavi—Muslim priest

milad—Muslim ceremonial celebration (Arabic)

Mountbatten, Lord—the last viceroy of India, supervised the partition of British India in 1947

murtadd—apostate from the Muslim faith (Arabic)

namaskar—greeting performed by joining the palms and moving them to touch the forehead (Hindu)

Nizami, Maulana Mohammad—general secretary of Jamat-i-Islami

paani—water (Arabic)

pishi—aunt

puja—Hindu religious service

Rama—Hindu god, hero of the sanskrit epic *Ramayana*

Rao, Narasimha—India's prime minister, leader of the Congress party

Rashtriya Swayamsevak Sangh, or RSS—Hindu fundamentalist organization

Section 144—under this law it is forbidden for people to gather in the streets. If people are caught gathering, the police or the army can shoot them.

Sheikh Mujibur Rahman—hero of the Bangladesh liberation war, considered the father of the nation. He was murdered in a military *coup d'état* in 1975. Leader of the Awami League.

Sheikh Hasina Wajed—the daughter of Sheikh Mujibur Rahman and his political heir. Leader of the Awami League.

Shiva—Hindu god

Tagore, Rabindranath—famous Bengali poet, composer and author. Nobel laureate in 1913.

taka—Bangladeshi currency

Tonk movement—movement by Hajong (tribe)

Uttar Pradesh—India's largest state in terms of population

Vishwa Hindu Parishad (VHP)—Hindu fundamentalist group

Zahannam—hell

Zia-ur-Rahman—president of Bangladesh, 1975–1981